Allied at the Altar

When only a convenient wife will do!

The face of Victorian London is changing. Innovation and reform is the order of the day. At the heart of this new Society are Conall Everard, Sutton Keynes, Camden Lithgow and Fortis Tresham.

These four dashing heroes are determined to make their mark on the world. But what starts out as four convenient marriages will change these gentlemen's lives forever...

Don't miss this new sexy quartet from Bronwyn Scott!

Read Conall and Sofia's story in
A Marriage Deal with the Viscount

Read Cam and Pavia's story in
One Night with the Major

Read Sutton and Elidh's story in
Tempted by His Secret Cinderella

And look out for the final book in

Allied at the Altar,

coming soon!

Author Note

Elidh and Sutton's story poses the question: "What will you do for love?" For Sutton, the answer revolves around whether or not he'll risk giving his heart again after a youthful disaster. For Elidh, the question is even more complex. What will she do out of love for her father? Will she risk his wild masquerade? When she meets Sutton, the question deepens. Love has torn her in two. Who does she choose? Sutton or her father? How can she possibly have them both? And then there's the issue of her own self-love and what she will do in order to love and be true to herself without hurting the two men she cares for.

Against the intricacies of these questions, a Cinderella story unfolds. But what makes the Cinderella story line engaging in any telling is what lies beneath the surface. The Cinderella story is more than a poor girl being rewarded for kindness with pumpkin coaches and glass slippers after enduring hardship; it's a love story on a far deeper level. So let me ask you: What will *you* do for love? For the chance to be transformed? I hope you enjoy Elidh and Sutton's story. For those who want a light read, the surface of the story will give you that. There's much to be enjoyed at Sutton's house party. For those looking for something more, you will find it. Beneath the first layer there is also a story here about human nature, morals and ethics, hard choices and much more to appeal to our inner philosopher.

BRONWYN SCOTT

*Tempted by His
Secret Cinderella*

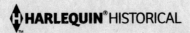

HARLEQUIN® HISTORICAL

Recycling programs
for this product may
not exist in your area.

ISBN-13: 978-1-335-63519-8

Tempted by His Secret Cinderella

Copyright © 2019 by Nikki Poppen

Printed in U.S.A.

Bronwyn Scott is a communications instructor at Pierce College in the United States and is the proud mother of three wonderful children—one boy and two girls. When she's not teaching or writing, she enjoys playing the piano, traveling—especially to Florence, Italy—and studying history and foreign languages. Readers can stay in touch on Bronwyn's website, bronwynnscott.com, or on her blog, bronwynswriting.blogspot.com. She loves to hear from readers.

Books by Bronwyn Scott

Harlequin Historical

Scandal at the Midsummer Ball
"The Debutante's Awakening"
Scandal at the Christmas Ball
"Dancing with the Duke's Heir"

Allied at the Altar

A Marriage Deal with the Viscount
One Night with the Major
Tempted by His Secret Cinderella

Russian Royals of Kuban

Compromised by the Prince's Touch
Innocent in the Prince's Bed
Awakened by the Prince's Passion
Seduced by the Prince's Kiss

Wallflowers to Wives

Unbuttoning the Innocent Miss
Awakening the Shy Miss
Claiming His Defiant Miss
Marrying the Rebellious Miss

Visit the Author Profile page
at Harlequin.com for more titles.

For Brony, who always has the best ideas when I get stuck. For Catie, who rescues anything on four legs, and for Rowan, my very own philosopher king, who contemplates the big questions.
A piece of each of you is in this story.

Chapter One

London—Friday, July 13th, 1855

Sutton Keynes considered himself a man of science, for whom all occurrences had a logical reason. There was little room in his well-ordered life for superstition. And what room *did* exist for such a novelty was quickly being filled to capacity as his uncle's ancient fossil of a solicitor, one Mr Barnes Esquire, leaned forward, joints creaking from the effort, and uttered thirteen of the unluckiest words ever spoken in succession to a bachelor who was quite happy with his single state.

'You have four weeks to wed if you want to claim the fortune.'

Four weeks to wed.

The words seemed to suck the very air out of the cramped little office in Poppins Court. Damn it all to hell. He thought he'd headed off such madness when he'd visited his uncle this spring. He'd made it very plain he didn't want his uncle's money. He'd even gone as far as to suggest that if his uncle wanted to keep the money out of his own son's hands he should tie it up in charitable annuities. His uncle had given it to him anyway. Sutton had not been nearly as persuasive as he'd thought.

Sutton reached for his teacup, wishing it held something stronger, and took a long swallow. He tried to appear neutral, as if his world hadn't just been upended. He was a man of reason. He should stay calm until he had all the details. Perhaps the pronouncement only seemed dire on the surface.

'Four weeks? That seems an exceptionally short amount of time in which to find a wife.' A partner for life. It was an enormous commitment, one he'd managed to put off because of its enormity, until now. These things, like any decently run experiment, could not be rushed. There would be specimens to collect, variables to account for, observations to make, information to collect and analyse, hypotheses to test and eliminate as he winnowed down the field. 'It would take at least a year to find a suitable bride.' Sutton put his cup down and Mr Barnes quickly refilled it, perhaps hoping to make up in quantity of drink what the tea lacked in quality—mainly that it wasn't brandy. 'Is there any significance to that deadline?' Sutton asked with a demeanour of equanimity, not wanting to give away his hand. He wasn't opposed to marriage, in theory, but he was opposed to undue haste. Haste increased one's margin for error exponentially. Surely he could argue for an extension unless there was a pre-determined reason for such immediate action.

His mind was already searching for a rationale behind his uncle's decision. His uncle liked to play with numerology among his many eccentricities. Four—the four archangels, the four gospels, the four sides of New Jerusalem in *Revelation*. Those things would appeal to his uncle, but Sutton couldn't see any relevance to this situation. Four, of which the square root was two, his scientific mind put forward. The four elements, the four phases of the moon, the four seasons, the four divisions of the day.

'It's the bank's provision, Mr Keynes,' Barnes explained. 'The bank your uncle's funds are invested with requires that all accounts be resolved within four weeks of the account holder's death.' But the rest of it, the marriage condition, was all his uncle's. In order to be a legitimate beneficiary of those funds, his uncle, *not the bank*, required him to be married first. It made sense now. Four. The square of two. Husband and wife. Completion. Two parts of a whole.

'And if I refuse to follow my uncle's dictates?' He watched Barnes's bushy grey eyebrows go up. It wasn't every day a man considered turning away a fortune handed to him.

'Then the fortune reverts to your cousin, Baxter Keynes.' Mr Barnes peered over his thick-rimmed glasses meaningfully.

'Of course. Bax.' Sutton gave a derisive chuckle. Bax was the one factor that could compel him to take up his uncle's challenge. There was much he would do to keep that amount of money out of Bax's control. What an unreasonable game this was becoming. He wasn't only being forced to marry, he was being forced to step into the metaphoric ring and compete against his cousin, his uncle's only child. 'Are you acquainted with my cousin, Mr Barnes?'

Barnes fixed Sutton with a strong stare. 'Yes, indeed I am, Mr Keynes. He was here this morning, in fact. He didn't stay long enough to have tea.' The man's tone was sharp, his gaze intuitive. For the first time since Sutton had entered the dingy office, the solicitor appeared to be more intelligent, more sane than Sutton had given him credit for. Most sane people struggled to do business with his uncle.

Baxter knew, then. That would make things interesting in a dangerous sort of way. Sutton picked up his tea and pondered that piece of information. 'Angry, was he?' His cousin had been left with nothing, although it couldn't have come as a surprise. Sutton's uncle had been threatening for years to pull something of this nature. The old man's title wasn't hereditary. The only thing he could leave Bax was his fortune and he hadn't. Instead, he'd left it to his nephew.

'Positively furious.' Barnes grimaced, nodding towards the cracked window pane.

Sutton offered a tight smile. 'If you've met him, you know there's not a choice. It's not a question of if I want to claim the fortune. I must. Baxter is not the sort of man to whom a fortune of that magnitude can be entrusted.' His cousin wasn't just reckless, spending money frivolously, although some of the fortune would indeed be squandered on harmless pursuits. Bax liked a good silk waistcoat and a fast horse as much as the next man. It wasn't the harmless pursuits Sutton was worried about. It was the more harmful ones; Bax was mixed up with slavers, the type that sold white women into the harems of the east in order to gain the favour of the Ottoman pashas, and arms dealers who sold guns for profit regardless of the cause, regardless of the side. In short, Bax played a deep game with powerful men. His involvement, of course, was most certainly not well known. For all intents and purposes, Bax, son of the eccentric Sir Leland, was a typical gentleman. But only on the surface. Beneath that surface, Bax inhabited a dark, dangerous world.

Barnes's old eyes sharpened for a moment over the rims of his glasses. 'We see each other plain, Mr Keynes. I assume you'll be marrying shortly, then.' It was not a question. Barnes tapped his papers into place and reached for another set of documents.

'I suppose I shall be.' Shortly. Quickly. Without the study necessary to make a quality decision. It was antithetical to his nature. Anabeth Morely had taught him that in his youth. He'd jumped into love with her head first only to find shallow water and grave disappointment. He'd not ventured forth since.

As a result, marriage was the last thing on his mind, right there at the bottom of the list of his priorities including his uncle's fortune. Whenever he thought about marriage, and that was hardly often enough to even qualify as seldom, it was as an amorphous something to pursue in a nebulous future, perhaps five years from now, once his camel dairy was firmly established in Newmarket. But not this summer. The summer was half over. He had his prized mare due to foal next month, he had next year's breeding programme to look over, bloodlines to study, the camel's milk studies to continue. The Newmarket Breeders Club would be expecting his report on the subject at the September meeting. He absolutely could not get married this year, not when there was so much to do.

It was bad enough his uncle's death had pulled him away from Newmarket this week. He'd be there now if it wasn't for the details of his uncle's will to sort through. In fact, he'd thought to leave for home as soon as the will was read, but today's revelations had put paid to that. Signing papers and looking over deeds would keep him in town another few days.

He far preferred the clean, straightforward living of Newmarket to the bustle and social politics of the London Season. He far preferred his animals to the matchmaking biddies of the *ton* and their feather-headed daughters. Some might consider him reclusive. They wouldn't be far wrong. He liked to think of himself as 'selective in his attentions'. He simply didn't have time for nonsense and London was notoriously full of it. He'd had plenty of its shenanigans when he'd first come up to town.

Now, however, his uncle's will threatened all that selective attention on a more permanent level. It didn't need to, though. Surely if there wasn't a way around the will, there was a way through it. His logical, scientist's mind turned itself to his options. He could make his marriage a temporary arrangement. Once the will was satisfied and the fortune was out of Bax's hands, they could separate.

'Ahem, Mr Keynes, are you listening?' No. He wasn't, in fact. He was too busy looking for loopholes. 'There are conditions attached to your marriage.' The solicitor raised his bushy brows again. 'I would listen closely if I were you. No sense in sacrificing oneself in marriage just to get it wrong.' Barnes had his attention now and he knew it. The old man smiled in satisfaction. 'If I may continue?' He cleared his throat. 'First, the bride must be from a noble family. Second, the marriage must last. It cannot be annulled or divorced or discontinued in any manner or the fortune is forfeit.'

Damn. Sutton had been counting on that—bear out the marriage for a couple of years and then cut his wife loose. Surely he could find a woman who would agree to those terms if she was handsomely paid. Sutton rethought his options. If divorce was out of the question, there was still a chance at informal separation, an 'open' marriage, as distasteful as the idea was to him. He had expectations, after all, loyalty and fidelity being two of them. His uncle's mandate, however, was playing havoc with those ideas along with everything else.

Sutton had no sooner contemplated the idea of the open marriage than the solicitor continued. 'Third, no separate lives, which means no separate residences and you may spend no more than a third of the year apart.' Well, so much for the wiggle room. That took care of it. The noose was tightening.

Sutton shifted in the hard wood chair and crossed a leg over his knee. His blasted teacup was empty again. 'It seems that I am well and truly roped into this, then.'

'Some would say you are well compensated for your sacrifice. All men marry in the end anyway,' the solicitor offered in an attempt to soften the blow.

'It's not the marriage I mind. It's the haste with which it must be done and the parameters placed on who it must be in order to claim a prize, a fortune I don't want except that it must not go to Bax. I have wealth of my own,' Sutton replied drily. That was the complete irony of the situation. His uncle had given a wealthy man a fortune, knowing full well the fortune itself held no allure. 'My uncle is blackmailing me from beyond the grave.' The dead bastard was getting everything he wanted: his fortune protected from his unscrupulous son and his nephew wed, the best his uncle could do to ensure the Keynes line continued, having all but officially disinherited Bax.

'I can't possibly consider refusing, for the greater good, as I am sure you know.' He couldn't possibly consider failing either. His canny uncle hadn't only made an ultimatum regarding his fortune, he'd made a game of it, one that pitted cousin against cousin. Bax would get the fortune if Sutton failed. Bax wouldn't sit idly by and leave the outcome of that game to chance. He would meddle and he would be dangerous, not only to Sutton but to whomever Sutton targeted as a bride. Bax would stop at nothing to prevent him from fulfilling the conditions of the will.

Barnes poured a third cup of tea. Sutton picked it

up and drank it down reflexively, his mind moving on to other issues like the pressing matter of a bride. It was one thing for him to marry in four weeks. He had a motive. But what bride of noble birth would marry him under such short notice? And the notice would only get shorter with every day that passed. Where was he going to find a bride in time? Especially one he could live with for the rest of his life?

The scientist in him shuddered to think at the flaws in collecting an adequate sample to base his decision on. The Season was more than halfway gone, but his bride would have to come from whoever was on hand in London and unclaimed at this point. He wondered if his uncle had thought about that? He supposed it could have been worse. His uncle could have died the end of August with Parliament out and everyone already absconded to their country homes. Where would he have found a bride then?

Barnes collected the pile of documents, making signs of dismissing him. But Sutton wasn't ready to leave yet. 'What about those papers? We haven't talked about everything in them yet.'

'And we won't until you have your bride,' Barnes said sternly, not appreciating the affront to his competence, as if he'd left something undone. 'Your uncle has left instructions to be read upon the announcement of your engagement. Then, and only then, shall we proceed. He was very thorough, Mr Keynes. As for you, there is a lot to think about, and do, if you choose, in a very limited amount of time. Please let me know if I can be of assistance.' It was about as blatant a dismissal as they came. The implication was clear: the clock was already ticking. The old man might as well have turned over an hourglass and started counting down the minutes towards four weeks.

'Thank you, I appreciate your time today, Mr Barnes.' Sutton rose and extended his hand. 'We will be in touch.'

Outside, the sun was still high, it was still July in the city, and it was still hot. Sutton ran a finger around the inside of his collar. It seemed unfair the world had not changed in the hour he'd spent in the solicitor's office. His life had changed. Shouldn't the world have changed as well? Sutton headed towards Ludgate Circus, pausing at the public urinals to relieve himself before he caught a hansom cab to Mayfair. Too much damn tea. Too much to think about, all of it circling back to focus on one critical issue: a bride. Without a bride, it wouldn't matter how willing he was to make the sacrifice.

Perhaps that was what he hated most about the whole arrangement. It required him to rely on someone beyond himself. It was not something he did easily or often, even with friends. To do so now with a woman he didn't know was preposterous. He liked to be the one who controlled the variables of any given experiment. Now, the critical variable was beyond him. Everything hinged on her, whoever she might be.

Sutton shook his head. No. He would not be the victim here. He would not focus on what he didn't control, but on what he did. He might not know a woman to marry, but he did know a woman who could help him: his mother. Before he could approach her, however, he needed a moment or two to think. He had the cab stop and let him out a few streets before he reached South Audley Street. By the time he reached number 71A a plan was forming. He would solve this situation as he solved every other puzzle placed before him—with logic and reason.

Chapter Two

'This is the most ridiculous, most scandalous thing your uncle has ever done. Wherever will you find a bride in four weeks and at the back end of the Season? People are thinking of *leaving* London, not lingering.' Catherine Keynes gave voice to the very thoughts that had plagued him from the ice-blue sofa in the drawing room where her at-home had just concluded.

'Those were my thoughts, exactly.' Sutton gave a wry chuckle. 'But you look well, Mother. Between the two of us, I am sure we're up to the task. I have a plan, but I will need an able assistant.' He studied his mother—a strong, shrewd woman who loved her family fiercely, if not maternally. He'd always thought, growing up, that she would have made a formidable queen in bygone years. He could imagine her navigating the dangerous intricacies of medieval court politics. His mother was the ablest person he knew for what he intended. Well connected, well experienced in society after thirty-two years among its ranks.

'I should have known you'd have a strategy.' She sighed. 'I don't suppose that strategy involves walking away from the fortune. You don't need it and I don't need it, in case you were thinking of taking it for my sake. I am comfortable enough with what your father left me. Who knows? I might even remarry at some point should the right man present himself, then you wouldn't need to worry over me at all.' It was a distinct possibility. His mother was still a handsome woman at fifty. This afternoon, she was dressed in a blue-and-silver gown of summer cotton that matched the drawing room decor, her still-dark honey hair coiffed in an intricate collection of braids. Her posture straight.

Sutton stopped pacing and leaned against the white Carrara marble mantel, imported from Italy and expensive, a further reminder that the Keyneses didn't need the money. They lived well enough on their own, Sutton's own father having made a fortune in the southeast Asian trade. Sutton shook his head. 'You know I can't just turn that money over to Bax.'

'It's not your job to save the world from him,' his mother argued the temptation that had crossed his mind in Barnes's office. He could walk away and it certainly made things easier. He could forgo a hasty, dramatic bridal search and retreat to the comfort of life as he knew it. But that was neither socially responsible, nor was it the honourable thing to do.

'"All it takes for evil to prosper is for good men to do nothing,"' he quoted. 'I have to do my part.' Sutton paced the length of his mother's drawing room, pushing a hand through his thick hair. He blew out a breath. 'The last girl Bax "importuned" killed herself last week. She washed up on the shores of the Thames with stones in her pockets.'

'Good lord.' His mother blanched. 'Will no one stop him?'

'He's too powerful. He owns too many secrets. But we can mitigate him and, in time, I can work against him and others like him. He's not alone in his corruption or his brand of it. For now, I can rob him of excess funds.'

'By making a scandal of a marriage?' his mother scolded, a furrow creasing her brow. 'A race to the altar can be nothing less than a spectacle.'

'Certainly it can't be *less* than a spectacle, but it can be *more*.' That was the plan anyway.

'I like the sound of that.' His mother held up the Wedgwood teapot in question. 'Tea, darling? While you lay out your grand plan?'

'No, no tea.' Sutton quickly waved away the pot. He'd had enough tea today to last him all week. 'Here's what I am thinking. If my marriage must be a spectacle, I want to make it one worth watching. I control if it becomes a scandal or not. I want to make it a grand event, create the perception of a whirlwind romance, love at first sight.' But it would be quite the exacting experiment beneath that frothy surface.

His mother smiled. 'You want to make it a fairy tale. I like the idea. It certainly softens the edge of scandal. You invite all the eligible girls to a house party at the Newmarket estate. Let them have a taste of the luxury that could be theirs. We'll put out the best china and polish the good silver to impress the mothers. We'll lay in champagne and French wine to impress the fathers. Hartswood always shows at its best in the summer. The girls can stroll and pose in their pretty dresses for you in the gardens while their fathers fish the river.'

Sutton laughed. 'You make it sound so easy.' He wished he had his mother's confidence when it came to his marriage. Some of the burden eased with the relief of having a partner in this. His mother did not challenge his decision, she simply got behind him and lent her considerable energies. 'I'm afraid it needs to be a bit more involved than pretty poses in the garden. I don't want to select a wife based on how she looks in a dress. I tried that once, a deviation from the norm, and a failure of an experiment, if you recall.' The disaster of Miss Anabeth Morely had been years ago in his youth, but he had no desire to repeat it.

Sutton moved on, refusing to dwell on the memory. 'We'll need a full slate of a variety of activities. I want to arrange to have time with each of the girls, to observe them in different settings, with different people, and with me. At the end of the house party, we'll hold a ball and I will announce my choice at midnight, the perfect ending to the fairy tale we'll create.'

'So, the party is to be your microscope? You'll be putting them under the lens of your scrutiny,' his mother surmised aptly.

'Yes. I suppose it is. But I am not the first to use a house party to such ends. There is no scandal in the setting I propose. It's quite traditional, really.' And it was efficient. He could gather everyone in a single space for his consideration.

'A setting and a task torn straight from the pages of a fairy tale,' his mother agreed. 'When is the party to be?'

'In five days. I don't think I can spare any more time than that if I'm to meet my uncle's deadline. Can you do it?' It wasn't the idea of the party that he doubted, it was the implementation. They had to act quickly, but extravagant entertainments took time. 'Can you arrange the activities, the details, the guests?' He was counting on her for this. His days would be taken up with paperwork and other legal details. Even so, he didn't know the first thing about planning a party of this magnitude.

'In five days' time? You want the impossible, but I think we can manage.' Her eyes danced, energised by the challenge. 'It's a mother's job to know how to arrange these things. If you are set on this, then I will help see it done.' She smiled softly. 'My son is getting married. Goodness knows you've made me wait long enough. I should start planning the wedding while I'm at it since time is of the essence.'

'Thank you, Mother.' He was an only child, out of poor luck in that department. His mother should have had legions of children to command: daughters to march out on the marriage mart, sons to organise into professions. Instead, she'd got him, a gentleman scientist who preferred his camels and horses to the social whirl. His one foray into that world had not recommended it. Some experiments didn't bear repeating.

There was one last piece to discuss. 'As to the guests, I am aware the Season is slowing down and so many of the girls are spoken for.' Sutton thought of the tea heiress, Pavia Honeysett, married now to his friend, Cam Lithgow. She would not have fit his uncle's criteria but she, a girl of mixed birth and not title, had caught the eye of a marquis before her marriage, general proof that girls had been swept up early this year and the competition for well-born wives was fierce.

'There's always someone to marry.' His mother was unbothered by his concern. 'People are looking for something new now that Ascot and the Regatta are behind us. I'll post an announcement in *The Times* and London will converge on Newmarket in five days.' She gave him a reassuring smile. 'Everyone will want to come.' Her eyes twinkled. 'And we'll let them; let them vie for your attention. *London* will wait upon your favour. You needn't beg, not with your good looks and the promise of that fortune.'

That's what he was worried about. He didn't want to limit his choices to the dregs, to wallflowers and fortune hunters, but he kept his thoughts to himself. There was only so much of the situation he could control, thanks to his uncle's stratagems. It wasn't the house party that would draw them, it was the mere presence of the fortune. Whether he was in Newmarket or in London wouldn't matter. At least in Newmarket he could control who he spent his time with. Here in London he'd be at the mercy of other people's guest lists. He bent to kiss his mother on the cheek and took his leave. He needed the sanctuary of his club, a drink and time to think. Who would want him, just him, now? Who would even *see* him, the man, standing there behind the fortune? In that regard, he'd just have to trust to luck that he'd be able to throw the net wide enough. But he was a scientist. Trusting to luck was not something he was used to doing.

There was a reason for that. Luck often failed and it was failing him spectacularly today. Sutton had barely set foot inside the asylum of his club before he realised his mistake. London had not waited for an announcement in *The Times*. From the buzz in the common room, it seemed the whole city already knew he had been named heir to Sir Leland Keynes's fortune. By four o'clock that afternoon, London fully grasped the import of that. The Season now had an eligible *parti nonpareil*.

Sutton was bombarded with men wanting to shake his hand, some of whom he hadn't seen since school days, others whom he'd never met at all but who claimed introduction through convoluted connections. Older men wanted to offer condolences on his uncle's passing, younger men wanted to renew acquaintances or establish them. *All* of them had sisters, daughters, nieces, cousins, wards or god-daughters. The preponderance of females offered up to him made his earlier observation about the dearth of candidates laughable. Apparently, marriageable females were thick on the ground when one was possessed of a fortune.

But his instant popularity reinforced his earlier worry. He'd become nothing but a placeholder, a gateway to a fortune. Sutton made his way to an empty, isolated chair in the corner and ordered a drink. He didn't kid himself the privacy of his seat would last long. He was a man no longer, but a thing to be used and manipulated for personal gain, the very reason he'd resisted the idea of marriage for so long. He didn't want an alliance. He didn't need an heiress's money or a debutante's father's political connections. He wanted something more.

Not love, necessarily. The idea of love was an illogical concept when it came to the science of successful pairings. Animals didn't mate for love or for alliances. They mated for strength, for compatibility. That's what he wanted. Compatibility. Someone who loved animals, who would enjoy working beside him with his camels and his horses, who might enjoy *him*. Those wishes were now officially relegated to the dustbin of impossibilities.

A pair of young men approached his sanctuary and invaded with oblivious bonhomie, taking advantage of a very casual connection. They'd met once or twice at Tattersall's. 'Keynes, so good to see you. Dare say we'll see more of you in London, these days.'

Sutton smiled and shook their hands, wondering just how long it would take them to mention the unattached women in their lives.

'My sister is with me this Season,' the first one said,

and Sutton restrained the urge to laugh. Of course she was. It had taken the man all of thirty seconds. A record, to be sure. If his uncle wasn't already dead, Sutton would kill him for this. His uncle had made his life a living hell.

Chapter Three

Bermondsey Street, south-east London—
Saturday, July 14th

The fast click of boot heels on the wooden treads of the boarding-house stairs alerted Elidh to her father's return. From the sound of those clicks, he was excited and in earnest. That worried her. It usually meant he had concocted a new scheme to lift them out of the encroaching poverty of their life. Elidh set aside her mending and steeled herself for whatever came through the door. With her father, one never knew. Sometimes he brought home people, sometimes he brought home ideas. Once he'd brought home a monkey. She wished he'd bring home money. They could use some right now. She'd economised all she could and it still wasn't enough. Not for the first time, she wished her father could be normal, that he would get up in the mornings and go to a clerking job for the Bank of London. A man could make a hundred pounds a year clerking and there was security. A clerk worked for life, until he chose to quit.

Right now a hundred pounds a year sounded like a fortune to her. They could move out of the dingy boarding house, even out of the dockside neighbourhoods, to a cottage, perhaps in Chelsea. They could eat their own meals instead of the general fare served downstairs in the dining room where they ate with the other boarders. But her father wasn't a clerk. Clerking was beneath him. Just ask him. He was a playwright, the leader of an acting troupe. At least he had been three years ago, when her mother was still alive and every day had been full of adventure.

Her mother was dead now, lost to tuberculosis, and her father might as well be, too, stumbling through life without his wife, his love, his *raison d'être*. He had moments. Moments when he was inspired to write his next big play. The moments lasted a few days, long enough to conjure hope that this time it might end differently, that he might complete a work, that it might actually be good enough to sell. But it always ended the same way. Crumpled papers on the floor, a mad rage in which he declared his latest work was rubbish and he vowed never to write again. But that had to change. They'd been close to broke before, but nothing like this. There'd always been something to sell, something to be done to get them by. This time, Elidh wasn't sure anything would save them. There wasn't anything left to pawn, no prospects left to hope on that a play might be finished, that a patron might emerge to purchase it. She had counted their funds this morning.

Counting her recent payment from a dress shop that gave her piecework during the Season, they had enough to pay the rent for another month, but that was an unreliable source, petering out when the Season ended. Such inconsistency made for long winters. When the money gave out this time, she didn't know what would happen next.

The door to their rooms crashed open, her father waving a newspaper excitedly in one hand. 'I've found it, Elidh! This will be the making of us!' He thrust the paper at her. 'Read!'

Elidh took the newspaper hesitantly. It was fresh, newly printed. She thought of the coin that had been spent on this luxury, precious shillings that could have been hoarded against the inevitable. She scanned the page her father had folded back. Her brow furrowed. It was the society page. Gossip, all of it, most of it about a Sutton Keynes and his newly acquired fortune. The reported amount staggered her. Just moments ago, she'd been thinking a hundred pounds a *year* would be heavenly. Lucky him. 'I don't see what this has to do with us.' She passed the paper back to her father.

'Don't you see, Daughter? The bloke needs to marry, quickly, or his fortune is forfeit. He's holding a house party to find a bride. Anyone is welcome.'

A tremor of angst rippled through Elidh. What was he planning? Her father couldn't possibly be thinking of going? Of passing her off as bride material? Had he looked at her recently? She was plain: blonde hair, nondescript eyes that vacillated between hazel and brown. The most interesting thing about her was her name. A man who could pick anyone would definitely not choose her. He probably wouldn't even *notice* her. She took back the newspaper, scanning it once more. 'Anyone who fits the standards, Father,' she corrected, feeling more confident she could scrap his airy plans. 'He needs a woman with a title.' There was nothing her father could do about that. There wasn't a title anywhere in their family tree. He was a playwright, her mother an actress.

'Then we'll make one.' Her father turned about the room, dancing with his imagination. He snapped his fingers, inspiration finding him. 'I know—you will be an Italian *principessa*! Where is my map of Italy?' He opened one of the trunks crowded into their small space, doubling as storage and furniture. The scent of cedar filled the air as he rummaged. 'Ah, here it is.' He shut the lid and unrolled the map, reaching for a mug and a plate to anchor the sides.

'Father, what are you doing?' Elidh crossed the room cautiously, fearfully even. She hoped she hadn't understood him aright. 'I can't be an Italian *principessa*.' Surely he wasn't thinking they'd impersonate royalty?

His finger stopped at a spot of the map. 'There—Fossano. You can be the Principessa of Fossano. Now, let me see. You need a name.' He thought for a moment. 'Chiara di Fossano. Principessa Chiara Balare di Fossano. I think that has a nice ring to it.'

Elidh grabbed for the map and rolled it up in a fury. 'Stop! This is nonsense. You want me to impersonate an Italian princess?' There'd been schemes before, little scams on the road when the troupe had been short on coin, but nothing like this. This was madness even for him.

'It's not really impersonation, Elidh. I don't think Chiara Balare actually exists,' her father reasoned as if creating a fiction was somehow better than pretending to be someone else.

'That's not the point.' Elidh lifted the trunk and put the map away. She wished she could put her father's ideas away as easily.

'What is the point, my dear? This man needs a wife to claim his fortune and we need a fortune.' For a moment, the light left her father's dark eyes. They were sober and sad. 'Don't you think I know how close we are to the edge? This time, we might very well fall off.' He took her hands and turned them over, surveying her palms. 'Thank goodness you haven't stooped to doing other people's laundry. Your hands aren't ruined. It would give you away immediately.'

Elidh sighed, summoning her patience. How like her father. Serious one minute and back to his schemes the next. It had been an enchanting quality in her childhood. It had made every day part-adventure, part-fairy tale. Her world had been magical. It wasn't any more. The enchantment had worn off long ago, leaving the realities of poverty and hopelessness in its wake. It was up to her to be the voice of reason. She took her father's hands and led him to a trunk. 'We have to think about this logically. To start, the premise is madness. You want us to infiltrate a party for nobles and impersonate Italian royalty.' Couldn't he hear the prepos-

terousness of his own suggestion? What he proposed
was impossible.

'We've done such things before, Elidh,' her father
chided as if *she* was somehow in the wrong. 'Do you
remember the time your mother and I pretended to be
an English lord and lady on a Grand Tour whose carriage had broken down?'

'Yes, of course I remember,' Elidh cut him off
swiftly with a polite smile. If he got to talking about
the old times, there'd be no reasoning with him. 'But
that was different. That was just for one night and it
was for a free meal.' Her father had promised to pay
once their luggage had been retrieved, which it never
was, and they'd scampered out of the inn before dawn to
avoid detection. 'This is about trapping a man into marriage.' There were so many things wrong with the idea,
she couldn't begin to put them into words. She began
with the most obvious. 'He'll be swarmed by women
who are actually eligible for the honour. The odds are
firmly against us, even if we were legitimately titled.
We can't risk so much on a gamble we have no hope of
winning. He wouldn't look twice at me and, if he did,
he'd look straight through me and know. I haven't the
demeanour.'

'The demeanour, bah! Do you remember when we
toured Italy, Daughter? We played all the places—
Naples, Florence, Rome, Turin, Milan.' She didn't
have the heart to correct him. They had played those
places. But not on the big city stages. The troupe
had roamed in their caravan through the countryside,

playing for various *conti* and *duchi* at their summer villas.

'I remember.' She remembered the warm nights, the lights in the darkness, the food, the wine. Her mother's laughter as she charmed the noblemen. Those were good times when she was innocent and thought they were untouchable. She wasn't so innocent any more.

'You spent the summer in Italy with nobles, you were sixteen then. You managed beautifully. It will come back to you and, if you make a mistake, you shrug and you say "it is different in Italy." Being foreign will cover a multitude of sins.'

'But not a lack of clothing.' Even if she could pull off the mannerisms, her wardrobe would give her away.

'Nonsense. We have your mother's costumes.' Her father rose and moved about the room, flipping open trunks as he went, pulling out gown after gown in a whirlwind of silks and satins emerging from their tissue wrappings until the little room was a harem of colours, rich and lush, at odds with the grey pallor of the walls. 'This one should do for an evening gown, there used to be a tiara that went with it.' He rummaged deep into the trunks. Out came the velvet sacks of paste jewels and headpieces. They winked and twinkled in the gloom, looking exquisite at a distance. Looking real. 'Rosie can help you alter them. She is still in Upper Clapton living with a sister. She can help us with costumes and maid duties. She played one often enough on stage, she should be an expert.' Rosie had been her mother's dresser and had played a maid both off and on stage.

Elidh was truly worried now. If her father was willing to alter her mother's sacred costumes, he must be desperate indeed, all that more committed to his latest scheme. When he had an idea, he clung to it with tenacity. It would make her job of persuading him that much harder. 'Father,' she warned, 'we'll never get away with it.' Perhaps the best way to reason with him was to play along, to pose obstacles carefully veiled as questions. 'I don't speak Italian, not much of it anyway.'

'No one else does either. They will compliment you on your English. Your accent was flawless when you played Juliet on stage in Tuscany that one summer,' her father said encouragingly, his eyes lighting again as he thought of the past. He held out his arms in an expansive gesture and turned about the room. 'Everything we need is here. We have all of your mother's costumes and our own ingenuity.'

Elidh tried one last time. 'Even if you are right, it's too much to risk on the hopes he'll look my way.'

Her father gave a nod and tapped a knowing finger to his temple. 'There's more than one way to win at this. We're not going solely for the young, rich eligible *parti*. That would be far too foolish. We will also be pursuing a patron. This party will gather the right sort of men I need access to in order to sell my play. If an Italian prince can convince them he's found an Englishman to rival Shakespeare, they'll listen.'

'But you don't have a play,' Elidh put in bluntly. This was getting crazier by the moment.

'Yes, I do. Nothing new, mind you, but I've given an old play a new title. It's been years since it was out and it was only performed on the Continent. I've been thinking I simply haven't had the chance to meet the right patron. After all, what sort of men buy plays in Bermondsey Street? My plan's not so risky now, is it? There's money to be made in the short term if nothing else, perhaps at cards if no one buys a play. I can wager some of our "jewels" for a stake.'

Dear heavens. Elidh wanted to reel and she was sitting down. Impersonating royalty, crashing an elite party, trying to court a wealthy man, trying to snare a patron, all the while fleecing people with the lure of false jewels on the side. Worst, her father was entirely convinced of his plan's merits. She could see it in his eyes. Elidh tried a new strategy. If she couldn't persuade him it was impossible to crash the party, perhaps she could persuade him about the dubious merits of actually succeeding. Success was not without consequences.

'It's mad genius to be sure, Father,' she said sweetly. 'Have you thought what happens, though, if we succeed? I would be trapping a man into marriage.' Her father was a romantic at heart. He'd loved her mother deeply—surely such sentiment would work against him here?

'Trapping him? It would hardly be that,' he scoffed. 'Being alone with a man in a garden with the sole intention of being caught kissing him is a trap. But when a man invites women to his home for the express *and* overt purpose of taking a wife, that is not a trap any more than the entire Season in London is a trap. Society doesn't call it the Marriage Trap, they call it the Marriage Mart. This is no different.' He wagged a finger at her. 'And we are no different, miss, than anyone else attending the party.' He talked as if going was a foregone conclusion.

'We'd be impersonating royalty,' Elidh reminded him once again. It was so easy to overlook that one detail amid all the madness surrounding it.

'If you think anyone going to the party is really being themselves, you're more naive than I thought.' Her father frowned. 'Those guests might bring their own names, but they'll be impersonating their better selves and leaving their real selves at home. Those sorts always do.'

'Then I pity this poor Sutton Keynes,' Elidh said defiantly. 'He has to choose from a room full of frauds and that's no choice at all. *If* he chose me, I'd be no different than them, a false front for someone he doesn't really know.'

'You see!' her father crowed. 'No different. That's what I've been saying. We're just levelling the playing pitch. We'd be no different than anyone else there.'

'If you're right, he'll fall in love with a princess.'

'If I'm right, he'll fall in love with *you.*'

Elidh studied the newspaper. 'If you're right, I'll cost him his fortune. He would hate me for it. Saving his fortune is the whole motive behind his party.' All the more reason her father's idea was the height of madness. This Sutton Keynes couldn't afford her.

Her father's features softened and he looked at her

gently. 'A man who chooses money over my daughter isn't the right man for her. It's the classic quandary, isn't it? Love or money? It's the stuff playwrights dream of.' Her father sighed happily, already imagining a hundred plots he would never write.

Long shadows filled the room. Elidh moved to light their candle stubs. She stopped to open the window and put out a dusting of breadcrumbs for the birds who gathered on the little sill. If she didn't go with him, she feared he'd go alone and goodness knew the trouble he'd get into without her.

'What's the worst that can happen if we try?' he cajoled as she worked about the room.

Elidh paused and looked up from the candles. 'We end up in Newgate? Fraud *is* a crime.' They'd be committing it on so many levels.

Her father looked thoughtful, hands folded across his stomach. She thought she might have reached him at last. 'We might end up there or somewhere like it anyway if we do nothing. If we stay the course, we are certainly doomed, Daughter, for the workhouse, for the streets.' He shook his head. 'We have nothing to lose as it is. We have to try. It's all we have left. Your mother would expect it of us. She wouldn't want us to give up.'

Her mother wouldn't want them defrauding an innocent man either. Elidh was sure of that. Well, *fairly* sure of that.

He met her gaze sombrely. 'I haven't anything left to give you but this one chance. I couldn't save your mother, I couldn't save the troupe, but maybe I can save you. Win this man's heart and you will have your freedom from penury. You will have a life of luxury I could never give you.' He paused, his eyes watering suspiciously. 'I'm not getting any younger. Last winter showed us both that. I want to know you're taken care of.' It was a lovely little monologue. Was he the actor in these moments or her father? It was so hard to tell. When she was little, she'd loved watching her parents on stage, playing out a scene from her father's latest work: her mother so beautiful and blonde, her father darkly handsome and intense. Even now, he could still deliver a speech with enough pathos to bring an audience to tears, even if it was only an audience of one.

'Don't talk like that, Father.' She couldn't bear the reality of his words. Elidh busied herself putting away her mother's costumes. Her father had nearly died last winter with a terrible cough that had lingered for months in his chest. What would happen if he took sick again this winter? What would happen if she lost him? He was all she had left. The thought was untenable.

It was a classic quandary indeed. What would *she* do for love? Would she risk it all on her father's mad plan? Not out of love for an unseen man with a fortune, but out of love for her father. She would risk for him what she would not risk for herself. But how best to do it? If her mother were here, she'd say to find the middle ground, that there were always more than two options to any dilemma.

Elidh put the last dress away, carefully tucking it into its tissues, her mind searching for that middle ground. She didn't have to win the bachelor's hand. She simply had to help her father secure a patron; if they could do that, perhaps it would prevent him from passing off fake jewellery as stakes at the tables. It seemed the best option. A patron's support would be enough to get them through the winter. She would worry about spring when it came. What harm could there be in the masquerade? It only had to last two weeks. Then the Principessa Chiara Balare di Fossano could disappear for good and no one would be the wiser. She turned to face her father. 'When do we leave?'

'In four days.'

Elidh nodded. 'You'd better call on Rosie, then. We have a lot of sewing to do.' It was a plan with flaws and consequences even if they succeeded, but she'd worry about that later, when and if they appeared. Now, she knew what she'd do for love and how far she'd go. All the way to Newmarket, apparently.

Chapter Four

Four days later, Principessa Chiara Balare di Fossano, accompanied by her maid and her father, Prince Lorenzo, stepped down from the hack that had driven them from the station in Newmarket, on to the hallowed grounds of Hartswood. Elidh had never been more nervous in her life. Perhaps it was fitting. This scheme was more outrageous than any other her father had cooked up. It was only right she should be more nervous. There was more to lose.

The concept of 'more' followed her everywhere like an unwanted stray. Her father was *more* audacious than he'd ever been, not only using their precious rent money for the carriage ride that took them from the station on All Saints to the estate, but he'd also purchased first-class accommodations for the journey from London and proudly introduced himself as Prince Lorenzo whenever asked. He reasoned no one would believe in a prince who travelled third class. If anyone made note of their arrival, he wanted to be prepared on all fronts. Elidh hoped they didn't regret the expenditure later.

Looking up at the sandstone façade of Hartswood, it appeared the audacity and luxury didn't end with her father. The estate was *more* opulent than anything Elidh had ever seen in England. That luxury was evident from the first turn into the long drive, featuring perfectly manicured lawns and leafy green trees overhead through which the sun filtered so artfully one had to wonder if the trees had been planted deliberately to get the effect. The circle at the end of the drive continued the theme, welcoming guests with an Italian fountain that burbled coolly in its centre while two sandstone staircases flanked the rising entrance to the double front doors of the estate, an elegant mix of English baroque and Italianate architecture.

The luxury didn't end there. Grooms had leapt to take the horses' heads as soon as the driver halted. A footman's hand had waited to help her down, his head respectfully inclined. There was no moment for hesitation or uncertainty on her part. Nerves or not, she was immediately 'on stage', immediately immersed into her role as the Princess, and no one assumed otherwise. Perhaps her father was right. People saw what they expected to see. Certainly, none of the servants suspected otherwise.

A maid was present to guide them up the staircases to the wide, cool, white-marbled entrance hall, through the house and out to the afternoon comfort of the back terrace. The walk itself was subtly orchestrated to show a guest the level of opulence they'd stepped into. Perhaps it was meant to remind everyone that despite the lack of a title, the Keynes family was not without funds.

It seemed she was not the only one with something to prove. Elidh filed the insight away for later.

She was grateful for her father's presence at her elbow. Whatever the message this home meant to send, it was intimidating to a girl who lived in a tiny two-room boarding-house suite on Bermondsey Street. Her father was, at least, known and familiar to her in this strange wonderland. 'Don't look around too much,' he whispered. 'A princess would expect such a setting. Our hosts are trying to separate the wheat from the chaff, Daughter.' He was playing his role of princely Italian royalty to the hilt, chin up, shoulders back, not a fearful iota in his gaze as they passed crystal-cut glass vases filled with armfuls of fresh flowers and open doors that allowed for surreptitious peeks into elegantly appointed rooms done in cool, pale colours.

Elidh could not argue with her father's reasoning. Out on the back terrace, young girls gaped shamelessly at the graduated water ladder running down the centre of the gardens, the strategically placed statuary, the topiary trees cut in animal shapes, the plants arranged in colourful designs to draw the eye. She thought their gaping could be excused. The garden was spectacular.

'Capability Brown's best work, I like to argue.' A stylishly dressed older woman with elaborately coiffed hair swanned up to them. 'The house has been in the family for three generations. I'm Catherine Keynes, Mr Keynes's mother and hostess for the party. Welcome to Hartswood.'

Elidh was immediately alert. Their hostess smiled politely, her tone gracious, but her eyes were sharp.

'Forgive me, I don't recognise you from London. You haven't been up for the Season otherwise I would know. I know everyone.' It was politely said, but the warning was unmistakable.

Elidh swallowed. This was their first test and their last if they failed it. But like any test, they'd prepared for it. They had a script, as her father liked to call it. He launched into that script now, bowing low and taking their hostess's hand. He was being lavish, placing a kiss on her knuckles, his eyes holding hers, his accent thick. '*Buongiorno*, Signora Keynes. The apology is all mine. I see we have come unannounced despite my best efforts. My note must have missed you in London. I am Prince Lorenzo Balare di Fossano. Please, allow me to present my daughter, the Principessa Chiara Balare.'

He relinquished her hand and swept their hostess another extravagant bow. 'We'd only just arrived in London when we saw the announcement and thought this would be a splendid opportunity to experience an English house party and to meet people.' He paused long enough to look troubled. 'I wrote, of course, enquiring about an invitation, but you'd already left. I hope we have not caused you any discomfort?'

It was cannily done; his wording already implied their appearance had been accepted. Elidh felt Catherine Keynes's gaze sweep her, assessing her from the wide straw brim of her hat to the peeping toes of her shoes, dyed to match her gown. She'd dressed carefully for this first impression in an afternoon gown of robin's-egg blue trimmed in expensive falls of cream lace at the short sleeves and a wide band of matching grosgrain ribbon at the waist. Rosie had outdone herself on this one. The transformation had astonished even Elidh. The fabric from her mother's Lady Macbeth dinner gown combined with yards of lace from one of Titania's filmy peignoirs. She was accessorised from head to toe, with tiny gold flower-shaped bobs at her ears, to the hand-painted fan at her wrist and the white sheer shawl looped through her arms. Nothing had been overlooked. She appeared both refined and fresh. Elidh wished she felt that way, too.

Assessment flickered in Catherine Keynes's sharp eyes. Elidh could see her weighing the advantages to an additional guest who was both pretty and hopefully as polished as she looked. Elidh held the woman's gaze with a confident smile, the sort of smile a princess would use, who did not doubt her acceptance anywhere. Catherine Keynes smiled back before she transferred her attentions to Elidh's father. 'It is no trouble at all, Your Highness.'

'Call me Prince Lorenzo, *per favore*.' Her father smiled graciously as if he was doing his hostess a favour by appearing at her party instead of discommoding her and creating the impossible task of finding two more rooms in a home that must already be filled to bursting if the number of girls on the back terrace was any indicator.

Catherine Keynes smiled, warmly this time, charmed by her father. 'Allow me to introduce you to some of our guests. Rooms will be ready after tea. You will have a chance to meet my son at supper tonight. We dine at eight, with drinks in the drawing room at seven.'

They had passed the first test. A bubble of elation welled up inside Elidh. But that elation was short-lived. The prize for winning entrance to the party was to be bombarded with a barrage of names and faces to remember. Lord this, Lady that, Miss Sarah Landon with blonde ringlets in the frothy pink gown, Lady Imogen Bettancourt in the peach confection, Miss Lila Partridge in blue, the Bissell twins, Leah and Rachel, both in a lime-green muslin dotted with cool white flowers. The list went on, and those were only the lovely girls. There were the requisite mothers, but there were men, too. Brothers, uncles, fathers, cousins, who had come as well to perhaps lend additional credence to their female relations' claims of eligibility. In short, a daunting field. The finest young girls in England were here, in a daunting home, undertaking a daunting task for which the outcome would be a single victor.

Well, it was a good thing she and her father had other goals to accomplish here. With so many pretty girls on hand, Elidh knew she didn't have a chance, even if she'd wanted one. Now, her father would know it, too. He'd have to recognise their first priority needed to be securing a patron now that they'd seen the field first-hand.

When their rooms were prepared, Elidh was more than ready to seek the sanctuary of hers.

Rosie was waiting for her, unpacking trunks. 'Did

you see him, yet?' She was vibrating with excited energy as she shook out a dinner gown.

'No, we won't see him until supper.' Elidh untied her hat. 'That's better. All these clothes are so hot. Help me get out of this dress.' She looked about the room as Rosie worked her laces loose. Even on short notice, the room carried the same opulence displayed throughout the house: pale blue walls, yards of flowing sheer white curtains at the long windows, wainscoting at the ceiling finished with intricately carved cornices, plush carpet beneath her feet, and a bed to die for—crisp linen, soft pillows, and a silk coverlet in easy-to-stain white, the ultimate in luxury.

'There's even a little chamber off your room for me to sleep in. My own room. That's so much better than sharing a bed with my nieces in Upper Clapton,' Rosie confided. 'I've never seen a place so posh.'

'I haven't either.' Doubt swamped Elidh. 'Do you think we're in over our heads, Rosie?' They could still pull out, leave at any time. There were numerous excuses they could give. It wasn't too late.

Rosie gathered up her gown and winked. 'Being in over our heads is half the fun. We'll manage, you'll see.'

'You're as crazy as my father.' Elidh stretched out on the bed.

'Maybe so, but he hasn't ever let us down,' Rosie answered. Elidh thought that was debatable. She supposed it depended on how one looked at it. Rosie began going through the wardrobe, sorting through the newly unpacked gowns. 'Do you remember when the troupe was in Prussia and the axel on the wagon broke?' She did remember, it had been November and there'd been an early snow. 'We had no money for rooms and repairs, so your father arranged for us to perform at the tavern in exchange for room and board. We never went hungry even when our pockets were to let.' They'd slept in the hayloft, all of them crammed together. There'd been little comfort and less privacy, as Elidh recalled. She'd picked hay out of her clothes for days afterwards. 'We always managed.' Rosie sighed with nostalgia. 'Now, what shall we wear tonight? I'll need to get it pressed and these new skirts with their yards and yards of fabric are the very devil.'

Elidh laughed. 'Spoken like a true lady's maid. You pick. You'll know what's best.' She would like to share Rosie's nostalgic view of the past. Once, she had done so, but from the vantage point of the last few years, all she could see was how close to the edge they'd lived, how risky the adventure of their lives had always been. There'd never been a time of plenty, of ease, where there wasn't a need to think about where the next meal came from. She envied the girl she'd once been, who hadn't feared that uncertainty, who hadn't been bothered by the unknown.

Elidh rolled to her side and stared out the window, listening to the ripple of the water ladder in the garden below. When had she changed? When had any risk become too much risk? When had she begun to crave certainty and stability? Goodness knew she wouldn't find any of those things here. This whole scheme was the antithesis of all that.

'What do you suppose Mr Keynes will be like?'

Rosie asked from the wardrobe. 'Do you suppose he's handsome?'

'He's certainly arrogant, to think he'll find a bride in two weeks.' Elidh sighed. 'He's audacious, too. How could he be otherwise, Rosie? I can't imagine a serious man engineering such a spectacle, not that I need to worry. He won't look twice at me, not with a house full of lovely girls.' The sooner Rosie and her father accepted the fact that she couldn't compete, the sooner they could set aside their fanciful notions.

But Rosie was undeterred. 'There will be no talk of defeat, not so soon and with a closet of new dresses waiting to be worn. Don't count yourself out yet. Now, come sit and let's start to work on your hair for dinner. You have to give old Rosie a chance to work her magic and you might just be surprised.'

'We have unexpected guests.' Sutton's mother met him in the hall outside the drawing room where the company was gathering before dinner, her voice low as she imparted the news. 'Italian royalty have arrived. I'll have them vetted of course. I'll make enquiries immediately.'

'I don't like surprises.' He'd had enough of those this week to last a lifetime.

His mother shot him a sharp look. 'You wouldn't be surprised if you'd been here to greet them.' He'd spent the afternoon in the dairy and the stables, pointedly avoiding the company converging on Hartswood until the very last minute, which was fast approaching. At the stroke of seven it would all begin—the countdown to his wedding.

'Why are they here? Does the Principessa want to try her luck?' Sutton joked drily with a nod towards the drawing room. How odd to think his future bride was in that room right now and he had no idea who she would be. The thought was enough to unnerve him.

'Hardly. They assure me they are here to experience an English house party. They saw the announcement in *The Times*.'

'How intriguing. Guests who aren't interested in the fortune.' Sutton held out his arm to his mother. 'Shall we? I can't put it off any longer.'

He halted at the doorway, taking in the scene before him, the drawing room so full of guests it might have been a ball. There was no question of the dining room accommodating everyone. Dinner would be served in the ballroom tonight at round tables of eight. His popularity had outstripped the capacity of traditional dining arrangements. He patted his mother's hand. 'You've done well. I think every eligible girl in London is here.'

She smiled up at him. 'And then some. The footmen have already evicted six ineligible candidates whose family trees weren't quite as strong as they purported them to be.' She shook her head. 'Granddaughters of earls simply won't hold up to scrutiny if your cousin contests the will or your marriage. We need the daughter of a titled father, a very clean, direct, connection. That's trouble we don't need.' She grimaced. 'Speaking of trouble, has there been any word from Baxter yet?'

'No.' But Sutton feared Baxter had eyes and ears at

this party and that his cousin was merely waiting for
him to single out a bride before he made his move. 'But
we'll see him before this is done. He won't let the money
go without a fight.' Sutton surveyed the room, taking
in all the girls, all of them looking frightfully young
and frightfully alike. 'Which one is she, do you think?'

'Your wife?' His mother laughed.

'No, the Italian Principessa.' He paused, his eyes
lighting on the woman by the long window; blonde
hair done up in artfully braided loops, her posture
straight, her gaze fixed on a point beyond the room as
she looked out into the gardens, and that dress, red—
startlingly so—against the backdrop of the room's virginal palette. There was something about her that made
his heart pound, as if she, too, were somehow apart
from this world he was forced to inhabit and he knew.
'It's her. That's the Principessa.'

'Yes, and she's not for you, my son. Come, let me
introduce you to the others.'

Sutton spent the next half-hour of drinks in the
drawing room, smiling and bowing to all the darling
daughters. There were plump ones, thin ones, blondes,
brunettes, redheads; girls with curls, with straight,
silky tresses; girls with blue eyes, brown eyes, pink
dresses, yellow dresses, satins and silks. The array
was dazzling, overwhelming. His drawing room was
crammed with girls waiting to meet him and his fortune. Not one of the girls held his attention. His attention was free to wander about the room at will. And it
did, stopping frequently on the slender, blonde woman

by the window, who stood alone sipping sherry in that stunning red dress.

By the time the butler summoned them for dinner, he'd come to a disappointing conclusion: as different as they were in appearance, the girls all shared two things in common—they giggled at everything he said even when it wasn't particularly witty and they all wanted his money.

'Give them time, Sutton,' his mother cajoled, reading his mind as he took her into the ballroom for supper. They'd decided beforehand that it would be an unfair advantage for him to take a girl into dinner the first night. 'The girls are young. The stakes are high for them. Their parents are watching their every move.'

'Once I see them in their natural habitats, playing the pianoforte or games, or picnicking, they'll start to act more like their true selves? Is that it?' The words came out more cynically than he intended.

'Dear lord, Sutton, "their natural habitats"? Really? You make this sound like a zoo.'

'Tell me I'm wrong.' He was starting to think his fabulous idea of a house party was a mistake and now his ballroom was full of dinner tables and moon-eyed girls. He'd never wanted to be back down in his stables so badly.

She tapped his sleeve with her fan as he walked her to her place. 'Cream will rise to the top, dear boy, just wait and see.' Sutton hoped there was enough time. In his experience at the dairy, cream took a while to separate. He wasn't sure he had that much time.

Sutton made his way to his table, disappointed to

find himself boxed in by Miss Lila Partridge on his left and Miss Imogen Bettancourt on his right, their beaming parents beside them ensuring his attention remained fixed on their daughters. A quick glance around the ballroom revealed even more disappointing news. The elusive lady in red was seated at a table near the door, lucky her. She could escape. He watched as she smiled to her tablemates, laughing as she leaned close to the gentleman beside her. She might be having the best time of anyone present and she was clearly not interested in him, not in the least, which suddenly made her, without doubt, the most intriguing woman in the room.

Chapter Five

The first thing Elidh noticed about Sutton Keynes was that he wasn't interested: in dinner, in the women around him, or in any of the proceedings. He most decidedly didn't want to be here and, unlike her, he was doing nothing to hide his displeasure over the situation. He was not the showman she'd anticipated. While she laughed and flirted and interspersed her comments with a handful of Italian exclamations, pretending to enjoy herself, he sat woodenly at his table, surrounded by pretty dolls who catered to his slightest indicator of interest.

He might as well have been a doll himself for all the responsiveness he showed. A very handsome doll, though. He had his mother's dark honey hair, thick with a hint of a wave that saved it from being straight. The candlelight in the ballroom picked up the honey hues, causing them to wink temptingly like veins of gold in a mine. And an open face. She liked that. The firm mouth, the strong nose, the eyes that expressed exactly how he felt at being here. Trapped. She couldn't see the colour of his eyes at this distance, but she could see how they felt. They were restless, always scanning the room as if he were seeking a way out.

It was an outlandish thought that made no sense. Why would he be wanting to escape his own party? A party he'd planned for the express purpose of finding a wife? If it was not escape he sought, perhaps it was a particular woman he was looking for? His gaze quartered the room again and Elidh felt a little rill of awareness tremble down her spine, accompanied by the sensation that he was looking for her. It took all her bravado not to sink down in her chair, to keep her eyes and attentions fixed on the men at her table, all of whom might be candidates for her father's play.

She'd felt his eyes on her in the drawing room, his gaze coming back to the window where she'd stood. She'd been careful not to turn around or to cultivate his attention just as she was careful now to be immersed here at her own table. Should he look in her direction, he would see a woman who was enjoying a good meal in a beautiful setting, and enjoying her popularity at her table, giving no thought to her wife-hunting host. But in both cases, it seemed her attempts to keep herself separate from the cluster of girls around him had created the opposite effect. Even now, she could feel his gaze stop on her table. She must put herself beyond his reach. Surely he would forget all about her soon enough if she wasn't there to be remembered, especially with so many other girls clamouring for his attentions.

Elidh rose from the table. The delicious supper was coming to a close and she felt a keen need to escape their host's gaze, keen enough to risk violating tradition. A lady didn't dare leave the table before the hostess gave the signal, but perhaps with the unconventional seating arrangements and her own table so close to the door, no one would notice. She chose to risk it. 'Gentlemen, if you will excuse me a moment. I feel slightly faint and in need of some air after such a lovely meal.' Eight courses. She and her father had never eaten so well. Sometimes they had eight meals all week.

Outside the ballroom, Elidh searched for a door, an exit, anything that led to fresh air and privacy. When she didn't find one, she settled for a velvet bench set before a large window at the end of the dark hall. No one would notice her there unless they were looking. She needed a moment alone, a moment to think before the post-supper activities began. Sutton Keynes's visual attentions had unnerved her. Perhaps she was being overdramatic. Perhaps she'd even imagined them simply because they were the one thing she didn't want. That was the deal she'd made with herself, despite her father's wishes.

She was here to help her father find a patron. Nothing more. As the Prince and Principessa, they could sing her father's praises incognito, secure a patron and disappear, resurfacing for the patron as themselves. The patron need never see the Italians again. Sutton Keynes's attentions made the latter harder to do. If he fixed his attentions on her, disappearing became not only a difficult feat, but a potentially dangerous one.

Perhaps she could blame tonight on the red dress and

Rosie's artful design of braids. She'd hardly recognised herself when she'd looked in the mirror. *That* woman had been stunning—sophisticated, self-assured. That woman could charm a patron and she had. She could not have done otherwise. She needed the gown, the hair, and the cosmetics to charm the table, to do her duty to her father and to herself. Their survival through the winter would depend on their success here. The gown had succeeded admirably in that regard. Men had been hard pressed to look away. Apparently, even Sutton Keynes, despite the fact they'd been seated on the opposite side of the ballroom.

Yes, that made sense. Tonight was all because of the dress. Without the red dress, she would likely have been invisible. Tomorrow, dressed in pastels like the other girls, she would not stand out and Keynes would forget about her. Elidh closed her eyes and drew a deep breath, starting to feel better. She would give herself just a few minutes more of solitude and she'd go back to the party. She was seeing trouble where there was none. She'd conjured a crisis when the man hadn't even crossed a room to meet her. He hadn't even spoken with her yet and it would stay that way.

'I thought I might find you out here.'

Elidh stiffened at the low voice in the dark. She was alone no longer. She opened her eyes slowly, careful not to jump or to show signs of being startled, careful to buy herself time, time to remember her role, time to hide her fear. A princess was never startled. A princess had the right to be wherever it was she wanted to be. Only guilty people startled when they were found in places they weren't supposed to be in. But there was no hiding the surprise from her eyes when she saw who was standing there: Sutton Keynes in all his restless-eyed glory.

'You've picked a beautiful place to hide. The view is lovely in the evening with the moon out and the lanterns lit.' He was so much taller close up. His shoulders broader, his face more handsome, his mouth friendlier than it had been at a distance, the woodenness of him gone, perhaps because now he was smiling. *At her* and it was dazzling. He bent forward in a bow. 'A rose for a rose,' he said gallantly, offering her his plucked offering, liberated from one of the centrepieces that decorated each table. 'You are a veritable rose in bloom tonight. I apologise for not introducing myself sooner.'

That was her invitation, her *cue*. Dear lord, it was show time, the curtain was going up on the next scene of this foolish play her father had crafted, and she wasn't ready: not for the azure eyes that sparked like flames in the dusky hall, or the commanding height of him, or that smile. She'd expected an arrogant man and she'd planned on not being attracted to him, because she couldn't be. She would garner a patron for her father and leave. She was not playing the same game as her host and as such, she was not prepared for this. She was a two-week wonder, nothing more. And yet, she could not deny the thrill that coursed through her as she took his rose. Perhaps this was how Cinderella felt in the story when the Prince had approached her at the ball—delighted, even knowing that the moment couldn't last, but excited at the idea of it all the same.

Elidh gathered her wits. This was no fairy tale. Later, when this scheme of her father's was finished, she could look back on the encounter and indulge in it. But not now. Now, she had to think and act like a princess. A princess wouldn't sit here and gape as if a handsome man had never spoken to her. A princess would take his attention as her due. 'Shouldn't you be in the ballroom with the others instead of playing truant in the hall?' she teased, once more the vivacious, confident woman from the table.

'Shouldn't *you*?' he responded easily, his blue-flame eyes turning merry. 'I think your table finds itself duller for the lack of your company.' So he had noticed. She'd not imagined it.

The hallway suddenly seemed overheated. Elidh flicked open her fan. Perhaps she could appear cool if she felt cool. 'My table will survive. *You* will be missed. I will not be. I dare say the ladies in the ballroom would be glad for one less woman in the room.'

'They will understand that I am the host and it's my duty to greet all my guests. If I am out here in the hall chasing you down, it's because you've eluded me, or is it that you've *avoided* me, Principessa?'

Elidh fluttered her fan, managing a look of sophisticated amusement. '*Allora*, an introduction is superfluous, then. You already know who I am and I already know who you are.'

'You have not answered my question, Principessa. Are you avoiding me?'

'You are already surrounded by so many admirers, you hardly need to add one more.' Elidh snapped her fan shut and speared him with a piercing stare full of haughty, royal contemplation. 'So, I will hazard another reason for your presence in the hall. You don't want to be in there. It's been written all over your face the whole evening. You were looking for a reason to escape and I gave you one.' Perhaps boldness would drive him into retreat.

Instead, the remark won her a laugh. 'You are beautiful *and* insightful, Principessa. I can see now why my mother thought you'd be a delightful addition to our party.' He offered his arm. 'Come walk with me and tell me how you find our part of the world. In exchange, I'll show you the portrait gallery, it's just up ahead. If you'd kept going, you would have run into it.'

Her mouth went dry at the request. Any other girl in the ballroom would have craved such an opportunity. But to her, it was a reminder of how real the game had become and how fast. 'Are you sure that's wise?' Elidh asked, but she was already slipping her arm through his and strolling down the corridor away from the faint clink of dishes and the murmur of indistinct conversation.

He arched a slim, dark brow. 'I don't know. Are you planning to compromise me?' It was a wicked joke. He lowered his voice to a mock whisper of conspiracy, making fun of the game he'd devised himself. 'I do suspect some desperate sorts might try, but not on the first night when everyone considers themselves still in the running.' It was further proof for her claim that he didn't want to be here, that he'd been looking for an escape. But still, how odd to have designed a scenario one loathed and then forced one's own self to play along with it.

He leaned close to her ear and she breathed in the pleasant scent of sandalwood and basil, all man and summer. It was enough to intoxicate any girl. Even her, Elidh feared. 'Perhaps I should tell you, Principessa, we have taken every security measure to ensure such a mishap doesn't happen. There are guards posted outside my bedchamber so that I am not surprised upon retiring. I assure you, that's not usually the case for most English house parties. Quite the opposite, in fact.'

His whispered confession coaxed a laugh from her. 'A necessary but unfortunate precaution under the circumstances, I'm afraid,' Elidh paused, remembering an incident from their travels. 'And not quite as unique as you might think, if that brings you any consolation. There was a *duc* we knew who had guards posted day and night outside his daughter's bedchamber the week before her wedding for fear of a kidnapping attempt by his rival.' The story was true, only the implications he'd draw from it were false. They hadn't been guests, but paid workers hired for entertainment. She gave a light laugh, enjoying too much the refreshing boldness of her role. The Principessa was a vivacious, charming young woman, so much fun to portray, so different than the self plain Elidh showed the world. It was like the inside of her had come to live on the outside. And yet, she must be cautious. Mr Keynes needed a reminder about her unsuitability.

She gave him a soft, reassuring gaze. 'You may rest easy, Mr Keynes. You needn't fear such antics from me. I will make no move to compromise you.'

He smiled, warm and charming, so charming she forgot to be nervous. After the woodenness he'd displayed at dinner it was surprising to find he could put a girl at ease. 'No, not from you. Perhaps that's why we're strolling the portrait gallery. I have nothing to fear from you. My mother said you were here to take in the house party, nothing more. Is that true?'

Elidh sensed a test in those words. His eyes were steady on her, looking for affirmation as he continued. 'You, Principessa, are a safe harbour in a veritable storm of female attentions.' There was a rueful tone about him now, as if he regretted the safety of her, as if he wished she might pose more of a danger to him. If he only knew, she was quite dangerous to him, to his fortune, more danger than he wanted in fact if he chose to pursue her. But that was not her intention, to encourage that pursuit. She would keep both of them safe by establishing her distance.

She faced him with another soft smile, making the implication of her words sound reassuring instead of cruel. 'It seems we are in agreement, then. You are safe for me as well.' Sutton Keynes would know precisely what she meant by that safety, that a title as lofty as hers could not be courted by a man who had only a fortune to offer. The Keynes were wealthy gentry and soon to be even wealthier, but they were not titled and they were not Italian. Her father would be reeling if he knew how the ruse he'd designed to attract the wealthy bachelor was now being used to push him away.

But subtlety was not her friend. If Sutton Keynes knew what she intended in that message, he did not let on. Instead, he held her gaze with blue eyes that sent butterflies fluttering in her stomach. 'What do you mean by that, Principessa?'

She was going to have to be blunt, and she would be, right after she calmed those butterflies. Elidh looked down where her gloved hand lay on his dark sleeve. It was not hard to feign a moment of awkwardness. Other than on stage with people who'd been like family to her, she'd never been this close to a man before, never flirted on her feet. She'd always had a script telling her what to do. But she was on her own in the hallway. 'Surely you already understand, I could never consider entertaining an offer such as the one you need to make at the end of the party.'

There. The words were out, gently spoken, and all the tawdry unspoken implications that went with them: that aside from the difference in their stations, his search for a wife in this manner was scandalous to a well *and* high-born girl of her rank, and that the conditions surrounding the attainment of his money were even more so. She was firmly waving him off, knowing that any girl in the ballroom would gasp at treating the rich Mr Keynes in such a manner. Then again, they'd come to play his game. She had not.

To his credit, Mr Keynes took the rebuke smoothly, as he apparently took all things, except ballrooms full of girls he'd invited but appeared not to want. 'Of course not. I would not think to presume. I appreciate the clarification.' He cleared his throat. 'May I ask, Principessa, are you always this plain-spoken?'

She glanced up with a coy smile on her lips. 'A necessary measure for one in my position, Mr Keynes. I find it prevents unpleasant surprises, much like your bedroom guards.'

'Touché.' He pressed his free hand over his heart in an exaggerated gesture, his eyes laughing as if to reassure her she had not truly hurt his feelings. 'Now that's settled, we can move on with our evening. Might I persuade you to call me Sutton?'

'Familiarity is dangerous, Mr Keynes. I thought we had established that,' Elidh cautioned.

'We've already established there is no danger here. We said nothing about first names,' he countered easily. 'Besides, I'm about to show you my…ancestors. Surely one can't get more familiar than that.' He was a dreadful tease. For a man who gave the appearance of eschewing crowds, he was extraordinarily confident and funny when he was alone. Yet one more thing she could add to the list of items she knew about Sutton Keynes. He was a charming man possessed of a sense of humour, who'd arranged a party he didn't want. There was a mystery in that. If she was smart, she would leave it alone. To solve it would be to know him and to know him might lead to other things she'd not come here for. She'd do best to leave the mystery alone, make her excuses and walk back into the ballroom. But that's not what Cinderella had done and it wasn't what she was going to do either. This was a moment out of thousands. Surely it would not endanger her masquerade entirely if she prolonged that moment, just this once.

Elidh laughed up at him. 'Well, if we're about to view your *ancestors*, you should call me Chiara.' She would take the middle ground and enjoy this interlude now and worry about it later.

He led her through the gallery, narrating with dry humour as they went. 'Shall we start with my uncle, the man who's caused this whole mad tangle? That's him right there just to the left, Sir Leland Keynes, my father's brother. He was knighted for establishing a British presence in the extremely lucrative Soojam Valley of Kashmir, a place noted for its sapphires. Too bad he hadn't found some more. He might have been made baron and this whole fiasco could have been avoided.'

Elidh furrowed her brow. 'How so?'

He looked surprised for a moment and she worried over a misstep. Should she have known? Was the reason obvious to anyone but her? 'Because everything would have been entailed,' he explained, 'Nothing could have stopped my cousin from getting his hands on it. Not even if I married the Queen herself.' The bitterness was self-evident in his tone. She didn't understand entirely why. The gossip column had only provided so much detail.

They started to stroll again, moving on to the next portrait, this one of a great-grandfather on his mother's side. 'You make it sound as if you don't want the money.' Elidh slid him a sideways glance. She couldn't imagine not wanting that much money or the security that came with it. 'Or is it the marrying you're opposed to?'

'Both, I suppose, but especially the latter. I doubt any one of those women in there is interested in me. I am just the living embodiment of British pound notes.' He chuckled drily, but she could see the admission bothered him. 'I am sure you understand.' He sighed, his blue eyes seeking hers, two sombre flames. Oh, how that gaze seared her with its attention, its intensity, a slice of his soul on display. His voice was quiet, thoughtful. 'It's ironic. You are a stranger to me, entirely. But you are the only one here I can confess that to who would know how it feels to lose their humanity, to become a representation of something other than who they truly are.'

Elidh was silent. For a moment, she mistook his meaning and thought he'd somehow guessed her ruse and seen through the disguise. Then she understood and the knife of guilt twisted a little deeper. She'd not come here to mislead this man. She hadn't her father's nerves for deep schemes. She tried to push the guilt away. An attractive man was showering her with attention. But that only made it worse. He was showering the Principessa with attention. Sutton Keynes would never look twice at plain, twiggy Elidh Easton, a girl who knew nothing about titles and fortunes, who was, in fact, the embodiment of what he professed to hate: a representation of something other than her true self.

Chapter Six

She'd been worth leaving the party for. The promise of that red dress had not disappointed. He'd feared it might, that she might be all dress and nothing else— a red-silk illusion best enjoyed at a distance, like the other girls who had nothing on the inside or, worse, like Anabeth Morely, who'd been all kinds of soft and beautiful on the outside but cruel on the inside. She'd had no qualms about destroying a young man's heart.

They stopped before another portrait, this one of a funny-looking gentleman with a long nose, protuber-ant, froglike eyes and a powdered wig, a toad of a man in demeanour and build, but highly ambitious and re-sourceful. 'Randolph Sutton Keynes, my namesake of sorts. His service to King George I earned him this house. It certainly wasn't his looks.' He tried for lev-ity and fell short. She was withdrawing and had been since his remark about being an object. He couldn't blame her. It was hardly the sort of conversation one had with a stranger at a party, nor was it the sort of conversation he was used to having with others. As a rule, he didn't make a habit of self-disclosing.

'Forgive me, I've made you uncomfortable. I've taken terrible advantage of you with my maudlin sentiments.' He was doing it again. Pouring out his thoughts. 'It's just that everything has happened so fast. Last week I could take refuge in my club like any other gentleman. Then the announcement came out and now I can't step foot anywhere, my club included, without someone approaching me with an introduction, or producing another female to meet.'

What was wrong with him? He blamed it on the dark intimacy of the hallway and the emotions of the week, and her own, welcoming boldness, not that a gentleman should ever take advantage of such a trait. She'd been open with him and he had been open with her in turn. She made him feel as if he could tell her anything. Perhaps it was because she'd made it clear she was not interested in the game of the party. Or perhaps it was because she was a stranger, someone he'd never see again. Maybe, in some way, that made it easier to pour out his heart. He sensed she would never take advantage of that knowledge, never tell another soul. Whereas, if he told anyone else in the ballroom, the news would circulate within minutes. London couldn't keep a secret if its life depended on it.

'I don't mind, truly. You've barely had time to grieve your uncle and yet there are expectations that must immediately be managed, regardless.'

Sutton shrugged. 'I suppose you're used to managing such things all the time. Tell me, does it get easier? Meeting others' expectations for you?'

She looked thoughtful for a moment. 'No, it certainly doesn't, especially if you want to please everyone. You're always playing a part, always alone. It's easy to lose yourself, to forget who you are.'

Just listening to her lifted his burden. She knew. This beautiful woman knew precisely what he carried with him. 'Until last week, I was content being a country gentleman. I still would be, if the world would allow it.' What would she think of his camel dairy and his brood mares? Would she laugh at him? Would she find such humble ambition too far beneath her as Anabeth had? Or would she understand because she had quiet ambitions, too, ambitions that she'd laid aside because the world demanded it. He suddenly wanted to know what they were. 'What would you do if you could do anything? Be anything?' he asked in a husky whisper, letting the semi-darkness of the gallery weave a spell around them as he watched her gaze soften with thought, as if no one had ever asked her such a thing before. Perhaps no one ever had. Maybe one did not ask princesses such questions. Maybe he didn't deserve an answer.

At any rate, he wasn't going to get one. His mother swept into the gallery. 'There you are! I've been looking for you.' She smiled, but her gaze drifted to Elidh, critical and full of speculation before returning to her son. 'Dinner has lingered far longer than it should have. Everyone is waiting for a signal from you to start the evening entertainments. Some of the girls have brought their musical instruments to play while we gather in the gardens to visit.'

Sutton met her gaze evenly, silently asserting his authority. 'I will be along shortly once we're finished with the gallery.' It was clear she did not approve of his departure or his reason for it. But he was not a young boy who needed his mother's approval for every little action.

The Principessa was more congenial. She stepped away from him and smiled at his mother. 'Ah, an Italian evening, just like at home. How wonderful,' she effused with good grace. Keynes applauded her for it. Here was a woman would not be intimidated by a man's mother no matter how strong his mother's stare. It was a rare woman who did not find his mother overwhelming. 'I do so enjoy a beautiful summer evening in a garden with strolling minstrels. Excuse me, Mr Keynes. Perhaps we can finish the gallery another time? My father will be wondering where I've got to. It was generous of you to devote yourself so singularly to me.'

'It was my pleasure.' He bowed as the only pleasure he was likely to have tonight disappeared into the ballroom.

'I see you've met our Italian guest,' his mother said coolly once the Principessa's red skirts were out of sight and her ears out of range.

'She is quite charming...refreshing, even,' Sutton replied with equal coolness, not pleased with his mother's interruption. She had chased away the best part of his evening and signalled his return to the hell of the ballroom, to a reality that would be harder to endure now that he'd had a brief slice of heaven for company.

'Charming? Well, I suppose she's as charming as a woman in a red dress can be in a room full of pastels,' she replied archly.

'What is that supposed to mean?' Sutton felt defensive on Chiara's behalf.

'It means she is not for you.'

'She would agree with you. She spent most of the conversation, in fact, making that same point.' A point that had done nothing to deter him from finding her fascinating. She'd shown him empathy and humour. Even now, the story about the *duc* brought a smile to his lips.

'And yet *she* has your attention while a ballroom full of girls do not.' His mother's tone gentled. 'The others will be jealous. It will be difficult for them to see that you mean nothing by it.' There was warning and instruction in her words.

'Perhaps giving her my attentions will raise the bar,' Sutton mused out loud. 'If those girls want my attentions, they need to claim them. Maybe I went looking for the Principessa because she knows how to hold a man's interest. The others are all milksops, Mother. If I am out of sorts, it's because I've discovered I don't need a two-week house party to deduce that.' All he'd needed had been two hours. These girls were as pale as their dresses. Whereas Chiara was as vibrant as her red skirts, red lips. Red, the colour of caution, the colour of passion. The colour of life.

'I've never known you to be unfair, Sutton,' his mother

scolded. 'Give them time. They'll improve, but as an experienced man, you have to help them. It's a gentleman's job to show a young girl how to go on in the world, how to find her own confidence once she steps out of the schoolroom and into society. You can't expect them to be dazzling when all you do is glower at them,' she pressed. 'Try to understand the pressure they're under. They all want to win, but there's only one you.' *Win.* What an awful word. They wanted to win *him.* The great prize. Not a man, but a thing to covet.

'The pressure *they're* under?' Sutton bristled. 'What about the pressure I'm under? No one here understands that.'

'But the Principessa does? Is that it?' his mother challenged. 'How convenient for her. Think about that, my son, the next time she contrives to get you alone, no matter what her father claims their reasons are for being here.' Her gaze softened. 'You're wrong. *I* understand the pressure you're under. Your uncle has asked you to make an impossible decision in an indecent amount of time if you want to do the right thing and protect that fortune. But I *am* here to help.'

She reached into the hidden pocket of her evening gown. 'I've drawn up a shortlist of the most viable girls as you've asked. Perhaps that will help minimise the "milksops" you have to deal with. I've also arranged, per your instruction, to have these young ladies put in close proximity to you at meals and during activities, so that you may get to know them especially.'

Good lord, the list. That, too, seemed like a poor

idea now, since Chiara Balare's name was probably not on it.

She snapped the list open. 'Isabelle Bradley, daughter of a baron, Eliza Fenworth, daughter of a viscount. She's here with her brother. Virginia Peckworth, Southmore's youngest, Alexandra Darnley, Eagerly's oldest, Ellen Hines, Wharton's girl in her third Season. Wharton's desperate. Philomena Whitely, Viscount Sheraton's daughter, and Imogen Bettancourt, the Marquis's daughter.' Her nose wrinkled in worry. 'She's young—'

'Yes, very,' Sutton cut her off. 'I met Lady Imogen at dinner already. Her parents all but cut her meat for her.' He sighed in apology. He was seldom sharp, but the whole affair had put him on edge. He just wanted to be down at the dairy. It was deuced difficult to be here, but not be able to indulge in his usual activities. 'I am sorry to be gruff, Mother. I know you're attempting to help. I do thank you.' He reached for the list and folded it, trying for graciousness. 'I will spend time with these girls—meanwhile, I would like to add the Principessa to the list.'

His mother gave him a stare that conveyed without words the message, *I thought we'd settled that.*

'Why ever for? These girls can give you more than your uncle's condition for nobility. Some of these girls like Imogen Bettancourt can give you access to a seat in Parliament, a seat you can choose to fill as you like, if you want legislative teeth to take action against Baxter.' There was a vehement edge to her tone that said she was frustrated with him.

'Mother, I haven't forgotten.' This marriage wasn't

only about keeping his cousin from the fortune, it was about using the fortune to stop him and others like him once and for all. That fortune would go towards standing for election, campaigning for laws that would stop the black market trafficking, an issue that had been overlooked to date because it affected so very few and because it affected the poorest among them, those who couldn't protect themselves and had no recourse to protest.

'Good. Then you need to get out to the garden and take Lady Imogen for a walk while the musicians play. It's all been arranged.' His mother's own temper was simmering close to the surface, too. They were alike in that way. But she needed to realise he wasn't five any more. Lines needed to be drawn before this went any further. Helping him was one thing, dictating to him was another.

'Thank you, Mother. I appreciate the arrangement tonight, but I am a grown man. I don't want to give anyone the impression otherwise.' Mostly her. He might not have any say in the matter of his uncle's will and its conditions, but he'd be damned if he'd let his mother spoon-feed him a bride.

It might have been the sense of rebellion his mother's assistance engendered in him, or it might simply have been the natural laws of attraction. Whatever the reason, Sutton could not take his eyes off Chiara. The more Imogen Bettancourt tried to make stuttering, youthful small talk as they strolled the lantern-lit garden, the more his eyes strayed to the Principessa.

He tried, truly he did, to give poor Imogen his attention. He asked questions but she had a habit of answering with a question of her own. If he asked what she liked to read she would say, 'I like to keep up on whatever is popular. And yourself?', until it became something of a private game to count how many times she used the phrase 'and yourself?' Meanwhile, Chiara was holding court at the fountain, a coterie of gentlemen gathered around her as the lantern light caught the facets of crystals in her tiara. What was she saying to those men to make them smile? To make them laugh? Was she telling them stories about guarded bedchambers?

'And yourself, Mr Keynes?' Imogen Bettancourt was gazing up at him expectantly with large brown eyes that reminded him of his favourite hound. She would be just as loyal and obedient, too, he was sure. She wouldn't know how to be otherwise. It wouldn't be a choice with her. She was trained for obedience, raised to it. Such devotion should inspire reciprocal devotion, but he'd missed her question. What had she asked him?

He brazenly overrode her question with an offer to disengage from the crowd. She would not miss the import of that, although she would misunderstand his motive. 'I was thinking, Lady Imogen, how much you might enjoy an evening tour of the topiary. They can be very beautiful by lantern-light, whimsical, I think.' He hoped that was the case. Perhaps away from the crowd, he would be able to focus more singularly on discovering Lady Imogen's charms without the distraction at the fountain. Despite his best intentions, his gaze managed one last look in Chiara's direction as they passed.

'He couldn't take his eyes off you!' Elidh's father slipped into her chambers as the hall clock struck one. The house had officially retired an hour ago, although Elidh wondered how many conversations just like this one were taking place in hushed bedrooms up and down the corridors; parents and daughters gathered to assess the fruits of the evening, to plot and strategise now that they'd seen the lay of the land. The Bettancourts were most certainly up and in alt since their daughter had been singled out for the evening walk.

'His eyes might have followed me, but he walked with Imogen,' Elidh reminded him before her father could celebrate too early. She didn't want to get her father's hopes up, especially when it would be for naught. She would continue to discourage Sutton Keynes if he persisted in seeking her out. She should have taken comfort in the sight of him with Lady Imogen. After all, she didn't want his attentions, yet Elidh couldn't deny there'd been a small sting of jealousy at the sight of them with their heads together, knowing Lady Imogen was breathing in the basil and sandalwood of his scent, knowing what it felt like to have his mouth so close to one's ear. Did Lady Imogen also feel that little trill of excitement as he whispered to her?

'He gave you a rose!' Rosie exclaimed, putting away the red gown. 'Was he handsome? Was he as arrogant as you thought?'

'Yes and no. He was handsome, but he was not arrogant. I was wrong about that.' Elidh played with the rose in her lap before setting it in a bud vase on her vanity.

Elidh looked around at Rosie and her father. They were all dressed for bed, Rosie in a simple, heavy cotton night-rail with a wrapper, her father in an elaborate damask banyan with a rolled silk collar and beaded pointed slippers that had once served in a production of *King Lear*. Each of them was dressed as befitted their stations, everyone acting their parts to the full. It reminded Elidh how deep their conspiracy went. Even in sleep, they couldn't let their guard down. Prince Lorenzo of Fossano wouldn't be caught dead in the drab grey-striped nightshirt her father wore at home.

No. Not home. They had no home any more. They'd given those boarding-house rooms up the day they'd left for Hartswood. There could be no going back because there was nothing to go back to. She hoped they weren't in over their heads. After tonight, she was more worried than ever before. 'How did the search for a patron go? I thought a few of the men at our table were promising.' That was the sort of talk she wanted to encourage, not discussion of Sutton Keynes. He was a pipe dream and she was glad her father had other reasons for coming. Tonight had shown her that in sharp relief. She had no hopes of winning Sutton and nothing to entice him with. It was more obvious to her now after an evening spent listening to men posturing and women jockeying for position. Everyone here had something to offer in exchange for Sutton's consideration: connections to power, connections to Parliament, investments, estates, land, even more money.

'Indeed, I think a few of them might be willing to engage a play for Twelfth Night, something to liven up their Christmas house parties.' Her father nodded. 'But we might not need them, not if Keynes keeps looking at you like he did.'

'I doubt that will continue. Lady Imogen's father is a marquis. He has political power,' Elidh said swiftly.

'Does that appeal to Keynes?' her father argued. 'We must discover what matters to him and then we cater to it. These people are indiscriminately throwing their merits before him and hoping something sticks. We will be more discerning, Daughter. We will discover what matters most to him and offer him that.' Her father smiled confidently.

Elidh found the prospect of deepening and pursuing that lie alarming. 'We don't have estates or seats in Parliament. We can't have the latter. We're supposed to be Italian.' They had paste jewels and trunks of remade costumes, hardly the stuff of enticement.

'Maybe what he wants most is not a thing at all.' Her father was not daunted. 'He walked with Imogen Bettancourt, but not because he enjoys her company the way he enjoys yours.'

Was that true? The alarms in her head rang loudly now. She'd glimpsed that man in the gallery, one who might indeed covet something different than a tangible thing. What had he said? *I doubt any one of those women is interested in me.* Only his money. That man had hinted at different expectations, different hopes for a marriage, that marriage might be a partnership of people and personalities instead of bank accounts and bloodlines. That man had her empathy and her concern. She needed to stay as far away as possible from him. She could not give him what he wanted. She would hurt him and that was not what she was here to do. She might be willing to go along with a scheme that netted them a patron for the winter, but she drew the line at hurting a man who didn't deserve it.

'As for estates, those can be fabricated.' Her father waved a hand as if he could conjure them out of thin air. 'We already have a villa in Sardinia for the summers. Delightful breezes off the sea. I may have mentioned it to Mrs Keynes during dessert.' He winked. 'She seems quite taken with Prince Lorenzo.' As did her father. Elidh hoped he'd remember the character was a fiction.

'Don't overdo it,' she cautioned. 'And remember to tell us what you invent so we don't confuse the facts.' Her father fabricated without worry, without concern for getting caught.

Her father rubbed his hands together, his face alert. 'Rosie, what's on the agenda for tomorrow?'

'Archery in the morning, then luncheon and a croquet tournament on the south lawn in the afternoon. People are drawing names for teams, the ladies' maids were all giggling about it below stairs tonight,' Rosie informed them. 'I've already laid out the white linen for tomorrow with the olive-green ribbon.'

'Perfect,' her father agreed. 'The Principessa would have done archery at our villa on Lake Maggiore.'

'Ahem. I am still here,' Elidh interrupted. They were arranging her like a player on a stage, blocking out her every move. 'It wasn't *our* villa on Lake Maggiore, it was the Duc's. We were merely invited to watch his sons shoot.' Sometimes she wondered if her father bothered to separate fact from fiction. The fiction came so easily to him. Maybe because the fiction was so much more pleasant.

'And they taught you to shoot afterwards,' her father added.

'I have shot precisely ten arrows in my entire life. That does not make me William Tell.' Any more than playing a princess on stage made her a princess in real life.

'Then, it provides a perfect opportunity to ask for help.' Rosie joined forces against her. 'It's a chance for a gentleman to have a legitimate reason to put his arms about a lady, his mouth close to her ear as he whispers instructions. Perhaps it's best if you don't know archery at all.' Rosie giggled like a schoolgirl and her father crowed. They were both enjoying this too much and at her expense. She'd never admit the thought of Sutton's arms about her brought a certain warmth to her cheeks. She didn't dare let the fantasy go any further. Tonight had been far enough.

Her father grinned confidently. 'Sit out the archery if you must. You'll redeem yourself at croquet. No skill necessary there. Just whack the ball with a mallet and stay as close to Keynes as you can.'

Chapter Seven

They were all cheating! It became quite evident half-way through the nine-wicket course of croquet that the female players were more interested in keeping their balls near Sutton's than going through the wickets and that the male competitors were patently ignoring such antics in the hopes of impressing a lady of their own. While such consensual conspiring certainly made Elidh's self-assigned task of avoiding Sutton easier, it did nothing for fair competition. The game itself had become nothing more than an excuse for men and women to be together.

She wasn't the only one who'd been encouraged by a parent to use the game to her advantage. It seemed every girl present had been counselled to do the same. Never mind that the party had been divided up into four teams, each team designated with a colourful ribbon tied around one's sleeve. Elidh was on the red team with Eliza Fenworth's brother, Louie, Michael Peckworth, and the lovely but shy Ellen Hines, daughter of Lord Wharton. Elidh's father was on the orange team and Lady Imogen had been relegated to the green team after having been awarded Sutton's attention for the morning of archery. Sutton was on the blue team with Philomena Whitely and Virginia Peckworth, who had, as best as Elidh could tell, been rotated in for Sutton's afternoon attentions. That didn't seem to be giving either girl any advantage. Girls assigned to other teams had not taken no for an answer.

Elidh blinked. Just a moment ago Lila Partridge had been standing by the tree at the edge of the course, quite alone in her exile where her ball had nearly gone out. Now, she stood to Sutton's left, significantly further up course and closer to their host. From the corner of her eye, Elidh caught the subtle swing of a skirt as Isabelle Bradley's hem discreetly covered Alexandra Darnley's ball long enough to give it a kick out of the way when Alexandra wasn't looking, only to have Alexandra slide her a venomous look. Retaliation wasn't far behind. On her turn, Alexandra opted to take aim for Isabelle's ball instead of making the wicket. With a solid whack, Alexandra sent Isabelle's ball sailing back towards the start, away from Sutton. Isabelle was effectively out of the game.

That seemed to give the other girls ideas. The area around Sutton suddenly became a veritable battlefield as the girls politely and with all the good breeding they possessed whacked away at their competition, sending ball after ball to other parts of the field. And poor Sutton! Elidh's heart went out to him, it truly did. He had to stand there, waiting his turn, making small talk with Virginia Peckworth, and pretend he didn't have a clue what was going on. All the while the girls made fools of themselves. It was an awkwardness only rivalled by Miss Peckworth's rather overt ploy for attention.

Virginia Peckworth frowned beside Sutton, asking him for advice with her brow wrinkled prettily as she contemplated her options for play. She begged Sutton to assist with her shot, knowing full well such assistance would require him to stand close behind her and place his hands over hers on the handle of the mallet. Elidh acknowledged it was a rather daring request on Miss Peckworth's part, but perhaps the girl reasoned it was a risk worth taking if it gave guests a chance to comment on how well they looked together or to whisper about what lovely children they might make. Indeed, Sutton with his height and his honey hair and Miss Peckworth with her own willowy height and dark hair looked quite handsome together. It was also a striking reminder to the other girls what they were up against when it came to superior looks.

Virginia said something over her shoulder to Sutton, something coy that came with a smile. She even gave a subtle wiggle of her hips as Sutton helped her line up the shot. It was a confident gesture, one that took full advantage of the situation. Elidh couldn't blame her. Miss Peckworth wouldn't be the first woman to make the most of croquet. That was one of its advantages, after all. Here was a sport men and women could play together out in the open and enjoy one another's company.

Who knew when Miss Peckworth would have Sutton's attention again? All the girls were eager for their turn and despite Catherine Keynes's best efforts to cycle the girls through, claim on Sutton's attentions had become nothing less than a free-for-all. The girls, it seemed, weren't willing to share or to wait for their turn. They were quickly taking matters into their own hands, or mallets in this case. It was further reason Elidh was glad she wasn't in contention. She couldn't compete in looks with Virginia Peckworth, nor was she mean enough to edge out another girl with deliberate sabotage. Surely her father would soon concede the best plan for the party was to simply engage a patron and leave. She could not compete with girls who'd been trained for the marriage mart since birth. Even if Rosie could turn her lovely with gowns and hairdos, she hadn't the 'skills' of a Lila Partridge or the 'tenacity' of an Alexandra Darnley.

Virginia made her shot, clapping wildly over her success and gushing over Sutton's part in it. Sutton managed a humble smile, either agitated or uncomfortable with the effusive praise, Elidh couldn't tell which. But she stared too long and Sutton's gaze caught hers. His eyes sent her a pleading a look. He was positively miserable. She smiled back in quiet commiseration.

It was her turn to play. Elidh picked up her mallet and considered the field. She'd been able to play well, probably because she'd concentrated on the game and not the man. As a result she was in the front of the field. She could either join the battlefield around Sutton and risk getting knocked out of the game or she could maintain her lead and take the final wicket. She smiled to herself. Maybe there was something she could do to liberate Sutton.

Her decision was made. Elidh lined up her shot with a coy look towards Lord Wharton, whose ball lay on the other side of her intended wicket, the only one standing between her and an unhindered pathway to victory. 'Lord Wharton, my apologies, but you are in my way.'

She cleared the wicket, knocked Wharton's ball and claimed a bonus shot. She cleared the next wicket and shot again through the double wickets baring the way to the finishing stake. She felt Sutton's eyes on her as Freddie Darnley called out, 'What will you do, Your Highness? Will you stake out or will you stay in play as a rover and help your team?'

'I'll play rover!' she declared, throwing a challenge of a smile in Sutton's direction. 'Never let it be said I left my team in distress.'

She was coming for his balls—his team's balls, that was. With a smile like that, it was the only conclusion a man could draw. The Principessa was on the warpath and charmingly so, flirting with each gentleman as she knocked them out of the way, blazing a path straight towards Sutton with a smile on her lips and laughter in her eyes. Was that smile for him or was it because he was the competitor who posed the greatest risk for her team? After last night, he couldn't be sure. She'd been clear about her position on this mad house party and on him. Yet there'd been a spark between them even as they'd set boundaries for their association. That spark was still there even if the red dress was gone.

Today, she'd worn white linen trimmed with olive-green ribbon, her sporting costume not unlike the other girls'. And yet he'd been aware of her. She had not blended into the background, proof that it hadn't been the dress alone that had drawn his eye, that his attraction to Chiara Balare was more than skin deep. That she was different.

'You wouldn't dare!' Sutton cried out good-naturedly as her ball approached, her intention to do damage clear.

'Oh, I would, Mr Keynes. Your ball threatens my teammate's.' She nodded with a laugh to where Louie Fenworth's ball lay on the lawn, just a strike away. 'Our team needs Mr Fenworth to score and he can't if you're in the way, or if you strike him on your turn.' She had a strong sense of strategy, of seeing the field as a whole. The idea that she would be magnificent at chess flashed through Sutton's mind unexpectedly. Around him, a few girls tittered nervously at the Principessa's bravado. While they had viciously dared to eliminate their competitors, none of them had dared to strike against him, even when it would have been in their team's best interest. Sutton knew why, of course. They didn't want to risk offending him or appearing unladylike. The Principessa needn't consider such things. She was free to be herself.

Prince Lorenzo strolled up, following his ball as it rolled to a stop beside Sutton's. 'Perhaps you'd like to rethink your play. If you knock him out now, Daughter, you will be in jeopardy from me.'

The Principessa laughed gaily at the teasing threat. 'I'll take my chances, Father.' Then she turned her attention to him one last time with a look that said 'beware' and sent her ball resoundingly into his while her team looked on with applause. 'Well done, Your Highness!' Louie Fenworth crowed, his own victory assured.

Well done indeed. Sutton grimaced. While Louie Fenworth was cleared to the final stake, his own ball rolled—no—*sailed* into the depths of the copse lining the edge of the lawn. That minx! 'I believe you've taken me out of the game, Principessa.' He gave her a small bow of good sportsmanship. 'If you will all excuse me, I must fetch back my ball.' *And if I have my way, I may be gone until dinner,* he added silently before it occurred to him that might have been what she'd intended all along.

She'd liberated him. But why? Was it only for the sake of the game or was there a larger reason? Was he reading too much into her choice because he wanted there to be a larger reason? This was why he eschewed society's games. They could drive a man to distraction with the need to always be guessing, always looking for the hidden nuance. The man who didn't look for such things made himself vulnerable. Animals were much more straightforward. When a stallion mated, there was no nuance.

Sutton had gone twenty-five paces into the woods, far enough back to be out of sight, when a cry of general laughter went up behind him from the game. Seconds later, a ball rolled past him, barely missing a clip to his ankles. A red ball. From the red team. Sutton smiled to himself. The Principessa was coming. Her father had made good on his threat. She'd be here any minute now. He trapped the runaway ball under his foot and leaned against a tree to wait.

She came crashing through the trees, laughing and breathless, and looking entirely lovely, entirely without artifice. 'Looking for something?' Sutton grinned and nudged her ball forward.

'Thank you.' She picked the ball up and brushed it off. 'It seems I'm out of the game, too.'

'Is that so bad? I was just thinking I should be thanking you. You've bought me a respite.'

She smiled her culpability. 'I thought you could use it. The girls were getting ridiculous. I caught at least one of them kicking their balls forward under the cover of their skirts.'

'Then they should be thanking you as well. You've saved them from making even larger fools of themselves.' Sutton doubted the girls would appreciate it, though, when Chiara's efforts resulted in taking him out of the public eye and putting him in her path alone. Any one of them would have given their right hand for a trip into the woods with him. How ironic it was that the one woman who claimed to not want such an advantage was the one who had it.

Silence drew out between them as both realised that irony. 'Well, thank you for finding my ball. I must return. Goodness knows what kind of trouble Mr Fenworth will get himself into if I'm not there to watch his back.' Chiara managed a laugh.

'Don't go. Stay.' The words slipped out before he could think better of it. 'Fenworth can take care of himself for a while.' Sutton pushed off the tree. 'But I'm not sure I can. My ball is still lost in here somewhere, no thanks to you, and so is yours.'

'What do you mean, mine is right—' The word 'here' died in a shriek as Sutton grabbed the ball from her hand with a grin and threw it deep into the woods. 'Sutton, what are you doing? It will take for ever to find it now!' she cried.

'That's the point. I'm giving you a reason stay.' He laughed. 'If you want it?' He felt young and carefree, like a boy in the woods with a girl for the first time. It had been ages since he'd felt that way. 'Come on, let's hunt some balls.' He held out his hand and she took it with a game smile. 'You called me Sutton just then. Might I hope that you've decided familiarity isn't so dangerous after all?' Being with her was intoxicating. He couldn't imagine any of the other girls using his first name, or teasing him, or knocking his ball out of play. In short, being themselves and letting him be himself.

So far, the caution in him warned. *What have you really shown her about yourself? What will she say when you do?*

'You're nothing like I thought you'd be.' Sutton helped her over a log. 'I thought an Italian *principessa* would be stuffy and arrogant. But here you are, tramping through the woods looking for croquet balls.'

What do you know of her? his conscience warned. *You know more about what she is not than what she is. It's a place to start, nothing more.*

She halted and stared at him, something inscrutable in her gaze. 'Are you disappointed?'

'No, on the contrary,' Sutton rushed to reassure her. 'I find it very refreshing to be with someone who is simply themselves. So few people are and no one here certainly is. They're too busy trying to be whatever it is they think *I* want them to be.'

A shadow passed over her face and she broke her gaze, directing her attention instead to a squirrel in the tree. 'Do you know me so well after only a day? There's still time, perhaps I will disappoint you yet.'

'I doubt that, Chiara. To disappoint, there would have to be expectations to begin with. We made it clear last night that between us there are none beyond the possibility of a fleeting friendship, if I am not too bold to suggest even that.' He stood close to her, following her fascination with the squirrel running the tree limbs. He could smell the unique scent of her, so fresh and crisp, like clean linen and apples. The smell was appealing after a day spent among the heavy floral fragrances of roses and lilacs liberally applied by girls who thought more was better.

'You are not too bold.' *Yet.* The quietness of her response suggested he was near the limits of that boldness, that they were flirting with something that might carry them beyond the borders of friendship. What would happen then? It made his pulse rush to consider the possibility: of taking her in his arms and kissing her, pulling out the pins one by one that held her beautiful braids in place, letting her hair spill over his arm, her body pressed to his.

He answered her in kind, his own voice matching the quietness of hers. The stillness of the woods created a sense of intimacy. They were alone in the world, the party momentarily forgotten. 'And if I *were* too bold?'

'Why would you be? There would be no purpose to it,' she answered firmly, not naively. She did not play the coquette like Virginia Peckworth who was looking to coerce a confession of love from him. Chiara was directness itself, a princess used to giving orders and being obeyed. 'We have already established there is no reason for "boldness" as you call it.'

'Perhaps because there is *no* reason. Perhaps because we are beyond it, we need not expect anything to come of it.' He paused. 'I did not think Italians were known for their directness.'

'Perhaps not in general, but I find it saves time.' Chiara's gaze slid his way. Despite her protestations that she was not here to play the marriage game, curiosity flickered in her eyes in answer to his unspoken question and he saw that she wondered, too. *What would it be like to kiss him? To be in his arms?* Proof that she felt it also, this pull between them. Was that pull the simple response to the pressures of the party and the belief those pressures didn't exist between them? That she could be his escape and he could be hers? Or was there something more to the pull? Something unique to them? They owed it to themselves to explore it.

His hands were at her shoulders, his mouth near her ear ready to make an overture. But she turned and pulled away. 'No, Sutton. It would ruin our "fleeting friendship".'

He chuckled, in part to hide his embarrassment over the polite rejection she'd just handed him. 'I think you might be the only woman at the party who doesn't want to kiss me.'

She laughed and reached for his hands. 'It's not that I don't want to. It's only that we don't want to find out, not yet anyway.' *Not yet.* There was hope, then.

She was right. He enjoyed her company. If he kissed her and there was no flare of passion, it would be disappointing. If there was a spark, it created other difficulties since nothing could come of it. Her decision was masterful. It created possibilities and prolonged the anticipation, while still rejecting him and giving him hope at the same time. A kiss would come. When? Tomorrow? Or the day after? Or the day after that? 'By chance, do you play chess?'

'No. Why do you ask?'

'Because I think you would be splendid at it. You're an excellent strategist.' His foot kicked at something near a tree root. 'Ah, we've found your ball.' She bent for it, but he was too quick and snatched it up. 'You must pay a forfeit if you want it back.'

She eyed him warily. 'We've already established I won't kiss you for it.'

'I'm not asking for a kiss. I'm asking for a question and I want your truthful answer. Did you orchestrate all of this to get me alone?'

Chiara laughed. 'You get one question and you waste it on one you already know the answer to.' She shook her head. 'I did it to rescue you.' She reached out and took the ball from him.

'And following me into the woods?' He held her gaze, looking for any telltale sign of manipulation, that this Italian *principessa* who'd dropped out of nowhere into his house party was too good to be true. Was she truly not interested in him as the other girls were? Why did he find that both refreshing and disappointing?

She held his gaze evenly, unbothered by his perusal. 'Ask yourself that question. You are the one who asked me to stay.'

She brushed past him then, her skirts flicking against his leg, the scent of linen and apples lingering behind as she left him.

She was right. His suspicions did her a disservice. Her ball *had* been in harm's way and she'd known the risk of her play. He couldn't blame her for that, couldn't see a conspiracy in it. And when pressed, when given the option to kiss him, a chance to advance her case if she was truly out to catch him, she had passed. Which both worried and reassured him. If she didn't want him, what did she want? Had Anabeth Morely ruined him so thoroughly he couldn't believe the truth when he heard it?

Chapter Eight

He did not want this. The afternoon had been a near disaster, with the girls cheating heavily just to be near him. Thank goodness archery had been in the morning before everyone's blood was up. Sutton couldn't imagine what might have happened with arrows available. Something drastic had to be done before the party disintegrated into anarchy.

Sutton paced the pale rose length of his mother's private sitting room. He had to take control of the situation or it would take control of him. When he'd envisioned a house party, he'd pictured a placid series of teas and picnics and boating parties on the lake. Now, he worried someone might drown on the lake if things kept going in their current direction. Cheating at croquet was just the tip of the iceberg.

His mother entered the room, a wry twist on her lips as she shut the door behind her. 'Lord Bradley has just offered me fifty pounds to have Isabelle seated beside you at dinner. I dare say we may have underestimated the determination of our guests to win a rich husband.'

She sank into a chair by the window, looking unusually fatigued. 'And it's only day two. I'm sure the price will go up as the party progresses.'

'That's precisely why we need to talk.' Sutton absently fingered a crystal paperweight on the desk, his thoughts coalescing around an idea, a rather radical idea. 'There are too many girls for me to meet on my own, no mattered how artfully the entertainments are arranged.'

His mother sighed. 'I've got them this far, but I am out of ideas, Sutton.'

'Well, I'm not. The ladies have made this into a competition, by refusing to wait their turn as demonstrated by their antics today, so I intend to further that theme. I propose to use our planned activities—the upcoming picnic, the boaters' luncheon, all of that—as a chance to focus on specific girls. Every evening, the girls who will spend time with me the next day will receive a bouquet and a note in their rooms.' The plan had come to him after his rather direct talk with Chiara in the woods. *I find it saves time.* And so this plan would, too. He could focus on finding a woman he could live with instead of finding himself besieged on all sides.

His mother hedged. 'I don't know, Sutton, it seems so calculated.' She waved an airy hand.

'*This* seems calculated? The whole party is a calculation and everyone knows it.' Sutton wasn't going to tolerate hesitation. 'Mother, I have guards at my bedroom door. How can I be expected to concentrate on finding a wife when I have to spend every moment alert to how I might protect myself from compromising shenanigans? That's not hyperbole. You've already turned away frauds attempting to infiltrate the party. People are willing to do anything.'

She nodded her assent and Sutton smiled. 'I will make the announcement at dinner tonight. The first bouquets will be delivered to bedrooms during the service of the evening tea cart. Now, please excuse me, I have notes I need to write.'

In the cool, dark-wood quiet of the study, with the door securely locked, Sutton sat behind the wide mahogany desk with a sense of relief at reasserting some control. His new plan didn't change the future that awaited him, but it did make it more manageable. It was imperative to all involved that he make a *good* decision when it came to choosing a wife. Not because the fortune demanded it, or because pushy mamas demanded it, but because his code of ethics demanded it.

Now, who might he put on the list? Who did he genuinely want to spend time with? Who might be compatible with him? If this was about his horses, he'd have straightforward bloodlines to help guide that decision. It would be helpful to have a neutral insider to coach him on the subject. That meant his mother was out of the running. She had her agenda and preferences, starting with Imogen Bettancourt. Sutton smiled, another name coming to him. Someone who had no interest in the proceedings other than being an observer. Would she do it?

Sutton opened the desk drawer and drew out a clean

sheet of paper, smoothing it on the surface of the desk. He reached for the fountain pen. At the top of the list he wrote the name Chiara Balare di Fossano.

She did not want this. Nothing was going as planned. Elidh stared at the note in her hand while her father and Rosie exclaimed over the bouquet of summer daisies left on her vanity. Well, Rosie exclaimed over the pretty bouquet. Her father exclaimed over what it meant.

'I knew we could do it! It must have been all that time you spent combing the woods today with him for his croquet ball, and last night in the gallery.' He elbowed her with a laugh. 'My manoeuvre at croquet was inspired today, was it not? I managed to get you into the forest alone with him. Genius!'

'You practically threw me at him,' Elidh scolded. 'It couldn't have been more obvious.' Being obvious was the last thing she needed or wanted. She'd not wanted to be alone in the woods with Sutton. It had been too tempting. He'd wanted to kiss her. She'd seen it in his eyes and for a moment she'd wanted that, too. It was hard to remember that whatever he thought he wanted with her, it was because he thought she was a princess. He'd not wanted to kiss Elidh Easton. He wanted to kiss a woman who didn't exist. And now this—Sutton's attempt to organise the girls into some semblance of order had landed her right in the centre of it. He officially wanted to see her again, which meant nothing was going as she planned. The harder she tried to push Sutton away, the more attracted he seemed to be. It was hardly the effect she'd been trying to cultivate.

'What does the note say?' Rosie peered over her shoulder after her father left, still crowing with delight and off to celebrate with the other fathers. Elidh didn't mind Rosie's intrusion. Rosie couldn't read. Her parts on stage had hardly ever come with lines.

'He wonders if I have a favourite book, and that he enjoys reading when he can't sleep.'

Rosie, always very literal, looked perplexed and began laying out her night things. 'I suppose it's good to know a little something personal about the man.'

'Yes.' Elidh folded the note. It was more than a piece of information. It was an invitation. Sutton wanted to meet her in the library after the house settled. Had he invited others? If she refused, would he not send a bouquet tomorrow? Knowing her luck, a refusal would bring him to her door in the middle of the night and that was hardly what she wanted. And yet well-bred girls didn't traipse through houses after midnight holding secret assignations with men.

Rosie helped her out of her evening gown and into an exquisite peignoir set of fine linen and silk. Her mother had worn it in its initial incarnation when she'd played Titania in *A Midsummer Night's Dream*. Rosie had transformed it into an elegant silk nightdress that flowed easily beneath a dreamy morning robe of linen that fell loosely from her shoulders.

'I want to go to the library and get a book before I go to bed. Just in case Mr Keynes asks me what I've been reading tomorrow.' But she was certain she'd find more than a book in the library. Part of her was excited by that, no matter how many warnings she gave herself. His touch in the woods today had sent a ripple of awareness through her—a new awareness of herself, an awareness of him. His words were thoughtful and, when he was alone with her, he was sincere in a manner that was not conveyed in a crowd. He was, in fact, very much himself, very much a temptation she was finding it hard to resist. Maybe she didn't have to resist him.

Elidh sat still as Rosie plaited her hair into a long, silky braid. They would be gone in two weeks whether they secured a patron or not. She'd told Sutton she had no intentions of pursuing the matrimony game, but did that mean she couldn't indulge in her own flirtation? If he wanted to steal a kiss, with the understanding it could lead nowhere, perhaps she should let him. There would be no harm to him or to her under those rules as long as she was careful not to let things get out of control. She could rationalise it as only a slight deviation from her original plan.

Her hair plaited, Elidh made her way to the library just after one. The house was quiet in the hallways. But she was not fooled. There would be the drama of celebrations and disappointments behind these doors tonight. *All the world's a stage,* she thought absently. Shakespeare had the right of it. The library was empty when she arrived. Good. It made coming here feel less like an assignation. She might truly look for a book.

She'd need to bring one back to her room or Rosie would be suspicious.

Elidh ran her hand over the spines, taking in the gold lettering, the expensive leather covers. What luxury it was to have a library like this. She'd heard of folks who had a monthly shipment of books sent to them. She couldn't begin to imagine having money for something like that. She knew she was lucky she could read. Her mother had taught her and her father had shared his love of books with her. They had a small library of ten books that travelled everywhere with them and the books looked it. They were worn, the spines cracked, some pages stained. Virgil, Homer, Aesop, Shakespeare, Aeschylus, Aristophanes, Socrates. 'All the classics,' her father liked to say.

At the great estates where they'd performed, there were occasional opportunities to borrow a book or two and there were always chances to acquire some unique skill that had created for her a rather incoherent but diverse education. She'd had fencing lessons, a variety of music lessons, vocal lessons, dancing lessons, all of which could be employed in various roles on stage. Before this ruse was done, she would need all those skills.

The door opened behind her and Elidh startled at the intrusion. She'd been further lost in thought than she realised. 'I thought I might find you here.' Sutton's voice was low.

'You invited me.' She turned from the bookshelf. 'I was just choosing a book to take back with me, if you don't mind.' Sutton was dressed for the night as well, a banyan in forest green thrown over his evening trousers and shirt. Gone were his jacket and waistcoat, his shirt open at the neck where his stock would have been, exposing a patch of tanned, bare skin, suggesting time in the outdoors, dressed casually. One's neck didn't tan covered up with a stock. How interesting. What had he done? What had he worn or *not* worn to acquire that piece of skin?

'Thank you for coming.' Sutton went to a console that held crystal decanters and poured a drink. 'Would you like anything?'

'No, thank you.'

Sutton motioned to the pair of chairs by the cold hearth. In the winter, it would be cosy to sit there beside the fire, reading and warm. There would be no draughts to contend with, no leaking roof. This room was full of luxuries: books, warmth, comfortable chairs that wanted to swallow you up for a day of reading. 'Since you prefer directness, I'll get right to it. I have a proposition I want to discuss with you, Chiara. I need your help.'

'I imagine so, after that announcement tonight.' What could she possibly help him with?

'I need someone who is neutral, someone I can confide in, someone who might advise me in turn.'

'You want me to help you pick your bride?' She was glad she hadn't anything to drink. She would have choked on it. The power such a position gave her was unfathomable. Her father would be in alt. She could see her father already plotting to get rid of the best options so that Sutton would all but beg her to marry him. That would not do.

Elidh narrowed her gaze. If he expected her to accept instantly, he would be disappointed. 'Why would you entrust such a task to me? You hardly know me. Two days ago, we'd never met. You would let a stranger pick your wife?'

Sutton chuckled. 'I said "advise me", not choose for me. I will do the picking.' She felt his gaze drift over her face. 'For the record, I don't feel we are strangers, Chiara. It is easy to be with you.'

'You know nothing about me other than I am a reckless croquet player.'

'I know more than that. You'd be surprised.' Sutton set aside his glass and leaned forward, hands on his knees, and her breath caught as all his attention fixed on her. 'I know you're loyal and honest. You played croquet without artifice. You played to win, not to advance an agenda with me. You knocked me into the woods, by Jove. No one else there had the guts to do it, not even when it was obviously the best choice for their team.' He paused, touching her with his eyes and it made her insides warm like melted chocolate she'd tasted once in Venice: delicious, silky and entirely becalmed. When he looked at her like that, the world faded. There were no troubles, no roles to perform, no deceptions to perpetrate. It was just the two of them, like it had been last night in the gallery.

'That's a lot to assume based on a single game.' Elidh had to look away for fear she'd betray the ruse. She used to be those things: honest, loyal, kind. The moment she'd put on the costumes and taken on this role, she could not claim those attributes any longer.

She supposed she was still all those things where her father was concerned. It was loyalty that had driven her to this and honesty. She was genuinely frightened about what would happen to her and her father if they didn't succeed here. But succeeding meant she couldn't be those things for Sutton Keynes. He could not have her honestly and, because of that, he could not have her at all. She was just starting to see the implications.

He reached for her hand, bringing her eyes back to his with his touch. He pleated his fingers through hers. 'Certainly, to conclude so much on a single observation is poor science, poor reasoning. There's more. You forget. When you had the chance to kiss me in the woods today, you were very careful with your decision because I think you knew it wasn't right for us, no matter how much we might have wanted to.' His thumb caressed her hand and her breath hitched. 'I admire that in a person, Chiara—someone who can see beyond themselves. That's what I am counting on. It's why I am asking you for this favour. Stay for the duration of the party. Be my advisor. Be my eyes and ears. I want to know which girls here have hopes elsewhere. I would not steal those hopes from them by claiming them in marriage. Which girls might have a true interest in me as a person and which are here for the money alone. Who might I make happy if given the chance? Marriage needn't be a legalised form of slavery for them.'

Elidh blew out a breath. 'Only for you? I think you are generous to consider the other party.'

'Marriage is only part of the shackle for me. My fetters come from familial attachment. So, will you help me sort through them?' Sutton smiled, intimately handsome in his banyan, his offer tempting. Perhaps this was a forerunner of what married life would look like—Sutton consulting his bride on household matters. The two of them making decisions together, sitting together late into the night, talking softly. Would it be with the lovely Virginia Peckworth? The brassy Isabelle Bradley with her glossy chestnut hair? Fenworth's sister? Who should she help him pick?

'Will you help me, Chiara?' Sutton prompted.

'Of course, I'd be delighted and honoured.' It was the right thing a friend would say. It overrode the little sliver of jealousy that had stabbed at her last night when she'd seen him walking with Lady Imogen after so recently having strolled the gallery with her. But that sliver stabbed again now. Harder this time and for no reason. She should not be jealous of these girls. She was not playing the game. She *could not* play the game. She was, as Sutton said, neutral. She had no choice. She was just starting to see that. It was not only a matter of protecting Sutton. It was a matter of protecting *herself* from him. The Principessa had to disappear in twelve days. No matter what. Ruses weren't made to last for ever and this one was no different.

Chapter Nine

By the fourth day, the house party was bristling with an unsuppressed tension, thanks to Sutton's bouquet brigade, as the guests began to call the footmen who delivered the evening arrangements and invitations. The routine of meeting with the girls was becoming more manageable even if it more fully called out the competitive aspects of the house party. Last night guards had caught a guest sneaking into his bedchamber.

Sutton had higher hopes for today's boating activities on the lake. The sky was blue, the weather perfect and he'd get to spend the entire day out of doors. If he couldn't be down at his dairy, this would have to do.

He'd opted to walk to the lake and, as a result, many of his guests had, too, including Isabelle Bradley, who'd claimed his right arm and not let go the entire mile. He smiled and tried to pay attention to her retelling of a boating incident gone wrong. Apparently, she thought her story of a capsizing would be humorous in advance of the outing. 'No one drowned, of course.' She shrugged with a smile to justify the inappropriate tale. 'So, that is why I prefer oars to sails,' Isabelle concluded with a light laugh. Those walking with them laughed along with her.

Sutton didn't see the humour. To be perverse, he said, 'I prefer sails. I like the science behind them and the challenge of matching my abilities to the wind.' Up ahead, he caught sight of Chiara's straw hat with the bright blue ribbon, walking with Virginia Peckworth's brother, Michael. Sutton wagered Peckworth wasn't telling stories of capsizing sailboats. Too bad. He didn't want her to find Peckworth too entertaining.

'I am sure you're a strong swimmer, too, Mr Keynes. That helps with one's confidence.' One of the Bissell twins—Leah, he thought—chimed in with a crooning compliment. He could never tell the twins apart and they insisted on dressing alike in identical gowns. 'It's easier to dare the elements when one feels in control.' She waved her parasol. 'I would positively drown if there was no one around to rescue me.'

'Oh, Miss Bissell, I'd never let you sink. Come sailing with me today,' Louie Fenworth offered, flirting cheerfully with youthful arrogance. 'I'll keep you perfectly safe and your sister, too.' Sutton stifled a groan. Had he ever been that brash? Fenworth oozed young cockiness. He hoped Fenworth knew what he was getting into. The Bissell twins weren't for the faint-hearted.

Miss Bissell blushed and dissembled as if that hadn't been precisely what she'd been angling for. 'What a kind offer. We will look forward to it, won't

we, Sister?' If she couldn't win the man with the fortune, she'd do just as well to capture an earl's young
heir. The twins swooped upon Louie, one on each side,
and looped their arms through his. Louie beamed at
the girls. 'I never can tell which of you is the most
beautiful.'

Chiara's laughter floated back to Sutton and he was
stabbed with something he'd call…curiosity. What was
Peckworth saying that was so amusing? Certainly he
wouldn't call the feeling jealousy. What was there to be
jealous about? Jealousy assumed he coveted the Principessa, that he wanted her for himself. He already had
her. He met with her each night in the privacy of the
library to discuss candidates worthy of pursuit and, of
course, to simply be with her. She was the most honest,
most enjoyable part of his days. She wanted nothing
from him but his fleeting friendship. He was happy to
give it and more if she would take it. She intrigued him.
But she'd made it plain on several occasions that she
would not. Perhaps she was the smart one. He hadn't
time for intrigue and perhaps not the fortitude for it.
Given his situation, he could not afford to invest too
much in unwrapping the mystery of her.

It was for the best, he supposed. She didn't really
know him. She saw a wealthy gentleman amid the luxury of his country estate. She didn't see the camel
dairyman, the man who loved animals and science.
On ordinary days he came home smelling of camel and
horse and manure, with straw sticking in his hair. He
couldn't imagine a refined woman like the Principessa
would find that terribly charming. And while she met

the technicalities of his uncle's will, there would be the practical logistics to work out about where to live. He doubted she'd leave her home in Italy for him and he could not contemplate leaving Newmarket. His whole life was here. That situation alone made her an impossible choice. And yet, he couldn't resist her.

The glimmer of the lake neared and Sutton picked up his pace, wanting to catch the group ahead of him, wanting to catch Chiara before they arrived. He would have her fleeting friendship for ten more days and then she would pass from his world. He intended to make the most of those days, starting right now.

At the lake shore, white canopies were set up for lunch and for relaxing; rowboats and sailboats lined the beach waiting for sportsmen and their passengers. There was a party atmosphere among the guests as people claimed their boats and their partners. Sutton wasted no time claiming his. He approached Chiara from her other side, engaging her bluntly before Peckworth could issue an invitation. 'Your Highness, would you sail with me?'

Chiara turned, a broad smile on her lips, looking pleasantly and honestly surprised as if sailing with him was a genuine treat. 'I would love to, Mr Keynes.' Then she sobered and turned back, remembering Michael Peckworth. 'If you don't mind?'

Peckworth made a small, gracious bow. 'Of course not, Your Highness. I am sure I will see you later.'

'Are you sure you want to sail with me?' Chiara tossed him a smile as he handed her on to the little skiff. 'The other girls will be jealous and you are losing a valuable opportunity to spend time alone with one of them.'

'Precisely. I'd be losing a valuable opportunity to spend time alone with *you*.' Sutton stooped to take off his shoes and roll up his trousers before he pushed the little boat into the water and splashed on board.

'Shall we row for a while?' Sutton settled himself at the rowlocks and went to work, enjoying the thrill of straining muscles. Exercise felt good. 'I feel like I've been cooped up for days.' He rowed hard, their little skiff gaining speed and distance from shore, from the party.

Chiara leaned back in the bow, the breeze of the lake toying with her hat. 'It goes without saying that I am not your best investment for this outing. I think Miss Ellen Hines will have her feelings hurt. I have reason to believe she felt it was her turn with you.' She reached up and undid the bow holding her hat in place and set it aside. She was stunning like this, her face exposed, the breeze ruffling her hair. Sutton almost forgot to row. When was the last time a woman had so completely stopped him in his tracks? When was the last time he couldn't have that woman?

'Today is too rare of a day to waste on house-party business.' Sutton pulled at the oars, directing the boat towards an island in the middle of the lake. He grinned, feeling alive as the breeze bathed his face and rippled his shirt. 'Besides, there's something I want to show you, just you.'

Just her. The thought was as intoxicating and as reckless as Sutton's grin. Too reckless. She should not have got in the boat with him, should not have taken off her hat and given herself over to the day. If she was really Princess Chiara Balare, really his advisor, she would have insisted he spend his time more wisely with a girl he could marry. But she'd done none of those things. She'd thrilled to the sound of his voice at her ear asking her to sail with him and it had all been a slippery slope to this.

They reached the little beach and Sutton splashed into the water. He pulled the boat to shore on the far side of the island where no one could see them. Then he came back for her. She was already busy shedding her stockings and shoes, leaving them beside her hat.

'Careful!' Sutton laughed as she stood, rocking the boat while she tied up her skirts. 'I'll carry you if you like.'

She tossed him a playful smile and jumped down beside him. 'I am *not* afraid of a little water.' The water came up over her ankles, cool and inviting against the sun; the pebbles on the lake bottom crunched beneath her feet.

'A wading princess? I am surprised once more.' Sutton gave her his hand for balance. 'I thought princesses were indoor girls.'

'Do you know many princesses?' She laughed, but perhaps this had been a misstep.

'No, I don't,' Sutton confessed. 'Just you.' They reached the shore and the sandy dirt was soft between her toes.

'Well, a princess is just a person like anyone else.' This was lovely. It had been ages since she'd been outside, lost in nature. London was a city full of soot and noise. Here, there was quiet, and dirt and green.

'I am just a person, too. Don't forget that, Chiara.' Sutton's voice was low, intimate, to match the silence that surrounded them. There was only the lap of small waves on the shore. She was reminded exactly how alone they were. She felt his eyes on her face. Her pulse pounded with the attention. 'Here on this island, Chiara, you and I might be just two people together.'

'And when we're off the island?' What was wrong with her? She was inviting trouble.

'No talk of that today. I don't want to think of any of them. Did you know Lila Partridge slipped into my bedchambers last night?' He took her hand and led her inland.

No, she hadn't. She supposed it wasn't the kind of thing people wanted to have gossiped about. 'Your guards remedied the situation?'

'Yes, but it's the desperation of the act that strikes me. The lengths people are willing to go to are astonishing when they feel they have nothing left to lose. That was how that poor girl felt last night, that the consequences of her action were worth the risk of being caught.'

Elidh swallowed. *Oh, you don't know the half of it. Some of us are willing to impersonate royalty to get into your party.* But the rest of it was real. She wasn't pretending anything when it came to his friendship. He could trust her advice, could trust her with his secrets whether she was Princess Chiara or Elidh Easton.

'Careful here, it's easy to turn an ankle.' He took

her hand again as they scrambled over boulders and rock, coming at last to a cave. 'This is what I wanted to show you.' He grinned and ducked inside. A match flared and a moment later a lantern came to life. She stepped into the cave beside him and gasped.

'It's amazing.' The walls were covered in crude drawings, of men with spears, of enormous elephant-like animals.

'They're original. Done by people who were here before us.' Sutton's voice was hushed at her ear. She shared that reverence as she turned about in a circle, taking it all in. Here before them was an understatement. Millennia before them.

'A mammoth hunt, I think,' Sutton told her, slowly moving the lantern across the wall face for her. 'It has a happy ending for the hunters, most of them anyway.' The lantern light stopped on the image of a fallen hunter.

'Not happy for him or for the mammoth,' Elidh remarked sombrely, feeling connected to these long-gone people. *I'm just a person.* They'd been just people. Ordinary like her, doing the best they could to make it through life. 'I wonder if anyone wept over him? If he left behind a wife? A family?' She traced the fallen figure with a gentle finger. 'I wonder what they'd think of our world. Our trains? Our cities and roads? We can travel to places in hours that would have taken them days on foot.'

'I wonder if things like marriage were as complicated for them as it is for us? Or if we've deliberately overcomplicated it?'

'If love was easy, everyone would fall. Is that it? Do you think in the modern day we've put ourselves beyond love?' she asked softly, wondering what was going on behind those blue eyes as he surveyed the cave. What was he wrestling with? His own impending choice? Was it the risk of that choice or the cost of it that he grappled with? Her curiosity did not do her credit. She should not be wondering about his opinions on love and marriage, it would only breed an unproductive interest in this man she needed to avoid.

'Are princesses "beyond love," as you put it? Are you spoken for, Chiara? Is there a dynastic marriage waiting for you to return from your travels?' Sutton was only half jesting. She heard the intrigue beneath the words. Apparently, she was not the only one with curiosity to satisfy. She should not encourage it from him any more than she should encourage it from herself, yet she could not drag herself away from the conversation any more than she could drag herself away from him. Both were captivating. What did a man like Sutton Keynes, a man with the world at his fingertips, think about such things?

'Not at this time.' If she was lucky, he'd accept the implication that a *principessa* was fated for such an alliance, that it was inevitable.

'But soon?' he pressed, choosing to ignore the implication. She didn't believe for a minute he was obtuse enough to not understand it. 'Is your father saving you for a grand alliance?'

'Yes.' There was truth in that. A grand alliance indeed, with the man standing in front of her. But she would not allow that to happen.

'Will there be love?' His gaze was intent on her, burning her with his eyes.

'One never knows. It's possible. One must always hope.' She'd spent her life hoping. It hadn't done her much good so far.

'I had once thought I'd have love. Now, I am not so sure. The world has taught me differently. My uncle's will has changed all that, taken the possibility away from me, even if the probability of it never existed.'

She heard the resignation in his voice, a resignation that indicated there might be more to that lesson than simply his uncle's will. But to probe further would be unseemly and it would invite the sort of interested speculation on his part that she wanted to avoid. All she could do was let her heart go out to him in sympathy. Whatever his hopes might have been, whatever his thoughts on love might have once been, this whole situation was not of his making even if the party was. 'When I met you that first night in the gallery, I wondered why a man who didn't want a party had thrown one for himself. Have you thought of giving up the fortune? Then you could marry where you chose and when you chose.'

'I can't, it's complicated. If I refuse the fortune, it goes to my cousin. He can't be trusted with the money. But there are times when I am tempted to do that very thing.' He stepped close to her, his hand cupping her head in his palm, her breath catching at his nearness. She could hardly think straight. Dear lord, he was going to kiss her.

'Sutton,' she made a breathless plea, whether for

or against what came next, she wasn't sure. Perhaps she tilted her chin up in invitation, perhaps he bent a fraction more until his mouth took hers, in a kiss that started gently, then evolved into something that lingered, that tasted, that drank from her lips, slowly, patiently, as if they had all the time in the world. She could feel his hand in her hair, drawing her closer until their bodies met.

He smiled down at her, his free hand skimming her cheek with his knuckles, his eyes soft. 'I've wanted to do that since the moment I saw you.'

She lowered her eyes, not wanting to give away all the emotion rushing through her. 'I thought we'd decided not to try this on.'

'We had,' Sutton acceded. 'But then I realised what a fleeting friendship meant. In ten days you'll be gone and I will have a bride. I found I could not put off kissing you any longer.' He kissed her again, hungrily this time, the strong hand behind her neck manoeuvring her to the cave wall, the press of his mouth hungry, and she answered it with a hunger of her own. Never mind her father's plans. Never mind that time and fate were against them. They had this moment. There would be time to regroup afterwards, time to remind herself she was not who he thought he was kissing, but for the present, there was only now.

A small squawk sounded near the cave, interrupting. It came again. Elidh pulled back, holding Sutton's face between her hands. 'Wait, did you hear that?' It came a third time, not a squawk exactly, but something between a cheep and a squeal. It was plaintive and alone, a singular sound. 'Are there birds on the island?' She was already moving past Sutton towards the cave entrance.

'Yes, there are geese, sometimes hawks.' Sutton blew out the lantern as they exited, and left it behind. For next time, perhaps? She didn't want to think of who he might bring, who he might kiss in the depths of the cave. Was this just another of his planned interludes? She'd thought not at the outset because they had their rules. She was not here for his game.

Elidh squatted down on the ground, parting the tall grasses and looking between the rocks. She waddled forward in an unladylike crouch, following the sound. 'Found him! Look, Sutton, it's a gosling.' The little baby cheeped and hopped, scared and trapped. 'It's his leg, it's tucked under one of the rocks.'

Sutton was beside her on his knees, carefully removing the rock while she cupped the gosling in her hand. 'He's hurt his foot.' Elidh held the little thing close, soothing it. 'The poor thing is frightened. Where's his mother?'

Sutton rose, dusting his hands on his trousers, his brow furrowed. 'Probably on the lake with the other babies. Geese can swim almost immediately after birth.' She heard the unspoken words: *but not this one*. This one, with its bad foot, wouldn't be able to paddle through the water, wouldn't be able to dive for insects and snails. Broken, imperfect creatures didn't fare well in the wild.

Elidh rose, the gosling cradled against her. 'We have to take it with us. It will starve. We'll bring it back when its foot heals and it can stand on its own.'

She started the trek towards the skiff at the shore defiantly, daring Sutton to argue with her. Another man would. Another man would tell her it was a hopeless cause, that this was the way of the wild, how nature winnowed out the weak. But instead, Sutton scrambled over the rocks, a hand at her elbow, gently guiding her and the baby gosling to safety. On the beach, he helped her into the boat and made a nest for the baby with his jacket.

'Thank you.' Elidh settled herself near the gosling, ready in case it needed her. The breeze caught her hair as they rowed out from shore. He stopped to put up the sails. 'We can take our time getting back.'

'Do you think we'll be missed?' Elidh shielded her eyes against the bright afternoon, taking in the distant shore. She was in no hurry to return, although she knew she should be. When it was just the two of them, it was becoming more difficult to remember who she really was, that the Princess was a fiction.

'Probably. I am missed if I go to the bathroom these days.' Sutton chuckled. 'If we're going to be missed anyway, we might as well make it worthwhile.' He settled into the bow beside her and the gosling, letting the wind take the skiff at its own pace. He smiled, the effort crinkling the corners of his eyes as he stroked the gosling with a finger. 'You've a kind heart, Chiara.'

'I can't bear to see anything in distress.' She shrugged. 'Not when I can help it.'

'Does that include me?' He gave a wry smile, his eyes still hot when they looked at her.

'Do you need rescuing?' She should not have said

it, should not have flirted or invited his confession. To know him would be to care for him. Leaving would be hard enough already without it.

'So much more than you know.' There was a dangerous hunger in those words.

That made two of them, then. If she didn't push him away fast, they'd both be in over their heads in no time.

Chapter Ten

'You shouldn't have kissed me,' Elidh said quietly.

'Didn't you like it?'

'Not like it? There was no question of not liking it.' If his touch made her feel like warm melted chocolate, then his kiss made her feel like chocolate lava. 'But we've already agreed it's not practical.' To feel the thrumming urgency of his hunger and his desire up against her body had been heady indeed, but he thought he was kissing someone else. She would never entice such a response from him.

'Not practical?' A wry smile curved the corner of his mouth.

'Because now we know.' Now they knew what was between them, what they could do to each other. They could burn each other with kisses that could go nowhere.

Sutton reached for her hand where it lay between them on the bench. 'Yes, now we know. The question is—what shall we do about it?' That was when Elidh knew the danger was real, no longer a cautionary figment of 'what if' existing only in her imagination. Was Sutton probing for a confirmation of interest on her part? What would he do if she gave it? Would he pursue a proposal? That must not happen. It was the last thing she'd come to this party wanting and, for Sutton's sake, it was the last thing she wanted still.

'We can do nothing about it except enjoy the moment, you said so yourself.'

'What if I am wrong about that? What if we could enjoy more than moments?' Sutton persisted.

'But, Sutton, you are *not* wrong. You've only known me a handful of days and your situation is every bit as desperate as Miss Partridge's when it comes down to it. You're simply reaching for me because you think I pose no threat to you, that I'm not competing for you, and that somehow makes me more honest, more real than the rest.' She smiled softly at him to soften the blow. 'You mistake my neutrality for something else, I think. It would be best if you don't.' She was pushing hard now, forcing him to see reason. This had to end. She was starting to fall for her own disguise, starting to forget who she really was and what she was doing there. She was someone else altogether when she was with him, not entirely Chiara, nor Elidh, and that was a very dangerous person to be.

The person in the mirror was ready for dinner, her hair done up in another elaborate, braided creation, her light blue skirts pressed to perfection, cosmetics delicately applied. But the girl on the bench before the vanity was not ready in the least, her insides in as much turmoil as her exterior was calm.

Rosie fastened a matching ribbon around Elidh's neck, pleased with her handiwork. 'You look like your mother. Blue was her best colour, too.'

That was the problem. Two problems, actually. Whether she looked like her mother or like Principessa Chiara, the truth was, she was neither and she was forgetting who that was. That was the second problem: the woman in the mirror was fast becoming far too real. Elidh was becoming too used to the illusion of being beautiful. It would be a hard fall to earth when the ruse was over if she didn't remember. Elidh fingered the ribbon. 'I'll never be as lovely as my mother.'

Rosie clucked disapprovingly. 'Your mother was pretty, but what made her stand out was who she was on the inside. She was good and kind to all those around her, just like you. Some of those girls downstairs would do better to remember that beauty comes from within. Isabelle Bradley's mother best take her in hand before it's too late.'

'What's too late?' Her father swept into the room, decked out for dinner in a lavish olive-coloured coat and rose waistcoat she recalled from *Hamlet*. His unruly greying waves were tamed and he looked dashing and in good humour. 'I've been playing cards.' He held up a jingly pouch of coins. 'Only lost once and all it cost me was the gold rose brooch.'

Elidh winced. In short, he'd lost nothing then. The brooch was gold plate over lead. It was pretty enough to look at, but she hoped the gold plate didn't chip until they were well away from here.

'I was wondering if it isn't too late to reconsider an early departure?' She stood and faced her father.

'Why ever would we want to do that? You spent the day on the lake with Keynes, I won at cards, I nearly have a patron lined up. We are that much closer to achieving all of our goals.' He beamed. 'Rosie should start designing your wedding dress from what I heard at the tables.' He grinned.

'That's what I fear. I can't marry him, Father, even if he were to ask.' She'd not thought to have this discussion. She'd not thought things would get this far. She'd meant to keep her distance, meant to do her job to help to secure a patron and nothing more. Her own plans had gone awry. 'Have you thought of what happens if we succeed?' In the beginning, she'd counted on the improbability of her father's plan coming to fruition to protect her, but that improbability was fading by the day. Now, she was forced to consider the consequences of succeeding.

Her father pinched her cheek in his good mood. 'We all live happily ever after with never again a financial worry.'

'But plenty of other worries,' she countered. She had to be firm here. 'If we get a patron we leave here and the Balares di Fossano disappear on their travels. No one ever need see us again. But, if the Principessa marries Sutton Keynes, the Balares di Fossano will exist for the rest of our lives. We can never stop the ruse. It must be sustained day and night.' How could she make him understand the horror of that? 'I would have to live a lie. I would have to lie to my husband. What kind of marriage could that ever be when it's started on a falsehood?'

It was no longer the improbability of the ruse that bothered her, it was the ethics of it. Her arguments in their rooms on Bermondsey Street had all been about the impossibilities of impersonating a princess. Her arguments now were more serious.

'If my husband were to find out, it would be disastrous. He would be compelled to divorce me or be complicit with the lie. Both are devastating.' If he divorced her, Sutton would lose the fortune he was marrying to protect. But if he chose to support the lie, she would lose him. Whatever hope they had for happiness or feeling would be gone. Those things could not exist without trust and honesty. 'We can't keep up the ruse indefinitely. There will come a point of discovery if we run it too long.' Two weeks was long enough. She couldn't imagine a lifetime of it.

'Well, we don't have a proposal yet, so let's say we'll cross that bridge when we come to it.' Her father smiled and cocked his arm. 'All we can do right now is go down to dinner and charm Lord Wharton into patronage.' He wasn't entirely wrong, but she recognised his ploy for what it was: a stalling technique. Her father wanted to believe true love conquered all, that she would win Sutton and his instantaneous love for her would override any and all considerations that might stand in their way. But the world didn't work that way.

Elidh took her father's arm and stiffened her resolve.

Things had got out of control today. She'd had her adventure. Now, it was time to make sure the adventure was over. To continue it was too dangerous.

There was no one more dangerous than Baxter Keynes on a vendetta and he was definitely on one now. Thanks to his cousin, damn him. Bax laced his hands over his midsection where rich living was beginning to take its toll and listened intently to his informant's report. For all intents and purposes, it appeared Sutton meant to see the farce of his father's will through to its disastrous conclusion.

It was galling to be just two miles from the house party of the Season and not be in attendance. Instead, he was relegated to using a false name and to snooping from a private parlour at a mediocre inn. And he couldn't even do that. He'd had to bribe his way to the information and hear it second-hand from a guest at the party.

His informant finished and Bax leaned forward, fingers tapping an edgy tattoo on the scarred table. 'Who are the leading contenders?' Perhaps he could help his cousin narrow the field even further. If he could get rid of the girls his cousin favoured, his cousin might lose his fortitude for the game, especially when faced with the possibility of marrying a girl he found unpalatable in the extreme. Such an obstacle didn't matter to him, personally. He'd marry a horse to secure a fortune of this size. But those things mattered to Sutton. As did other people. Sutton was a protector. If he thought these girls were in jeopardy, he might call it off altogether.

His informant, a young, well-dressed man, was the brother of one of the hopeful girls. From the looks of him, he probably spent far beyond the means of his allowance. The boy shifted nervously in his seat, suddenly concerned about propriety. 'What are you going to do to them? I don't want anyone hurt.' His conscience was waking up too late. The boy had already proven he could be bought.

'Who said anything about hurting anyone?' Bax replied smoothly. He motioned for the serving girl. 'A bottle of brandy if you have it.' People shared information better after a drink or two. This boy was green enough to be impressed with taking an expensive drink with his new friend. The bottle came and Bax poured two generous servings. 'I simply want to know.' He leaned forward across the table, his voice dropping. 'A man can make some money if he guesses the bride. The betting book at White's is full of opportunities.'

All true. Bets were being made across London over who would be Sutton's final choice. 'I could place a bet for you when I return to the city,' Bax offered. He'd given the boy brandy *and* money; how much more enticing could he be?

The younger man perked up at that, seeing the possibilities for his own gain. 'Well, if that's all you want the names for.'

'It is.' Bax smiled. 'What did you think I wanted them for? Serial murders? You, Fenworth, have a very dark mind.' He chuckled conspiratorially at his hyperbole. Really, young Fenworth was inspired. Was that such a bad idea? Killing off the competition? No one would think of marrying Sutton then. But who knew? It was still a lot of money. Bax supposed there'd always be someone willing to dice with the devil. Goodness knew, he was.

If there was to be a murder, though, Bax would save it for the finale. If a bride stood between him and his father's fortune, he'd take whatever measures were needed. Extreme measures came with extreme consequences. One always had to be sure they were necessary before embarking on such courses. The problem with murder was that it wasn't incredibly sophisticated. Why murder someone—that was so very final, so very irrevocable—when a simple kidnapping often rendered more leverage? Someone could only die once, but a kidnapping could keep giving and giving if a man was smart. Bax was smart. 'About the girls, Fenworth?' Bax smiled, man to man, and pushed a few pound notes across the table.

Fenworth put the notes in his pocket and drew out a folded sheet of paper in exchange, glancing surreptitiously at the few patrons peopling the afternoon taproom.

'Here's a hint, Fenworth,' Bax noted wryly. 'If you don't act like you're doing anything wrong, no one will think you are.' Fenworth was ultimately corruptible, but, by Jove, the boy was naive. All the more fun to ruin. Bax hid a grin as he scanned the list. There was nothing he loved more than watching the golden ones fall from their pedestals. He could turn Fenworth into a drunkard, a gambler, maybe even an opium addict within weeks. He'd have Fenworth gambling off more than a list of innocent girls' names in order to recoup his losses or pay for his next pipe of the poppy.

Bax raised his dark brows. 'Your sister's name is on the list.' He smiled in an older brotherly fashion. 'Eliza, is it? Congratulations. I am sure your father will be impressed with the results so far. I take it he sent you to watch over her? Guide her?' Eliza Fenworth was Viscount Weston's only daughter, a lovely but quiet girl who was pretty to look at, but not very interesting to talk to. She went on about music and composers until a man wanted to smash a violin.

Fenworth puffed up his chest, the little popinjay. 'Yes, absolutely. One can't go marrying one's sister to a man who possesses no title without serious consideration. Keynes would be a step down for her, for the family.'

'His money wouldn't be,' Bax said bluntly. Viscount Weston needed the funds. Who didn't need the money? For that amount, people would contemplate a great many steps down. He smiled to take the edge off his comment, to make Fenworth forget his comment insulted him as well. 'Does your sister have a chance? What is your father greasing Keynes's palm with?' Surely the girls at the top of the list were there because they offered his cousin something in exchange for access to the money.

Bax pushed a few more pound notes over to Fenworth, watching the reality come to him that selling information was very lucrative. 'Father has seats in Parliament.'

'Not as many as Lady Imogen Bettancourt's father,

and he's a marquis. His title is better, too,' Bax pointed out. 'So, your father and Bettancourt have seats, as do a few others on the list.' He tapped another name. 'Ellen Hines, Wharton's daughter. No seats there that make her stand out. What's the attraction?'

'Land. Wharton has estates everywhere.' Good. The boy was a quick study.

'Miss Peckworth? Southmore's youngest?' Bax queried.

'He's connected to the Foreign Office. Diplomatic opportunities.'

'And Miss Whitely?'

'East India Company connections,' Fenworth supplied, proving how easily he could be bought. In fifteen minutes Fenworth had gone from being concerned over how the information would be used to giving up not only a list of names, but a veritable biography as well. All for a few pounds. Still, it did call into question Fenworth's loyalty. People who were easily bought were easily bought by anyone. Bax wanted to ensure he was the only one buying Fenworth's information.

Bax poured another round of brandy for them. 'We have to keep your sister in the game, for both our sakes.' That seemed unlikely. Eliza was pretty, but Weston had little to offer in the way of enticements. 'Frankly, if it were up to me, I'd pick the Marquis's daughter and be done with it.' So why was his cousin lingering? The field might not be overly narrow at this point, but it was narrow enough to see the cream starting to rise.

Fenworth chuckled smugly with a confidence Bax

didn't care for. 'You have not seen the Italian Principessa. If you want to know why your cousin lingers in his decision, that's why.'

The one name on the list he'd not asked about because there was no reason to. A foreigner would have little to offer Sutton other than a technical title and one never knew how legitimate those European titles were. Italian princes and French counts were littered everywhere these days, many of them dispossessed, or struggling to maintain their titles in the wake of nationalism. It was not a good time to be European royalty. 'All right, I'll bite.' Bax leaned back in his seat. Fenworth was holding out on him. Perhaps he'd misjudged the boy. Untutored, perhaps, but not as naive as he'd thought. 'Tell me about the Princess.'

Fenworth's eyes glinted. 'Now, that, my friend, will cost you.'

Chapter Eleven

'Tell me again about your violin, Miss Fenworth.' Sutton sat beside the pretty blonde on the sofa, more out of guilt than out of any true desire to hear about her violin. She was quiet, notoriously so, unless, Chiara had informed him, she was talking about music. Then she became quite animated. He wanted her animated now. Her silence had made her easy to neglect. It had also made her palatable. It was easy to keep her at the top of his list because he didn't have to worry about Miss Fenworth sneaking into his chambers or hanging on his arm every time he walked somewhere.

Lord, what was happening to him? Assessing a woman as if she were a commodity. Which, the logician in him argued, she was. A wife was a means to an end, just as he was a means to an end for every woman in this room. Except one, his prickly conscience reminded him. Chiara. But she didn't count, by her own volition. His volition, however, wanted to change that decision, more so each day.

'It's new. It's a Jacob Diehl from Hamburg.' Eliza

Fenworth held out her prized instrument to him. He took it with a smile, trying to recapture his humanity, or perhaps apologise for the lack of it. The house party was turning him into a man he scarcely recognised, and all for a fortune he didn't want but felt compelled to protect. Maybe it was true. Money changed a man even when he tried to do good.

'See the wide soundholes and how Diehl placed the bridge? His violins are known for their long corners and their flat bridges,' she explained, her face coming alive with her talk of music. Chiara was right. The girl effused vitality all of a sudden. Her eyes sparked and she seemed to glow, her beauty becoming three-dimensional now. He wasn't going to marry her for it. But he knew a man who should—a Quentin Burbage, the second son of a baron, who spent his days in the Strand making instruments while his father raced the family string in Newmarket. He'd come for a few long weekends last year to see the horses and Sutton had enjoyed him—a kind, gentle, intelligent man. Perhaps he would write to Burbage and tell him about Miss Fenworth when all this was over. Eliza Fenworth had been one of the few to conduct herself properly this week. She'd not begged for his attentions and, in doing so, she deserved a prize she'd actually enjoy. He sensed Eliza didn't want to be married to him any more than he wanted to be married to her, or anyone else present.

Except Chiara. There it was again—that errant, wicked thought. Sutton passed the instrument carefully back to Miss Fenworth. It seemed Chiara had become the exception to everything since he'd kissed her in the cave. He only felt like himself when he was with her. He wasn't playing a role, wasn't pandering to parents and falsely flattering their daughters. Yet he'd shown so little of himself to her that to draw such a conclusion bordered on hasty generalisation.

By the piano, his mother called for attention and everyone took their seats. Tonight, the girls would entertain them with musical skills. Sutton surveyed the collection of aspiring musicians, a pit growing in his stomach. They were all lovely, all talented in some way, all desperate in others, put up to this farce by their parents or their own vanity. But who among them could he marry? Who among them did he see himself spending the rest of his life with? Isabelle Bradley with her incessant chatter? Did the girl ever stop? Eliza Fenworth, who was just the opposite? Virginia Peckworth, who spent more time watching herself in any available mirror? Each of them had their flaws. Which flaws could he live with? Could he live with any of them and still keep himself intact or would he lose himself entirely, completing the process the house party had already begun?

Always, his eye went to Chiara. Tonight, she sat among the pastel-gowned girls, dressed in her red gown once more. Tonight, she was a rose among daisies, a guitar in hand—a somewhat new and unconventional instrument compared to the traditional choices of piano, violins and Miss Peckworth's flute. It only heightened his already considerable interest in her.

Virginia Peckworth performed first. Sutton took
care to show attention, but his thoughts never strayed
from Chiara. It had been a day since she'd tucked up
her skirts and waded through the water, since she'd
walked on the island barefoot, since her eyes had gone
wide with awe in the cave, since she'd clutched the
gosling to her, determined to save it. Since he'd kissed
her.

Alexandra Darnley on her violin was next. Sutton redirected his thoughts long enough to notice she
played a simple folk song. Then he was back at it, still
debating whether he should have kissed Chiara or not.
He refused to regret it. They'd both enjoyed it, both
wanted it when all was said and done. They'd been
holding their curiosities at bay since they'd met and
now those curiosities had been satisfied. However,
other curiosities, other hungers had been awakened
in their place. The kiss had solved nothing.

The other performers paraded past the piano, ren-
dering their performances, the evening slipping into a
blur of songs, one after another. The only performance
that held any interest for him was Chiara's. She and
Eliza were the last two to play. Eliza stood before the
guests, dressed in a pale pink, with a confidence he'd
not seen her display before this evening. He understood. Tonight, she was offering him the best of her.
Never mind that she was quieter than the other girls,
never mind she did not want to marry him. It was not
her choice. She knew what was at stake for her family
and knew tonight was her best chance. For once, she
would be superior to all the other girls. It increased Sut-

ton's resolve to write to Burbage. A girl ought not to be put to such use for family against her will. She raised her bow and began to play, brilliantly, flawlessly, performing Vivaldi's Violin Concerto in E flat with such perfection that when it ended the guests came to their feet. His mother caught his eye and raised an enquiring brow as if to say *Perhaps she's the one. She has some fire in her, after all.*

Suddenly, Sutton wished Chiara had played before her. He feared her piece would be anticlimactic now. How could anything compare? But Chiara rose with her guitar, drawing all eyes to her red dress as she came forward, undaunted by Eliza Fenworth's performance. Then again, why should she be intimidated? She was the only one among them, himself included, who had nothing to lose.

Elidh had nothing left to lose as she plucked the plaintive, opening notes of another Vivaldi piece, the Adagio in D minor. She let the notes draw the audience to her, provocative in their simplicity, inviting the audience to lose themselves in the music's dreamy spell, inviting Sutton. He was in agony tonight. She could tell by the smile on his face as he'd talked with Miss Fenworth. Eliza Fenworth was not the source of his agony, though. The party was taking its toll on him and her heart ached. She knew something akin to how that toll felt. She was paying, too, for a kiss she should not have stolen, a boat ride she should not have taken, a stroll in the gallery she should not have allowed, a walk in the woods she should not have accepted.

Whatever objectivity she'd once hoped to maintain for this mad scheme of her father's had been undone subtly and slowly over the last days until it lay unavoidably naked before her in its truth. She liked Sutton Keynes. Perhaps even more than liked him. It was the last and worst thing that could happen. She had not wanted to like him, to know him. *I am just a man.* His words whispered through her mind. And what a man he was; a man who saved goslings and walked barefoot on beaches, who was awed by ancient drawings in a cave, a man who was socially far above the daughter of an actress and a washed-up playwright who could barely afford rooms on Bermondsey Street among dock workers.

She glanced Sutton's way, letting her eyes linger and lock with his for a brief moment. The music was working its magic, the languorous tones seductive, full of longing as she caressed each one from the strings. She could see its effect on his face. It was what she loved about the Adagio; it could be a lover's seduction, a mother's lullaby, or a mournful farewell depending on how one played it, depending on how one needed it. She'd needed it in all ways, once, after her mother died. The piece might not have the overt technical sophistication of Eliza's violin concerto, but it had emotional depth.

The key changed and the tenor of the piece altered, becoming, deeper, darker, more mysterious. She allowed herself another glance in Sutton's direction. What she saw nearly undid her. There was no escaping the look of intense rapture on his face. His eyes were closed now, the tiniest furrow creased his brow as if drinking in the music brought him a special kind of pleasure–pain that he could not resist. She knew. When it came to him, she could not resist it either. Perhaps he kept his eyes shut because it was too dangerous to do otherwise. What would she see if he opened them? What would *he* see?

Elidh finished the last lingering notes of the Adagio and moved into the overtly provocative rhythm of a gypsy song, the fast, strumming chords conjuring up images of campfires and starlit seductions. Then she began to dance as she played. How could one not? It was impossible to be still to such a tune, made for swaying hips and dancing feet. Sutton's eyes were open and on her now, closed in reflection no longer. She had everyone's eyes, in fact. Elidh gave full vent to the emotion of the dance, letting it wipe away her worries, her cares. For a few moments she was free. Was this how her mother had felt on stage, a queen in her gowns? As if the world could not touch her here? She gave herself, body and soul, over to the music, each riff faster, more frantic than the last.

There was silence when she finished. The audience was mesmerised, perhaps shocked. But she beamed at them, breathless and warm with a bead of sweat glistening at her temple, her hair coming down from Rosie's careful pins. Then Sutton rose and the applause began, ending only when the tea cart rolled in to signal the close of the evening. That was her cue to exit. Elidh used its arrival to escape to the balcony and cooler air. Now, it was her turn to close her eyes, to give over to reflection and savour the remnants of elation and cool evening air on hot cheeks.

She did not hear the French doors open behind her. Nor did she notice his presence until Sutton's sleeve brushed against her as he leaned at the railing. 'If you ever tire of being a princess you can always be a travelling minstrel.' For a moment she didn't hear the joke in his voice. The remark was too close to reality. Her first thought was fear—driven by the thought that somehow he knew.

'Sorry, not funny, I suppose.' Sutton misunderstood her stare. 'You can no more lay down your burdens than I can. Yet, tonight I did for a while when you played and I think you did, too.' He reached for her hand. Touching and talking had become almost second nature to them. How had that happened? How had she let that happen?

'Sutton, you should be inside wooing the other girls,' Elidh warned, too aware that she had claimed the lion's share of his attentions these last two days. 'Your guests won't believe my father and I are simply here for the experience. They'll think I'm determined to steal you for myself.' It was too easy in the moment to get caught up in him, to forget the promises she'd made privately to keep herself apart from the game.

'They feel threatened by you?' Sutton chuckled, but he didn't release her hand.

'I understand how they must see things. For a girl not hunting the fortune, I've had more opportunities to claim it than they have had. They're keeping score and they're not appreciative.' Tonight's performance wouldn't help in that regard. 'You don't want to give them the wrong impression.'

'I think I already have,' Sutton confessed, looking out over the gardens, his gaze tinged with reflection, his voice laced with the hint of regret. 'Not with you, of course. I didn't mean to imply that. I meant that I've given them the wrong impression of me.' His grip on her hand tightened. 'Sometimes I feel as if my uncle's fortune will swallow me whole and, if it doesn't, marriage to any of these girls will finish the job. The irony of it is that I have no one to blame but myself.'

Elidh squeezed his hand in silent sympathy. She knew exactly how that felt.

Chapter Twelve

Sutton was serious. He honestly saw the situation as his fault. Elidh could see the frustrated tension in the beautiful lines of his profile. Whatever peace her music had brought him, it was gone now. 'How can you blame yourself? You didn't design your uncle's will.'

'No, but I planned the party. I made the conditions of my marriage clear. Logically, it all made sense. I needed to gather all the eligible girls in one place, efficiently, quickly. I knew they would come. The money would bring them. I knew that, too. I knew the money would attract them, not the man. How could it be otherwise? Rationally, I understood that. I invited them knowing all of this and now I resent them for adhering to *my* plan.' He leaned on the balustrade. 'I'd not be the first to marry for convenience, yet I find myself in a conundrum. I am a scientist, a man of logic, or so I thought. But this week, I've come to see myself as a man of contradictions. I built a plan on logic, but it has failed me.'

'Why is that?' she ventured cautiously, thrilling to what the answer might be, and fearing it, too.

'When I look at you, Chiara, I find I want more than what logic can give me.'

'You hardly know me.' It was a weak defence. Her insides were jelly, quivering with the knowledge that she had undone this man. Only in her dreams had she ever imagined such a moment and she let it linger too long. Sutton took advantage of her pause.

'True, but I'd like to know you.' It was a heady and dangerous proposition. 'I want you to tell me, point-blank, Chiara, that what's between us is not a game.' He was challenging her, forcing her to confess the attraction was not his alone. She groped for middle ground. She could not deny the attraction outright. He would know it was a lie and he would press on, but she could not encourage his subtle advance.

'Why? What for, Sutton? Nothing can come of it. You still have to choose a bride and I will move on with my travels.'

'Perhaps for that very reason. Maybe I want to have something to hold against the days that will come? Maybe you do, too? Otherwise, I'll need you to explain to me why you looked at me the way you did while you played tonight.'

'Are you suggesting an *affaire*?' Elidh threw the words like a bucket of cold water, hoping to scandalise him sober, out of this nonsense and into reason. But the words were laced with a wicked temptation of their own. Why not say yes? When would she ever feel this way again about someone? When would she ever know someone like him? Perhaps he was right; they would have something to hold on to, a keepsake. An *affaire* implied there would be an ending, that recognised she would leave.

'I believe you're the one doing that,' Sutton replied, voice dropping low and husky, the air around them charged with a tension that crackled with intensity. Was she really contemplating such a thing? She had to stop this; making rules and breaking them with her flimsy justifications just to get what she wanted in the moment, forgetting that the moment wasn't real and neither were the circumstances. Everything about this house party was manufactured, designed to engineer romantic feelings, to move him towards such a decision.

'However, I will answer your hypothetical question for the sake of argument, or curiosity,' Sutton drawled, his voice at her ear making her shiver. 'An *affaire* is rather sordid. You should know by now I am a discreet man, Chiara, and a respectful one. I would never presume to dishonour you.'

'And yet, what you suggest is not much different— that there's a way to be together and yet not be together. But I don't see it, Sutton. Under the circumstances, we cannot simply be just friends. You are a man with a fortune, hunting a bride, and I am a princess.' Would he be so mortified about dishonouring her if she was plain Elidh Easton, a woman who was far below him in station? 'I fear I've become a distraction for you.'

He ran his thumb over her knuckles. 'I forget our

positions sometimes. To me, you are just Chiara. I prefer to see you without your title, perhaps because I prefer people see me without my fortune, even though I am discovering daily how difficult it is for them to do just that.'

If ever there was a moment to confess, this was it and, oh, how she was tempted to lay down the disguise and spill her secret at his feet. To blurt out the words, 'I am Elidh Easton and have no claim to nobility,' would solve all her problems concerning him. It would put her beyond him, the temptation of Sutton Keynes removed for good. He could not consider her then, nor would he want to. In fact, he'd help her pack. At least then the danger she posed to his fortune would be gone. But not the danger he posed to her heart. She supposed it might be too late for that.

'Is there no chance, then? To get to know you?' Sutton returned the conversation to the original question. She should give him a direct no and find some way to avoid him from here on out, but he was stroking her cheek, tipping her chin up to meet his gaze, his eyes on her lips, and the moment blurred. 'All I am asking for is your time. Surely that's no great threat to whatever you're trying to protect?' He paused and considered her for a long moment, a thought coming to him, clouding his eyes. Oh-oh, her heart seemed to thump. 'But perhaps you resist on moral grounds? Is that it, Chiara? Do you resist whatever is between us because you feel disloyal to someone else? A secret love at home in Fossano? I know I asked that day on the island if you were engaged in a dynastic alliance.

Since then, it has occurred to me, I might have asked the question incorrectly.'

She shook her head. She could tell the truth in this at least. 'No, I am not engaged elsewhere, officially or otherwise. Neither are my affections, not unless you count the gosling in my room.' She tried for humour, wondering suddenly if a lie might have served her better. A fictional betrothal might have achieved the distance she needed.

'Then why do I sense resistance, Chiara? I confess I've racked my brain trying to come up with a reason.'

'Because nothing here is real! Perhaps not even what you find intriguing about me. For fourteen days, everyone's world is narrowed down on the singular pursuit of a husband, or, in your case, a bride. Every activity, every interaction is aimed at that goal. Every walk, every game—archery, croquet, musical performances—all of it is designed with that goal in mind. Nothing is real, you said so yourself.'

'I am real. You are real. *We* are real, at least to each other,' Sutton argued quietly but firmly. 'This is real.' He reached for her then, his hand turning her face to his, his intentions clear.

'Sutton,' she breathed his name as his mouth took hers in a long sweet kiss reminiscent of the Adagio with its lingering notes. But it was more than that. It was a marking, a claiming. Elidh shivered despite the warmth of his presence. *Il bacio della morte.* The kiss of death. A Judas kiss.

One kiss changed everything, including the atmosphere in the music room when they re-entered.

Expressions communicated disapproval and distrust without words when Elidh stepped inside, Sutton behind her. She realised, too late, the illusion of privacy beyond those French doors. The glass panes blocked the sound of conversation, but they did not block the sight. The entire interaction had been visible for anyone who cared to look and apparently everyone had. Elidh felt her face flush, the final confirmation anyone needed if they'd doubted. She hated the thought of such a private, perfect moment having an audience.

Yet, the press of his mouth against hers lingered on her lips. It took all her willpower to resist tracing them with her finger, to touch where he'd touched. Isabelle Bradley pierced her with a stare that called her a liar in all but words as she passed on her way to the tea cart. Reactions warred inside her. Part of her wanted to run, but part of her refused to be ashamed. A princess would not be cowed by a middle-ranking nobleman's daughter.

But you're not a princess—not really...not any more than you are pretty. Both are illusions. Take away the pins and the silks and what is left?

Elidh held her head high and took a teacup from the cart, making it clear to any onlooker that she was going to stay and enjoy her tea. She wasn't alone. Her father came to her side and smiled at her, fondness lighting his eyes. 'You look so much like your mother tonight. She could command a room like no other woman I knew. I think you have come into your own.' The compliment disappointed her. She didn't want to be her mother or a princess in order to be noticed, to be liked—by her father, by Sutton. She just wanted to be herself. But their attentions, it seemed, were contingent. Her father nodded to Lord Wharton as he passed. Wharton's eyes were coldly polite. Battle lines were drawn, to her regret. She knew what her father was thinking—that she was the front runner, that he was close to winning his largest gamble. 'Now, drink your tea, my dear, and smile like this doesn't scare the hell out of you. That's what I am doing.'

'You? Prince Lorenzo Balare di Fossano? Scared?' she whispered. Perhaps there was still time to talk him into leaving right now. Only her heart wasn't in it, it was too busy savouring the grand moments of the evening and forgetting the danger each moment was wrapped in.

The two of them said nothing more until they were back in her room, the door closed behind them. They took up their usual places: her father on the tufted stool at her vanity, she cross-legged on the big bed, the gosling on her lap, Rosie on the window seat. The three of them stared at each other, gathering their thoughts in the silence.

'Bad news?' Rosie asked at last. 'Did the performance not go well?'

'On the contrary. Chiara has won his favour,' her father said solemnly. 'She was spectacular tonight.'

Rosie looked between them in confusion. 'Then this is cause for celebration? We're going to be rich!'

'We're going to be liars for ever,' Elidh said softly. 'This will never be over. If we're found out, it will

ruin not only us, but Sutton, too. He will lose the fortune if he doesn't wed a woman of noble birth, or he'll
have to support the lie.' How had this happened? She
wasn't even playing the game and yet she'd emerged
tonight as the perceived front runner for Sutton's attentions.

'Then we make sure he never finds out. After a
while, it will cease to matter. He'll be so in love with
his new bride. It's not as if he suspects anything as it
is,' Rosie reasoned.

'It's not him I'm most worried about,' her father
put in. 'The others will try to bring us down now that
his preference is public. I am sure many a parent will
be burning the midnight oil with hasty letters back to
London, making enquiries now that the Principessa
is a threat to their daughters. Rosie, we need all the
servants' gossip you can hear. I will personally assign
myself to Catherine Keynes to head off any trouble
on that end.' He fixed them with a general's stare, the
one he'd used in *Julius Caesar*. 'The real fight begins
now. We must be more vigilant than ever to ensure no
one gets inside our defences.'

'I can intercept the letters,' Rosie said. 'It's easy
enough. They're all collected on a plate, waiting for
the footman to take them, once they've been franked.'

'Or we can leave now,' Elidh interjected firmly.
Rosie and her father were building schemes upon
schemes now, talking of intercepting and stealing letters. Even if only one letter slipped through, the risk
of discovery would be great. 'What will people find
in London, Father, if enquiries are made?'

'Nothing but one late-arrived letter,' her father replied thoughtfully. 'The one letter I told Catherine Keynes I'd sent asking for permission to join the party. The one that arrived purposely late, which confirms our story. We have nothing to fear from London, because there's nothing there. Why ever would we leave now when we are so close to winning?'

Because they couldn't win, Elidh thought desperately. Even if they won, they lost. This ruse could not and should not be sustained. Elidh sighed. It was up to her, then, to put a stop to the madness and there were only two ways to do it. Either leave or tell Sutton the truth.

He was getting close to the truth and now the damn trail was cold, just when Bax had wagered a significant sum on his cousin proposing to a woman who didn't exist. The best runners in London couldn't find her and no peer of note had ever heard of the Principessa Chiara Balare di Fossano.

Bax ordered another brandy. Something was afoot, something that would hopefully justify this journey back into town. Before his cousin's house party, it seemed, no one in London, high society or low, had ever known of or encountered the Principessa except a young ticket seller who'd sold Prince Lorenzo Balare di Fossano first-class accommodations the day of the party.

Hell and damnation. Bax opened the slim file again, hoping to see something new in the information, something he hadn't seen before. But the file was scant.

There was one sheet inside. It contained two lines. His eyes fixed on the line that mattered.

It is the conclusion of this investigation that be-yond the sale of the tickets there is no record of the person you have enquired after.

No record. Nothing.

The runner had tried to explain to him that 'no record' simply meant there was no criminal record. Police weren't interested in ordinary citizens who committed no crimes, and certainly not foreigners visiting for a short time. He'd dismissed the runner and gone to the club to think—not White's. God, no. White's was too pristine, too clean for him, populated by men who gave themselves pristine airs as well.

Bax preferred a different sort of club—the Tartarus, located in Covent Garden where the population of gentlemen who frequented clubs was a wilder set. One could see all nature of interesting human behaviours outside these windows and there were rooms in the back where there were no windows. Peepholes. Maybe. Well, most likely. The Tartarus didn't skimp when it came to depravity and predilections. It was not the sort of place Sutton would ever frequent. Oh, no, his perfect cousin was going to marry a princess. Sutton had the world's best luck, it seemed. Forced to marry a noblewoman within four weeks and a beautiful Italian princess drops into his lap.

But not if Bax could help it. He was a big believer in the idea that when something looked too good to be true, it definitely was. Usually, people vanished *into* thin air. But the Princess had appeared *out of* thin air and conveniently just in time to win a fortune. How interesting. One wouldn't think a princess would be intrigued by a fortune. Normally, they came with fortunes of their own. Of course, Fenworth had told him she was only at the party as an observer, so perhaps that explained it. *Perhaps.* Bax wasn't buying it. He took a swallow of his drink, letting the brandy burn down his throat. It was a cut cheaper than what White's would serve, but he liked the edge. It kept him sharp. He had business to conduct in a while. But first he wanted to poke a few holes in this mystery.

The dregs of London had no record of her. What of society? Surely the upper class had records? The police kept note of criminals but society kept note of princesses. Surely she would have caught the *haut ton*'s attention? Surely she would have been mentioned in society pages, raving beauty that she was? It was this piece that mystified him more than the lack of a criminal record. Successful frauds didn't have records anyway and one would have to be extremely successful to escape his aunt's detection. But how to prove it? Maybe he didn't have to prove it. Perhaps a brazen stab in the dark with a little blackmail would be enough to send her running off into the night. It might be time to put in an appearance at the party and conduct a little fishing expedition. He could leave London on the morning train.

A man approached the table, well dressed but with

an air of roughness about him. Breeding would always tell, Bax thought, no matter how expensive the suit. He'd made this man rich, but he couldn't make him a gentleman. 'The cargo's ready. Did you want to inspect it one last time?'

Bax tossed down the rest of his drink and stood. 'They're clean? We have a doctor certifying they don't have the pox?' That was a mistake he couldn't afford to make—giving an eastern pasha the pox. It would be tantamount to a declaration of war. England wouldn't thank him for it if the Ottoman Empire accused him of infecting their royalty. It would expose the whole arrangement and him.

'Yes, sir, and everyone made their marks on the papers saying they chose to do this freely.' That was critical. It was the one thing he could use as proof that this wasn't slavery, that these women, most of them prostitutes, had chosen to take his offer to send them to Turkey. It was an enticing offer the way he presented it: to live in the luxury of a harem, to have clothes, food, shelter all their days. All they had to do was what they were already doing, only they didn't have to settle for the next sailor off the boat. They could have a king. That wasn't entirely true but the distinctions of Ottoman royalty would be lost on them. Bax didn't even try.

'Hopefully it wasn't too much trouble?' Bax asked, following the man to one of the back rooms.

'No more than usual. There's always a couple who resist, but we took care of that,' his man assured him. It was to be expected. It was a lot like net-fishing—

a few unexpected fish were pulled in with the usual catch, but the ends justified the means and if Bax sent a few girls east that might otherwise not have gone, he didn't worry over it.

Chapter Thirteen

His mother looked worried. Sutton glanced up from his correspondence. He'd stolen a few moments after breakfast to sift through the mounting pile of letters that had accumulated during the house party. 'What is it, Mother? Have the guards thrown another girl out of my chambers?' He smiled, but his mother didn't laugh.

'I want to talk about Princess Chiara. You were indiscreet last night at the musicale. I have been entertaining arguments all morning from concerned and angry parents. Lord Wharton has been most vociferous.' His mother took the chair across the desk. Her gaze was steady, but she looked drawn, giving truth that her words were not exaggerated. 'She offers you nothing, Sutton, but a distraction from the real task at hand. It insults the other guests.'

Sutton sat back in his chair, ready to defend his position. '*If* I was staking a claim to her, she is noble— that's all she needs to offer. It seems people are too quick to admit defeat if they're already assuming I'll marry the Italian Principessa.' The Marquis and Lord Wharton would only be too thrilled to know Chiara had resisted his efforts to court her affections. They'd rest far easier if they'd heard the conversation on the balcony last night instead of seen it. 'For the record, however, you're wrong on the other account, too. She does offer me more than just a title that satisfies my uncle's will.' How did he describe what she offered? There was peace in her presence, a chance to be himself, to express himself in ways he did not share with others. He tried to explain. 'We have things in common. Surprising things. She makes me laugh, she speaks her mind. She's the one girl here who appears to like *me*, not my money.'

A tempting realisation flickered to life, taking shape from the amorphous, nameless something that had flared between them from the start. *I could be happy with her. We could build a life.*

His mother read the trajectory of his thoughts. 'Can you truly see a princess rusticating with your camels at your dairy?'

Sutton did not hesitate. 'Yes. Not any princess, but I can see her. She rescued a gosling on our boating expedition. His foot was hurt and she scooped him in up in her palm and brought him home.' The more he argued, the more the idea grew and took form.

His mother arched a brow coolly. 'A gosling is not a stable full of camels. It's not like you to be irrational. Think, Sutton, how unnecessarily complicated it would be. How would you live together and satisfy your uncle's conditions? Your uncle's will doesn't allow for more than three months apart. Will she give up living in Italy? Will she expect you to spend part of the year at one of their many villas? You can't even spend two weeks away from your stable. You're chafing to be down there even now. How would you manage months at a time?' She gave him a pitying stare. It wasn't that the stable needed him. A manager could handle it. It was that *he* needed the stables. *He* couldn't be away from it. He was always drawn back to it. These last days, being so near and yet unable to be at the stables as he usually was, had been difficult.

Sutton said nothing. His mother was sowing the beginnings of doubt, as he was sure she'd intended to do. Chiara's question last night ran through his mind. *Why? What could come of it?* Perhaps, like his mother, she also saw the impossibilities of anything beyond the moment, no matter how great the attraction. What was happening to him that he had not? He, with his great mind for logic and his past, should have been the first to see them.

'Perhaps you should consider these things if you insist on singling her out and kissing her in front of everyone,' his mother warned.

'I did not single her out,' Sutton growled. 'Any more than I kissed her in front of everyone. People need to mind their own business. It was a private conversation. Voyeurs were not invited.'

'Yet it does not change the fact that, under other circumstances, the situation was nothing short of compromising. If it had happened at a London ball, you'd have been forced to the altar.' His mother did not back down. 'The only thing protecting you now is that no one in that room last night wants you to marry her. They want you to marry their daughters and you can't if you're caught compromising the Principessa.' His mother's eyes blazed. 'Sutton, you know nothing about her, about where she comes from, who her people are. She makes you laugh? That is not enough.'

'It was enough for you and Father,' Sutton argued. 'Why shouldn't my marriage be held to the same standard of happiness and mutual respect? Love, even, if we can find it.' There it was again, the contradiction he'd tried to explain to Chiara last night. The logic of choosing a mate had failed him. Like was supposed to attract like, that's how it worked in the animal kingdom. There were indicators that guided one's choosing and those indicators were ironclad. But not for him. The straightforward methods of the animal kingdom had failed him, superseded by an illogical emotion, something he'd thought he'd given up long ago after the debacle with Anabeth Morely. More to the point, something he should not revisit, if he had any sense. Emotion had served him poorly once. There was no reason to believe it would serve him any better a second time around. With so much at stake, he could not afford to lose his head over Chiara Balare. He knew that much at least, even if it seemed he was having difficulty from stopping himself from the action of doing it, proof that simply knowing wasn't preventative enough.

'You have different standards, now. Your uncle has seen to it.' She looked down at her hands. 'Since Leland's death, I have wondered if this is his way of getting revenge against me at last for not choosing him…' she looked up at him '…the sins of the father being visited on the son and all that.' Sutton knew this story, the love triangle between the brothers and the lovely Catherine Allwise in the Season of 1829. She'd chosen the second son, to the first's everlasting dismay, a dismay that coloured his marriage a year later to the wealthy East India Company heiress, Rose Hampton. His mother's idea wasn't outside the realm of possibility. His uncle was keen on revenge in general—the will was proof of it, subtly pitting cousin against cousin in a race for the fortune.

'No, Mother, I don't think this is about revenge against you,' Sutton offered. His mother wasn't looking for approbation, she was looking for absolution and he would give it to her. He'd been looking for something of the same last night on the balcony. Was this whole debacle truly his fault? 'Love doesn't work that way. If Uncle Leland had loved you, he would only have wanted your happiness even if it wasn't with him.'

She smiled. 'I appreciate your thoughts. I do *want* the same for you, I am just not sure the Princess is the one you can find it with.' She was holding back, debating whether or not to speak. For a woman who didn't usually hesitate to be direct, this offered a level of intrigue and concern.

'What is it, Mother? You have reservations. I hear it in what you're not saying. Do you know something?' His stomach clenched, a horrible hypothesis forming. What if he *couldn't* choose Chiara? What if there was

some impediment that prevented her from satisfying
his uncle's conditions? He ran through the conditions
in his mind. There'd been no stipulation that the bride
had to be English. Any nobility would suffice. But he
was going to need more than the usual persuasion. Her
eligibility might not matter if he could not overcome
her resistance.

'I fear she's not who she says she is.'

'Has there been word from your enquiries?' He
would pursue this logically. He would not let emotion
ride him, but the knot in his stomach drew tighter, making him regret the extra sausage he'd had at breakfast.

She shook her head. 'No. Nothing yet. But I am not
the only one making enquiries. Wharton has written
to friends and I suspect, after last night, others will
write as well.'

'So, there's no proof.' The knot began to relax. It
was all jealous supposition.

'Not yet. I just need you to be prepared, to have a
second choice in mind. Don't alienate the other girls.
Remember that no one likes to be second place. You
will lose Imogen Bettancourt. The Marquis will not
settle for his daughter to be a runner-up and to marry
a man with no title. His pride will not allow it. Others
will feel the same way. If you make them mad enough,
they might join forces and leave you holding an empty
bag, force you to surrender the fortune because you
snubbed their girls when you had the chance.'

Ah, so his mother had come with worries *and* warnings this morning. What if Chiara refused him at the
last? What if someone designed an obstacle that for-

bade him from choosing her? Choosing Chiara had suddenly become dangerous, not only for her, but for him.

'So the lords have gone from bribing us for our approval to threatening us for it,' Sutton mused over the birth of this new strategy. It was in direct response to his actions last night. Sweet heavens, they might as well put up a board like the one at the Newmarket race track displaying all the odds. He could imagine where the most pressure for this threat was coming from: Wharton, the Marquis, and Isabelle Bradley's father. 'Then it's time for us to divide and conquer.'

Sutton ran through in his mind the allies he needed most and who could be sidelined. In other words, which girls did he have to keep hopeful? Louie Fenworth didn't have the balls for confrontation and what balls he had were likely engaged on behalf of the Bissell twins as opposed to his poor sister, Eliza. But he would keep the Fenworths hopeful just because it was no trouble. Alexandra Darnley and Virginia Peckworth would easily find matches when they returned to London, matches their families might benefit from more in other, non-financial ways. They wouldn't protest much and neither would their parents. Moving them to the back of the pack would satisfy Wharton's little coterie by suggesting their own daughters were rising. 'Let Wharton and the Marquis know their daughters are still in contention. I'll spend time with them both today on the shopping trip to the village. We'll take the barouche, just the three of us.'

His mother nodded, her agile mind sifting through

his decision with approval. He reached for the next letter on the pile and casually scanned it. He reread it, this time far less casually. It was from the stable.

'What is it?' His mother leaned forward in concern.

'The mare, the one in foal.' It had turned into a high-risk pregnancy. The mare was only eight, but she'd not taken the other two times she'd been bred. Now, he feared she'd taken too well. 'I think it's twins.' It would be a rare occurrence, but he'd sworn he'd felt two babies and the mare's size was tremendous. 'She wasn't due until the end of August.' After all this business was done. The party would be over and he'd be wed. By August, he'd have the consolation of returning to normal life. But now, the mare was in labour three weeks early. He stood up, his decision made. 'I have to go. I'll leave immediately. Please make my apologies. I'll be back when the crisis has passed.' He knew that wasn't much of an answer. It could be anywhere from a few hours to a couple of days.

'Sutton! You can't walk out on your own gathering.' His mother was aghast. 'This is unorthodox, even for you. Wharton and the others will not tolerate this. They will sink you.'

'I cannot do otherwise. The mare needs my help. She won't make it without me.' She might not make it anyway if there were complications. Sutton halted at the door. 'Quietly tell Wharton, the Marquis, the Bradleys and the Fenworths they are front runners. That should placate them.'

'But the shopping trip!' his mother cried. 'Wharton will be furious.'

Sutton smiled. 'You planned an amazing house party in five days that drew England's finest. I have every confidence, Mother, you can smooth Wharton's feathers.' He slipped out the door. There was no more time for protests. He would change clothes and be at the barn within the half-hour.

She wanted to be gone from here! Elidh pressed her back up against the corridor wall, trying to be invisible. She clutched the basket holding her gosling tight to her chest. She shouldn't have eavesdropped, but once she'd started she couldn't stop, horrible as it was. She was supposed to join the girls for a morning of correspondence writing in the blue sitting room but when she'd approached, the gossip had stopped her short. They were talking about *her*.

'She's a fortune hunter and a liar, telling all of us she was just here to see an English house party.' That voice belonged Isabelle Bradley. Elidh would know that spoilt whine anywhere. 'But she's no different than the rest of us.'

'Maybe even worse.' That dart came from Imogen Bettancourt, who was always happy to parrot the opinions of others since she seemed to have none of her own.

'What do you mean?' someone asked in feigned shock designed to invite disclosure, and Imogen complied, eager to be the centre of attention for once on her own merits instead of her father's. Even Elidh found herself craning to hear.

'You know those foreign types. The Continental

nobility is wrecked. A Continental *conte* isn't worth nearly as much as an English viscount, for instance. Everyone knows English titles are the only ones with any real weight. The Princess and her father are probably paupers when it comes down to it, nothing but a title to recommend them.' Oh, that girl was cruel! Elidh winced at the words.

'That might be true.' Isabelle was back at it. 'She's worn that red dress twice.'

'I thought the dress was lovely,' A shy voice spoke up. Eliza Fenworth, Elidh thought. 'Besides, she's travelling. She doesn't have her whole wardrobe with her. It just proves she wasn't planning on coming. If I was allowed a red dress like hers, I'd wear it every day. I think the Princess has such beautiful, colourful clothes.'

Elidh smiled at Eliza's kindness. But her smile faded almost instantly. 'Colourful. Like her morals, no doubt.' That was one of the Bissell twins. Leah. She had a lower voice than her sister, not that anyone ever noticed. But Elidh did. It came in handy telling them apart. 'Italy is a land of passion and I dare say she's indulged. You can tell. That music she played last night, the dancing. The way she kissed Mr Keynes on the balcony.' *She* kissed? Sutton had kissed her. They had that part wrong.

'She's always throwing herself at him, it's shameless, really. She went off in the woods with him for croquet and then last night…'

'Don't forget the boating.' That was the higher-pitched twin, Rachel. Elidh stomped her foot. Didn't they remember *he* had asked her? That she hadn't even walked down to the lake with them. She'd walked ahead with Michael Peckworth. 'They were out on the lake for ages,' Rachel continued in a scandalised tone, 'and they even disappeared.'

'Slut.' Isabelle Bradley made a knife out of a single word. 'I don't know what he sees in her.'

'Don't be naive, Isabelle.' Leah laughed. 'All men want the same thing. I know exactly what he sees in her. A tumble to entertain himself with while he decides on a wife. She's easy and he's...hard.' She giggled at her wicked juxtaposition.

Virginia Peckworth spoke up, sounding pious. 'Be careful, Leah. You're not much better, you and Rachel, going off with Louie Fenworth. You don't want to end up tarred with the same brush.'

Leah snickered. 'You've been sweet on Louie for months and he's never noticed you. You're just jealous.'

'Well, it's common knowledge that Englishmen will flirt with easy girls like the Princess, but they will marry a respectable, *English* virgin.' Virginia preened. Elidh could almost see her sitting up straighter, tossing her glossy chestnut curls.

'Even your brother, apparently.' Leah wasn't ready to concede the field to Virginia. 'He was quite taken with the Italian slut before she ignored him for Keynes.' She laughed meanly. 'I guess size does matter. Your brother's...er...*fortune* can't match Keynes's.' An ominous silence followed. Elidh held her breath, hoping no one came stomping out of the room. She'd be seen for sure and they would all know she had heard. Perhaps they didn't care. She could imagine Virginia's brown eyes shooting darts at Leah. She half wished Virginia would do more than stare her down. Maybe stab her with a fountain pen. But that thought was petty and hardly worthy of her. It was a sign of how the masquerade was getting to her and how much the situation with Sutton was spiralling out of her control into emotions she didn't want to feel.

'Ladies, we shouldn't fight,' Alexandra Darnley, a friend to both the Bissell twins and Virginia, intervened. 'We should be united against a common enemy. Whatever she's done, it's working for her. She has Mr Keynes's attention and we don't. We have to neutralise her if any of us are to stand a chance. But look at us, we're fighting among ourselves and she's not even here. Do we *know* where she is? Has she somehow wangled yet more time with Mr Keynes while we sit here dutifully writing letters to our aunts? This is war, my friends, and we are being defeated. The Princess must be eliminated.'

Chapter Fourteen

Eliminated. What an awful word. The gosling began to cheep, restless in his basket. She would have to move on soon or risk discovery.

'We can't kill her, Alexandra!' someone cried. Elidh was beyond caring who.

'Heavens, no.' Alexandra was a cool customer. 'But we can minimise her. I have a plan.' The voices dropped to whispers and Elidh squeezed her eyes shut against the tears. They hated her. She could not go in there. This was naked female aggression unveiled. She didn't want to go anywhere they might be. *Eliminate. Neutralise. Minimise.* She was tired of being brave, tired of pretending she could face them down and win. There were simply too many of them.

She turned and ran, hoping to make the sanctuary of her room before the tears fell. Princesses didn't cry. Princesses were not intimidated by the likes of Alexandra Darnley. But she couldn't be a princess right now. It felt as if she was besieged from all sides: girls who thought she was competing against them; her father who was scamming everyone, even her, by pushing her forward in this competition she wanted no part of; even Sutton was against her in his own irresistible way, with his insistence about spending time with her, with that ill-advised kiss he'd stolen last night. She was fighting on all fronts and she just couldn't keep it up. She took the first corner and ran straight into a wall—a wall with arms, a wall that had also been moving in a distracted hurry.

'Where are you going in such a rush?' Sutton steadied her, taking in her stricken face. 'Chiara, what's happened?'

She couldn't breathe for a moment from the impact. But it was long enough to gather her wits and to take in the fact that he'd been running, too, his own breathing uneven. 'Where are *you* going?' Far better to ask a question than to answer the one he'd asked.

'To the stables, I must leave immediately. A mare is in distress.' And so was he. It registered now that he'd changed clothes. He was dressed in a work shirt and old breeches. She forgot about her problems and focused on his concern. She'd yet to see him worked up over anything like this, but he was definitely upset. 'I have to save her and her foals.' The concern was etched all over his face as the words tumbled out. He'd been distracted, it was why he hadn't seen her sooner. Elidh made a split-second decision.

'I am coming with you.' It would be an escape and perhaps she could do some good.

'Chiara, there's no time to lose. I cannot wait for

you to get ready.' He was setting her away from him even as he spoke, his urgency driving him to bluntness.

She held up her basket with the gosling inside. 'Then stop arguing. I have everything I need. Let's go.'

It was the most impulsive decision she'd ever made in her life. It was the kind of decision her father would make: rash, well intentioned, but with unlooked-for side effects such as being thrown up on Sutton's big gelding, Sutton's body behind her on the saddle, his arms about her as he took the reins and kicked the big bay into motion with only the tersest of warnings— 'Hold on'—something easier said than done when holding a basket with a baby goose in it. Then they were off, galloping across the estate to stables she hadn't known existed.

That had been her first miscalculation. She'd assumed they were going to the stables closer to the house, where Sutton's gelding and the guests' mounts were boarded for easy access along with the carriages. But these stables were working stables and further away on the edge of an estate that encompassed acres upon acres of land.

Distance was her second. Her impulsive decision to accompany him might have secured escape from the girls, but it had also played into their gossip. She was unchaperoned and alone with their host, flying across fields between Sutton's legs. Frightening as the ride itself was—Elidh wasn't much of a rider—she could not overlook the intimacy of the experience, something she was reminded of frequently as she jounced between his thighs—his rock-hard, well-muscled thighs that she suspected flexed endlessly to keep them both in the saddle. Whatever the girls had accused her of, she'd certainly given them cause. She knew exactly how this would look if anyone discovered she'd left with him. It would not look altruistic and there wouldn't be anyone who'd believe she'd thought they were just going to the riding stables and checking on a mare.

With relief, she saw the stables come into view and, shortly after, Sutton reined his horse to a halt in the yard. He dismounted with efficient athleticism and helped her down, a somewhat less athletic dismount on her part. A man raced out to greet him. The two of them were already in deep conversation, striding towards the barn, leaving her to trail behind at her own pace as a boy came to take the gelding.

The first thing Elidh noticed when she entered the barn was the overwhelming smell of manure and urine, which was a fairly significant thing to notice considering the stable floor was brushed clean, not a stick of errant straw in the aisle, and exotic camels lined the stalls, their long necks poking over their half-doors. Out of reflex, in defence against the smell, she pulled out her handkerchief. Ahead of her, Sutton strode unbothered by the stink. Camels! She'd never seen one up close, but there was no time to explore the excitement of that if she wanted to keep up with Sutton, who was nearing the end of a long stable. The smell was better here. Camels gave way to horses in the stalls until they reached the end where a mare lay on her side in a big box stall full of hay.

'How long as she been like this?' Sutton asked the

groom as he knelt beside the mare's head, crooning soft words.

'Since this morning when we brought the hay. She was sweating for a while and I thought she might foal, but nothing has happened and she's stopped sweating.'

'Foaling in the morning would be unusual,' Sutton mused, moving to reach over her back to feel her belly, careful to stay away from any sudden flailing hooves.

Elidh watched in the silence as he conducted his examination. 'What is wrong?' she asked softly once he'd finished and they were alone.

'If she was in labour, there'd be contractions. I don't like that they seem to have stopped.' Sutton furrowed his brow, his usually neatly combed hair falling forward over his face. He pushed it back and ran a hand over his mouth in thought. His gaze met hers. 'I think she might be carrying twins.'

Elidh worried her lip. One didn't need to know horses to know delivering twins of any sort was dangerous. 'Perhaps if we get her up, have her move around, that might wake the babies up,' Elidh suggested. 'It could be that the grooms mistook kicking for contractions.' They'd had a goat once, which the troupe had used first as a prop for *A Midsummer Night's Dream* and later kept on for milk. The goat had been one of her father's more impulsive purchases, but Elidh had loved that animal. The troupe had discovered rather unexpectedly the goat was pregnant. A farmer who'd let them camp on his land had recommended they walk her as labour neared.

Sutton nodded. 'Stand at her head and help me get her up. When I give the signal, tug at her halter.'

Horses were bigger than goats. A lot bigger. But Elidh didn't hesitate. The mare's distress overrode her own fears. This was no time to be afraid. The mare was clearly uncomfortable, clearly in need of help, and Elidh's heart went out to her, much as it had gone out to the goat years before and the gosling snuggled in the basket. On the third try, they got the mare up, Elidh pulling at the halter and Sutton pushing from behind. The horse came to its feet in an unsteady lurch, bulky and unwieldy. Sutton was beside her, attaching a lead rope to the halter and clucking to the mare. 'We'll take her outside and walk, nice and slow.'

The fresh air helped. The mare seemed more relaxed and Sutton did, too. They walked slowly, one on each side of the mare. Under other circumstances, the outing would be ideal. The weather was warm, the sky blue, a perfect July day. But Sutton was worried about the mare and she knew there were other things on his mind as well. 'Tell me about the camels,' she asked in hopes that, for just a few moments, she could take his mind from his troubles.

'They're my project.' He smiled across the mare's nose. 'I am studying the effects of their milk across breeds. I am a proponent of feeding camel's milk to thoroughbred foals as a supplement to their usual diet after the first month to enhance their nutrition and strengthen their bones. Maybe even help them grow faster, stronger. In the past, it hasn't been uncommon to feed camel's milk as a substitute to foals, but I'd like to see if its properties can be more than a substitute. I think camel's milk could be good for humans, too.'

Elidh wrinkled her nose playfully. 'They smell.' She couldn't imagine drinking something that came from such smelly creatures.

'It's because they recycle their urine internally. It causes them to give off an odour…it permeates, or infiltrates their skin.'

'Recycled urine? Lovely,' she choked out. Well, that certainly explained the smell at the other end of the barn.

Sutton laughed. 'You should see the look on your face.' Then he sobered. 'I am sorry, I have shocked you. At last, I have found Princess Chiara's limits of good sense.' The remark stole the joy from him.

'Oh, no! Don't think that. It's just a rather new concept.' She smiled, embarrassed that she'd not responded better. His face had lit up when he'd spoken of his camels. She should have known. 'So, do you drink camel's milk?' That seemed to be a safer topic to return to.

'Yes, absolutely.' He was grinning again and it was infectious. His joy had returned.

'What does it taste like?' Elidh asked with cautious curiosity. 'I'd like to try it sometime.' She'd drink anything to see him smile, further proof of how far she'd fallen where this man was concerned, this man she wasn't supposed to feel anything for, whom she wasn't even supposed to have noticed.

'It tastes like milk, of course.' He laughed. 'It's creamy like cow's milk, maybe a little saltier, a little more filling.' They stopped at a white painted fence and let the mare rest. Sutton leaned against it, a booted foot on the lowest railing, the breeze ruffling his hair. He looked good, despite his worry. Natural even, in a way that was different from the confidence he exuded in dark evening clothes. There was an informal confidence that emanated from him as if he knew he'd found his place in the world.

'You belong here.' The words slipped from her without conscious thought. It was a conclusion as intuitive as breathing, and as obvious. He did belong here, with the horses and the camels, here among the paddocks and stables. There was an ease to him that was missing from the man he'd been at the party. 'I've only seen a glimpse of you until now, I think,' Elidh said softly, still in quiet awe of her discovery. Then she made another one. 'It must be hard to be away from it.' No wonder he resented the party so much.

'More than you know,' came the reply. 'Sometimes I think I am better with animals than people.'

'That's not true!' she protested quickly, automatically. 'You're very good with people when you want to be. You were so kind to Eliza last night.' Elidh remembered how he'd taken time to sit with Eliza when she'd been alone on the sofa before the musicale started.

'Yet I was far happier chasing a croquet ball in the woods than returning to the party,' he corrected with a laugh. 'When given the chance to socialise, I'll always choose animals over people.'

'Why is that, do you suppose?' she asked softly. This was a new piece of him he'd not yet revealed, a new layer to turn back. Certainly, he'd made no secret of resenting the conditions surrounding the party and he'd made no secret to her of his disappointment with the girls. But this was a new layer, a layer that might explain the reason for his reticence to socialise despite the fact that he was equipped for it in both looks and manners.

Her comment drew his gaze. He shook his head with a sad smile. 'I suppose it's because animals are more honest. One always knows where one stands with them. Even if they don't like you, at least you're clear on it. I was disappointed in love once. There was a girl who turned out to be less than I had hoped. It was a painful lesson in the nuances of society. I'd never felt that way about anyone before and it hurt for a long while. That was reason enough to withdraw, but when I stopped licking my wounds, I simply couldn't find a reason to go back. Why would I spend my time among frauds and hypocrites, where everyone tries so very hard to be something other than themselves?' He gave a little chuckle. 'Now you see why I resent this party so much. It seems everything has come full circle and I must choose one of them. I must play the games I despise. Worst of all, it forces me to become a thing I hate.'

Yes, now she saw not only the source of his resentment, but so much more. She could never tell him her truth. *Never.* That option was firmly gone. Whatever hurt this other girl had meted out to him, her betrayal would be so much worse because it would be the second time. He might never allow himself to love again. She could not be responsible for that. Sutton Keynes was a good man, caught in an untenable position. He deserved better. He deserved a chance to find love. His words had stung. *Why would I spend my time among frauds and hypocrites?* There was one standing right beside him and he'd bared his soul to her.

She was touched that he'd shared something so deeply personal and yet panicked by the revelation, too. Sutton was not a man who would tell just anyone such a thing. It was sign of his growing esteem for her, as if she needed another painful reminder. There were kisses between them and now there were secrets, private disclosures of the heart. 'I'm sorry you were hurt,' she offered gently. What else could she say?

He shrugged. 'I survived. Enough about me. What about you?' Some of the sparkle returned to his eyes. 'Have you ever been in love, Chiara?'

She laughed to cover her embarrassment. 'What a bold question!'

He nudged her foot with his boot. 'Come on, tell me. I've told you a secret, it's only fair you respond in kind.'

'No. I haven't been in love before.'

'That's it? Just no? No explanation? That's not fair,' Sutton teased. 'I poured myself out to you. Why not? Hasn't anyone captured your fancy?'

No one but you. You with your honesty and blue eyes, she thought. But that was another truth she couldn't speak out loud.

Chapter Fifteen

'There hasn't been time.' Elidh groped for a suitable answer and found this one to be true. Who would she have met? Who would have claimed her heart the way Sutton had claimed it in so short a time?

'Time?' Sutton persisted with a probing smile, inviting her to say more.

She slid him a nervous smile. Like him, she seldom talked about herself. Her life was taken up with other things; rent, the stress of their meagre finances, and Bermondsey Street didn't boast a social whirl she enjoyed. 'As you've noted, people take a lot of work.'

His chuckle encouraged her. They started walking again along the fence line as she talked. 'My father, for instance, he takes a lot of work. Ever since my mother died, I have a new appreciation for how she kept him in line. We both miss her. She brought balance to our little family. I've tried my best, but I can't compete. I'm not her.' Not in temperament, not in looks.

'I miss my father, too. It will be five years this autumn. He died in India. He caught a fever on a business trip. Now, I feel I need to be there for my mother, to take care of her the way he took care of her.'

'I don't think your mother needs looking after,' Elidh put in. Catherine Keynes always appeared in charge. She was quite intimidating at times, in fact.

'She doesn't, not in an obvious way,' Sutton acceded. 'But I don't like her to worry. I don't want her to be alone. She will always have a place with me at Hartswood. Father would have wanted that. But I'm not him. He loved adventure, the risk of a business gamble, but that's not me at all.' He gestured to the field around them. 'I like it here. I'd be content to stay in Newmarket for ever and never leave.' He gave a self-deprecating laugh. 'That must sound boring to you. You travel.'

'Only because circumstances demand it.' It was true as far as it went. 'My father needed to get away and I can't imagine leaving my father on his own. It would be a disaster.'

Sutton turned the mare back towards the stables and a slid her a warm look that nearly melted her. 'Your father, my mother, your goose, my mare, my camels—we have quite the menagerie between us.' And more than that. Here was a man who shared her love of home, of permanence, of the people in their lives. Both of them were very intentional about who received their attentions and affections.

'That's the sort of people we are. We collect those in need,' Elidh offered.

The mare stopped and heaved, swaying for a moment from hoof to hoof as a contraction took her. Sutton flashed her a smile of gratitude. 'How did you know to walk her?'

'We had a goat when I was growing up.' The words were out before she could rethink them. Her relief had made her careless and Sutton noticed.

He arched a dark brow. 'Really? A princess had a goat for a pet?'

'Well, you have camels,' she shot back with a directness that was becoming second nature. Perhaps she'd keep that quality once the ruse was over. 'I told you my father is a handful, always has been. He brought home a monkey once.'

They settled the mare back in her stall, careful to keep her on her feet lest the foals settle down once more and labour fail to progress. Sutton leaned against the stall door. 'Thank you, for being here, for being stubborn enough to make me bring you. It will be a while now. Labour can last up to eight hours and horses prefer to foal at night, the later the better, it seems. Would you like to go back to the house? I can have someone drive you up in the pony cart.'

'If you're staying here, I am staying, too.' Elidh stroked the mare's long nose and murmured to the horse, 'You're going to be all right. You're going to be a mother soon and I am not going anywhere until that happens.'

Sutton shifted uncomfortably. 'I appreciate the sentiment, but perhaps staying isn't the best idea. You'll ruin your...'

'Reputation?' Elidh put in.

'I was going to say "your dress," but reputation, yes.' Sutton looked serious. 'We're here alone.'

'Surrounded by your grooms,' Elidh argued. In truth, she was loath to go, reputation in question or not. She felt as if she'd finally discovered the real Sutton.

'Still, we're here alone. Away from the guests,' he pointed out.

'I think it's too late to worry about my reputation,' Elidh said honestly. 'Last night sealed it. The girls did not take kindly to my performance or yours.'

'Is that why you were upset this morning?' Sutton asked. She told him about her eavesdropping and he shrugged apologetically. 'I suppose you're angry with me?'

'I should be. But I'm not, truly.' She could not summon any anger for this man who'd also been thrust into an unwanted situation, this man who loved his mother as she loved her father, this man who gave his heart to those around him who needed him.

When it came to giving hearts, she might be in grave jeopardy of giving her own. As they stood there, stroking the mare, it occurred to Elidh she was going to leave with a broken heart when this all ended, and it would. The end was in sight, the party nearly down to its final stretch. What would happen to her then? How would she survive leaving Sutton? The mare shook with another contraction. 'It will be all right,' Elidh soothed the horse. But the words and the hopes they engendered were just as much for herself.

Everything was all right. For a while. Through the long afternoon of waiting, she and Sutton sat on hay bales outside the mare's stall and talked away the afternoon. He told her about his camels and his horses, how horses only feared camels if they weren't raised with them and all kinds of sundry trivia. She didn't mind. He could talk about camels all he wanted. It was becoming increasingly obvious that his joy was her joy. Elidh preferred to let him talk. It was best if they didn't talk about her, best if she didn't have to spin lies about a life she didn't really live.

They looked after the gosling, setting him down to waddle around the stable floor as evening fell. His foot was getting better. 'Soon he'll be able to go back to the lake.' A look passed between them, her words raising thoughts of other returns that would have to be made. The gosling wasn't the only one faced with going back. Sutton would have to make decisions soon. She would leave before that. She didn't think she could stay and watch him choose a girl, knowing what it cost them both.

'Who will you choose?' Elidh asked softly, picking up the unspoken conversation between them. After today, after seeing him in the stables, she couldn't imagine him with any of the other girls. Not for a lifetime.

'I don't know, truly, I don't.' Resignation shadowed his eyes and the sight of it pained her. 'Chiara, what if—' he began, and she cut him off swiftly, afraid of what he might ask her.

'You could give the fortune up. Perhaps marriage is too high a price to pay to protect your cousin from fiscal irresponsibility. He has to grow up at some point.' She couldn't save herself, but perhaps she could save him, persuade him that he didn't have to fulfil the conditions of the will. 'Let him fritter away money on fine clothes and luxuries if it buys you your freedom, your happiness.'

Sutton shook his head. 'If only it were just that. It's more than an abundance of fine living. To put it delicately, my cousin is entirely without morals. He will use the money to perpetuate a level of corruption I hesitate to discuss openly. My uncle knew this.' He was being delicate. Elidh heard it in his careful word choice. 'I am committed to this path, even if I am not committed to my choice.'

Behind them in the stall, the mare gave a groan. Sutton was on his feet and beside the horse. The mare went to her knees and on to her side. Sutton's hand was on her belly. He checked her flanks. 'She's sweating.' There was excitement in his voice. 'I think this is it. It won't be long now.'

'Shall I get anything?' Elidh asked.

'No, mares don't need any assistance unless something goes wrong.' He patted the mare's neck. 'She'll do fine. Horses have been doing this for thousands of years.'

But the mare wasn't fine. An hour later, there'd been no progress and the horse was clearly pushing. 'Hold her head,' he instructed softly, moving behind the mare. A few moments later, he swore softly. 'The placenta is coming first. The foal can't breathe. I need scissors.'

Elidh rose, 'I'll get them.' She raced to the tack room and found them hanging on a wall. When she returned, Sutton was working with the mare, his hands on her belly, competent hands, strong hands, tracing the outline of the foals while his voice murmured soothing words. She let the sight of him imprint on her mind: all that gentleness, all that love. She wanted to carry this image of him with her always. Perhaps this was the moment, watching him lavish the mare with his attentions and care, that she knew the hard truth. She loved *him*, this man who drank camel's milk and disdained society. It was going to hurt like hell to lose him. She'd come to that realisation, too, throughout the long day. She was going to lose him sooner or later. But before that happened, she wanted to have him, just once.

He would not lose her! By God, he would save the mare and the babies, too. Sutton took the scissors from Chiara with a grateful, grim nod and went to work. The next few minutes were critical. The foal would suffocate if he could not free it. With single-minded determination, Sutton set about cutting the placenta, careful not to nick the foal. Then it was time to reach, to guide the foal out into the world so it could breathe on its own. He shut his eyes, letting touch guide him. He could hear Chiara's calming voice at the mare's head, her lovely accent soothing the distraught animal. She'd been more help today than she knew. Her presence alone had brought him peace of mind while he waited for the mare to deliver. He was glad she was here now, never mind how unpleasant the situation. She hadn't flinched once.

There! He felt the foal's leg. At last the foal was in

the perfect position. Sutton drew out one leg, then the other, then gently reached for the head and finally the foal was out. 'Chiara, take him, settle him with his mother, let her clean her baby up,' Sutton instructed. There was no time to celebrate yet, not while there was the other foal to save, a foal who'd had no choice but to survive without oxygen slightly longer than his brother.

He closed his eyes and reached once more, aware only that Chiara had come for the colt. He could hear the rustle of hay as she settled it with the mare. He found the foot. He didn't like where it was positioned, it was as if the foal hadn't quite completed its turn. Not necessarily unusual given that space was a premium when two foals shared an area meant for one. Still, it made delivery difficult. He brought the leg forward and then the other, moving the foal bit by careful bit, caution and urgency warring within him. Too much caution on his part meant more time without oxygen for the foal. Too much urgency on his part risked the mare.

'Hold on, hold on, just a little longer, hold on,' he muttered the litany under his breath, encouragement for the unseen foal, encouragement for himself. He felt Chiara with him, standing beside him.

'You can do it, Sutton,' she said softly, lending him strength with her confidence that he could do anything. He hoped she was right. Then the foal was out, smaller than his brother, stiller than his brother. No, he wasn't too late, he hadn't been too slow. No, he would not accept that. Sutton took the foal to the mare, helping her to clear the amnion from the baby in hopes it would help with breathing. Precious seconds seemed to turn into minutes, then the colt's chest moved, haltingly, sputtering at first, becoming steady.

'He's breathing, Sutton. He's alive.' Chiara was crying, overwhelmed with joy, her response equal to the emotion of the moment. 'You did it, Sutton, you saved them!' She was in his arms then and they were laughing together, crying together, never mind that his clothes were covered in grime. Chiara's dress had fared only marginally better after a day in the barn. It didn't matter. The foals were here, alive, and whatever it was between he and Chiara was alive as well. The truth of it thrummed through his veins. She was the one he wanted, the one he could build a life with. Even at the dangerous end of the birth, she'd believed in *him*, never doubted him, and it filled him with a certain, confident euphoria that overrode common sense, that overrode the scars of Anabeth Morely's betrayal and the fear of giving his heart again. If he could, he would choose her. Would she choose him? In the moment, the other end of that equation seemed irrelevant. It was enough to hold her, to celebrate with her.

The first foal found his legs and staggered over to nurse. The second did not. Sutton felt Chiara's grip on him tighten in worry and anticipation. The mare nudged the little foal, encouraging him to move, to stand and then a little miracle happened. The first foal turned back to his brother and nuzzled him with his nose as his mother pushed once more, the two of them coaxing. The second foal tried once, twice, three times, and stood on trembling legs, his brother leading him to nurse.

Chiara's eyes shone up at Sutton with a glow that had nothing to do with the size of his bank account, but the size of his heart, the size of what they'd witnessed and participated in tonight, and the realisation moved him. Her arms were about his neck, her head tilted up to him, a smile that brimmed with life and love and a celebration of both on her beautiful lips just before she kissed him, hard and full on his mouth.

She was intoxicating like this, her hair down, her dress a mess beyond saving. She'd never looked less like a princess or more lovely. Her hips moved against him and he had her face in his hands, the kiss deepening, intensifying as the emotions of the night swept over them both. He should have stopped it there, should have known better. But he didn't. Perhaps it was the thrill of saving a life, or the potency of witnessing the great miracle of birth, the creation of a family, that pushed him to recklessness, or maybe it was something more he wasn't willing to name yet, and neither was she.

When Chiara breathed the words, 'I don't want to go back tonight', he didn't insist on reasoning with her. He knew what she was asking, what she wanted. They were of one mind on that account. After this afternoon, it seemed inevitable that their day would end like this. He led her to the small apartment he kept above the stables for all those nights when he didn't want to go back either.

Chapter Sixteen

Inside the small room, Sutton lit the lamp, casting shadows on the walls, illuminating the bed and the chest of drawers, the only furniture in the room. He turned to set the lamp down and Chiara touched his arm, her voice husky. 'Let me be clear. I want you to stay with me, Sutton.' Heaven bless her directness. She thought he meant to leave, that he'd taken her request literally.

'I know.' His voice rivalled hers for huskiness. The walk to the apartment had not dimmed his ardour, but it had reasserted his sense of honour. It wasn't enough for him to want this. She had to want this, too. 'I mean to stay, if you're sure?'

She nodded. 'I've never been more sure.'

Sutton grinned. 'Good. Me, too.' Then, as if to demonstrate, he pulled his filthy shirt over his head and threw it into a corner and stood before her, bare-chested and ready. She came to him, tracing the contours of his chest with her finger, the touch of her sending a wave of heat through him.

'You're tan. I wondered about that,' she breathed. She touched him, reverently, with awe as if she found him beautiful. He'd never thought of himself that way. Attractive, certainly. But beautiful? Worthy of a woman's awe? It was heady to see himself through her eyes, this woman who had no doubt been courted by Italy's finest men despite her claims to have not found love. It flattered him deeply that he would be her first naked man. Her first man. Period.

It did not escape him that for all her directness, she was as virginal as the other girls here. A young *principessa* from a Catholic Italy would be a virgin. It would be a paramount condition of her marriage to an Italian prince. He was cognisant, too, that there would be no Italian prince now. There would be him. Only him. He would be her first and last lover. The only man ever in her bed. He was that sure of *them*. That this was a decision neither of them had taken lightly. They both had too much at stake.

Untried she might be, but Chiara was not without curiosity. A glimmer of mischief sparked playfully in her eyes, her hands resting on the waistband of his breeches. 'Are you tan everywhere?'

He answered with a playful smile of his own. 'Let's find out.'

He was tanned everywhere. And he was beautiful, this man who calmed mares and saved foals, this man who looked at her with play and passion in his gaze as he stood before her naked, his boots and breeches discarded. Her imagination already conjured a hundred erotic scenarios as her eyes roved the length of him: the sculpted muscle of his arms, the smooth strength of his chest, the leanness of his hips, his powerful thighs and what lay between them, that utterly masculine part of him, so rigid and *hearty*. Robust came to mind, as did beautiful once again. Roughly beautiful, a contrast to his elegant beauty, and a reminder that, at his core, all refinement stripped away, he was an earthy man. 'How do you manage it? To be tan all over?'

'I don't spend my summers in London, for a start.' Sutton smiled. Even his smile looked different naked. 'I swim in the lake, I sail without my shirt on, there's a hot spring I like not far from the stables. I take a dip in it after a long day.'

'In short, you run around your property naked,' she surmised with a laugh. She liked this peeling back of the layers of the proper gentleman. He was an outdoorsman, a nature lover, an animal lover, a man who, despite his strengths, was vulnerable in his own way.

'Yes, I suppose you could say that.' He laughed. 'There's no one here to see, usually. So why not?' It was another reminder as to how much he must despise the intrusion of the house party on so many levels. It had upended everything about his life, from the grand scheme of it to his private, daily activities. 'Some women find men with tans to be common, ungentlemanly.'

She stepped towards him, wanting to feel with her hands the power she'd seen with her eyes. 'I am not one of them.' Beneath the good looks, the fine clothes and finer manners, he was a lot like her. Elidh had not thought to encounter such qualities in a man when she'd begun this. And yet day by day, as he revealed a little more of himself to her, she discovered they were more and more alike in thought, in temperament, than she'd believed possible. She touched him then, her hands skimming the defined expanse of his chest, tracing the ridges and planes of his musculature in fascination. This was new territory. Women's bodies, her body, didn't have this definition of form. A kernel of fear lodged in her belly. She hadn't her mother's lushness of figure. Would he be disappointed in her? All her deficiencies came roaring back to her. It was easy to forget them when she was with him. He made her feel beautiful—so beautiful, in fact, that she'd nearly forgotten to think poorly of her slimness, her flatness.

His hand was on the ribbon of her bodice, his voice a low, seductive husk as he chuckled. 'Your turn, I think. One of us is overdressed for the occasion.' She was suddenly shy. She covered his hand and removed it from the ribbon. She'd not thought this through. There was little chance her lack of cleavage would escape notice now.

'Did you think we'd make love with our clothes on?' It was kindly said. Intuitively, she knew Sutton would never be cruel about intimacy. But it was exactly what she'd thought when she'd imagined it, when she'd mentally committed to it in the long afternoon of waiting. She'd thought to have him once before she lost him. She'd thought a lot of things. But not that she'd end up here in an apartment with all the privacy she could desire, a whole night spread out before her with Sutton.

It was an embarrassment of riches as far as her fantasy went. Only, it seemed her fantasy had run ahead of her imagination. Her expression gave her away. She had indeed thought it might be managed clothed.

'It's not uncommon to think so,' Sutton offered with a smile. 'Many do, especially those of our class. I don't recommend it, however.' Of course not; he ran around his estate naked. 'I don't think there's much quality to those sorts of interludes. Keeping one's clothes on is efficient, speedy. I don't like to apply those adjectives to lovemaking.' He was kissing her again, small, tender kisses that started at her ear and ended at her throat, all designed to render her senseless, but not him. Sutton was the gentleman, even when he stood before her naked, his own commitment to this, to her, evident and ready. 'Do you want this, Chiara?'

In that moment, Elidh hated that name. It had come to represent every lie that lay between them, everything that would one day soon drive them apart. She wanted to hear her name on his lips. He was not bedding the woman he thought she was. But this was the compromise she had to make, the price she had to pay if she wanted to have him. She could only have him as the Principessa and even then the ruse could not protect her for long.

She stepped back, her hand fingering the ribbon of her bodice in a nervous fidget. 'I don't want you to be disappointed.' She would be honest in this, if nothing else.

He reached for her, untying, unlacing, loosening her ruined gown until it fell away. 'You *are* a beauti-

ful woman, Chiara, so elegantly turned out every day
with your hair, your cosmetics, your clothes and jewels. You dazzle men effortlessly with all of that. But
I pity the man who loves you for your hairstyles and
clothes. That man doesn't see your real beauty—your
heart, your passion for living. That man misses the
spark in your eye when you tease, when you play your
guitar.' His hands competently unlaced her corset and
stripped away the last of her undergarments until she
stood before him in all her honesty.

'No, don't cover yourself.' He coaxed away her
hands. 'Let me look at you.' His hands reached last
for the few remaining pins in her hair, pulling them
out one at a time. Her hair fell entirely free now, no
longer half-up, half-down, no longer an unruly mess
from the day's exertions. 'Your hair reminds me of soft
butter,' Sutton said as the last tress fell about her shoulders like a cloak. He held her gaze, his own, blue and
hot, communicating his desire long before his words.
'Come and lie beside me, Chiara.' The low rumble of
those words made her tremble with want. She slipped
her hand into his and let him lead her to the bed. This
room, this man, this moment, was the sum of the world.
Nothing else mattered. She would think of nothing but
these feelings. She would let nothing ruin this. Tonight,
they could not hurt each other.

It wasn't so much a lying beside one another as it
was a covering, his gloriously muscled arms bracketing her head, taking his weight as his length enveloped
her, the power of his body surrounding her. She was
safe here beneath him, where nothing could touch her,

not even the truth. His mouth, his hands made love to every inch of her; ears and lips, throat and neck, each breast in turn the recipient of his wicked tongue, his gentle mouth, as he sucked and licked. Although there was no gentleness in the reaction his lovemaking provoked. Her pulse raced, her body positively begged for more, each little gasp asking for more kisses, more caresses, more mouth, more hands, more him.

Sutton kissed her navel and looked up at her. It was a look meant to undo a woman, two hot, burning-blue coals looking up at her from her stomach. Elidh had never felt so completely on fire, never understood what it meant to burn until this moment. She gave a frustrated cry of pleasure partially fulfilled, partially denied. She only knew that she wanted and wanted and wanted.

Chiara writhed beneath him, fire writhed within him, passion's flames licking at the very core of his restraint as he came up over her once more. They were both more than ready for this. This time, she opened for him, her legs bracketing him, hips, thighs and all, as his arms bracketed her head, taking his weight. They were mirrors of one another, their bodies cradling one another. He moved against her, his manhood strong and hard at her thigh, a reminder of his power, as his fingers worked at her entrance. He would be a considerate lover in all ways, from her comfort to her pleasure.

'Are you ready for me?' One last huskily voiced request for permission, for consent.

'More than ready,' came her whispered reply, a

breathy rasp. He levered himself up once more and this time he took her, entering her slowly, his eyes closed against the exquisite torture of taking her, of feeling her stretching around him, her body welcoming him. This was sweet heaven and a sweet hell. He couldn't go too fast, couldn't stretch her too much too soon, no matter how his body wanted to rush.

He withdrew and pressed forward again and again, each effort bringing him closer to her core, closer to completion. He reached her core and felt her hips lift, welcoming him, *wanting* him. A begging mewl escaped her, her legs wrapped around him, holding him as she found his rhythm and joined him. A smile took her face as the pain of the newness, the presence of him, faded into pleasure.

He increased the tempo; desire had free rein now for them both. He felt the strain in his arms, in the clench of his buttocks as he thrust. His body tightened and he let release sweep him in a pounding wave that took them both, Chiara wrapped about him, legs at his waist, arms at his neck, her cries muffled against his shoulder for these extraordinary seconds. He closed his eyes and breathed deep, willing the seconds to slow and stretch, willing the pleasure to last as he held her.

Sutton was aware of everything in those precious moments—his world was a vibrant kaleidoscope of the senses. He felt the rapid rise and fall of her body, the race of her pulse and then its slowing as she recovered; smelled the sweet, tart scent of arousal on her skin as it mixed with his sweat. This was glorious in a way a purely physical coupling was not. She was his, would always be his, just as soon as he could marry her.

Sutton rolled on to his back, settling Chiara against his shoulder. He was the luckiest man alive. He held a princess in his arms, a woman he needed to marry for legalities, but a woman he *wanted* to marry for love. He'd not thought to find such a blessing. Yet here she was, an uninvited guest who'd dropped in unexpectedly with no intention of engaging in the game. It seemed too good to be true. He'd not believed in serendipity before. He was a man of science, but after tonight, he might have to rethink that.

Chapter Seventeen

The note was waiting for her when Elidh got back to her room the next morning, deliciously bleary-eyed, her mind still wrapped in fantasy's fog from the night before, and the day. Had it only been a day? Had it only been a quick journey to the stable at the other end of the estate? It felt as if it had been a journey to the other end of the earth. Everything had changed and yet nothing had changed, nor could it. There was a bitter sweetness to the notion if she lived outside the moment.

Elidh hummed a bit to herself as she picked up the note, wondering and marvelling at how Sutton had managed to get a note up to the house without her knowing. Perhaps he'd written it in the night while she'd dozed.

Rosie emerged from her little chamber, groggy. 'You're back, I see. Does this mean Mr Keynes has proposed? I certainly hope so if you were gone all night,' she harrumphed protectively.

'I sent a note to tell you where I was,' Elidh chided. 'A mare was in labour with twins.' She smiled just at the thought of it, remembering the colts as they'd left them this morning, satisfied and snuggled up against their mother, bellies full of milk. She and Sutton had checked on them before they'd ridden up to the house. This time the ride had been more leisurely and she'd been reluctant to see it end. She'd enjoyed the slow motion of his horse, the warmth of Sutton's body about her in the crispness of the early summer morning. She was determined to enjoy the sensation of being with him for as long as she could before the real world intruded, which would be all too soon.

'Don't expect me to believe that's all the two of you were doing, not with the way he looks at you and contrives to spend every daylight hour with you, and some not-so-daylight hours either.' Rosie speared her with a knowing mother-hen look. 'I suppose it doesn't matter, now that he's going to marry you.'

'There's been no talk of marriage,' Elidh cut in. The sooner she could disabuse Rosie and her father of the idea, the better. 'He will choose another. He has to. An Italian *principessa* isn't practical for him.'

'Since when has love ever been practical?' Rosie unbuttoned her ruined gown. 'We'll have to throw it away, I don't think I can get the stains out.'

'Since now, Rosie. It's not practical for him or for me. Father will have to face the fact that we can't risk trying to sustain our ruse indefinitely.' To try such a thing would hurt Sutton too badly. It was better for both parties if they left.

Rosie slipped off to the wardrobe to retrieve a morning dress and Elidh opened the envelope, a smile already playing at her lips as she wondered what she and Sutton might do today. She hoped it included a trip to the stables. She unfolded the note and froze, all idea of pleasure fading. The message was so entirely the opposite of what she'd anticipated she couldn't comprehend it at first. She studied it, reread it. The note fluttered to the floor as she took an involuntary step back from it, so mortifying was it. 'Rosie, Rosie!' Elidh gasped, reaching behind her for the security of the bed and sitting down hard.

'What is it, Lamb?' Rosie came running, gowns draped over her arms.

'Get Father. Someone knows.'

I know.

Two individually harmless words, but when put together and delivered in this context, they became a dangerous weapon in the wrong hands. Heaven forbid Sutton learned of her duplicity from someone else or that he learned of it at all. Sutton would be devastated. *She* would be devastated. He could not find out. Not now, when their time together was so short as it was. She only had, only *wanted*, a few more days. She might not be able to afford even that. There was nothing for it.

'We have to leave,' Elidh said as her father scanned the offending note. It wasn't from Sutton. She'd found the courage to look at the note again and it was decidedly not his handwriting. Sutton's writing had a firm, up-and-down stroke to it while this one was slanted left.

Her father looked up from the note sharply. 'We will do no such thing.' Elidh looked at him in disbelief. He couldn't actually be contemplating staying while the risk of being exposed lurked?

'We cannot do otherwise,' she argued. 'We will lose everything. You now have your patron, Lord Wharton is willing to take on a playwright for the winter holidays.'

'That is a temporary solution. We'd be throwing away a far bigger fish. Keynes is about to declare for you. We only have to brazen it out a little longer and we'll have everything we've ever wanted.'

'We don't know that. It's too big of a gamble.' And not one she'd ever wanted to take. That it had got this far despite her best efforts was a mystery to her and an even larger worry. If he was about to declare, it was all the more reason to run now while they could.

Her father came to her, kneeling and taking her hands. 'Daughter, what do we have if we walk away now? A patron, perhaps. We have what's left of the rent money and nowhere to go. How long do you think that will last? Then, we'll be back where we started—looking for a supporter.'

'I don't know,' Elidh said honestly, casting her mind about for options. 'We could look for work. I could wait tables in a pub, we could live over a stable until we have saved enough for a cottage. Rosie can go back to Upper Clapton.' Living out in the country was simpler, cheaper than in town, although there'd be no avenue for finding another patron hidden away in the country. But there'd also be no chance of Sutton finding her.

'I will not!' Rosie was indignant. 'Maybe I could find work, too, in a pub or with a seamstress in a small town.'

'We could sell some of these dresses, the paste jewels. It would gain us a little time until we found a place to settle and some work,' Elidh improvised. It wasn't much of a plan. She was grasping at straws here.

'Sell your mother's gowns?' Her father rose, affronted. 'Settling? That's what it would be, all right. Is that what you want? To disappear into the country, scraping for a living in a tiny cottage, *working*? Do you even know what you're suggesting? Waiting tables? Sewing for others? This is not the glamour of the stage where we practise by day and become gods at night. This is menial labour you're talking about.'

'It's honest. It hurts no one, misleads no one.' She glared at him, willing him to see sense.

'A princess would never run.' Her father paced the room, expending energy in thought. 'It's tantamount to an admission of guilt, that we have something to hide.'

'I am not a princess and we *do* have something to hide.' Something that could land them afoul of the law with no one to protect them. The law only protected the powerful. She was nothing, really. Just a girl from Bermondsey Street whose only possessions were a crazy father and trunks full of costumes and paste jewels. It was an icy dash of cold water after last night. She'd had everything. In Sutton's arms she'd been someone. She'd been cherished, worshipped, beautiful without artifice. There'd been no acting, no pretence.

'We can win this!' her father hissed. 'We are not going to go to ground because someone thinks they can threaten us.' He waved the note in the air. 'This is very vague, when you think about it. What do they know?

How do they know it? Can they support it? Who will believe them? Sutton Keynes, who is madly in love with you? Who is *he* going to believe? You or a jealous family who resents their daughter wasn't chosen? I tell you, we are still safe.'

Elidh sat silent, letting her father's surprisingly pragmatic assessment sweep over her, but it wasn't the pragmatism that overwhelmed her. It was the realisation beneath it: Sutton loved her, or, if not loved her, was *falling* in love with her, enough to defend her. It was an inconvenient truth, perhaps, one she might be guilty of avoiding or ignoring because of the jeopardy it put her in—a jeopardy that had little to do with discovery and ruses unveiled, and everything to do with her heart. She didn't want to hurt Sutton any more than she wanted to hurt herself. To acknowledge the depth of Sutton's feelings also forced her to admit how deeply she cared for him, too. Sutton was not alone in his growing feelings. Every bone in her body wanted to run from the acknowledgement. To stay would only give those feelings a chance to grow, to become more dangerous and, ultimately, more destructive, but her father was right.

She'd jumped to the worst possible conclusion. While they couldn't rule that out, entirely, they also couldn't panic, but it didn't change the need to leave soon enough as it was. At least they wouldn't have to leave today. She could have one more night, perhaps two. 'All right,' she relented, 'we can stay, on one condition. If this gets more dangerous, we leave immediately.' It was easier to stay a while longer. It was what her heart wanted: to stay with Sutton as long as possible. She wanted her

father to be right, that this was nothing more than a
jealous girl who'd been snubbed and who'd found out
something she thought would be scandalous to expose.
Elidh had heard first-hand a room full of culprits. It
could be any one of them.

Her father left the room, feeling the situation settled.
Elidh let Rosie put up her hair and dress her in the lavender gown, a carefree confection fashioned from one
of her own Juliet gowns. There was a youthfulness to
it, an innocence and calmness that suited the image
she needed to represent downstairs. She wished she
felt as calm as she appeared. She wished she had her
father's bold confidence that this was nothing more
than a young girl's attempt at revenge. But one thing
niggled about that. If a girl wanted to imply she'd done
something dishonourable, she couldn't possibly expose
it publicly without the risk of losing Sutton entirely.
To implicate Principessa Chiara would be to implicate Sutton.

A compromised gentleman could do no less than
offer marriage to save the compromised girl's honour.
That could hardly be what the blackmailer wanted,
which only served to lead her back to her original worries. This wasn't about girlish spite. Someone knew
who they were, or, more importantly, who they weren't.

Bax arrived. Finally. As Sutton knew he would. He'd
just rather have not had it be this morning. He was not
having a good morning as it was. Aside from waking up with Chiara in his arms, the morning had gone
downhill the moment he'd returned to the house. Lord

Wharton had demanded a private breakfast meeting and proceeded to suggest that Sutton needed guidance in the absence of a father. To which he'd responded that Wharton was not the man to provide such guidance. Wharton had not taken kindly to his response. Now, there was his cousin to face.

Sutton watched Bax help himself to the decanters on the sideboard in the estate office even though it was barely past eleven. Good lord, the man was a reprobate.

'Can I get you something?' Bax held up an empty tumbler in offer.

'No, I prefer to do my drinking after five,' Sutton said pointedly. The ease with which he poured a full glass suggested the hour on the clock had long since ceased to matter to Bax when it came to drinking. A lot had ceased to matter to Bax. Sutton supposed drinking before noon was the least of it.

'Suit yourself.' Bax took the chair across from the desk. 'Beautiful place you've got here. I've always admired Hartswood. Great location, especially now that the railroad can bring folks out for race day in Newmarket.'

'Thank you. Now, why don't you tell me why you've come? I imagine it must be important if it's dragged you away from the entertainments of the Season.'

'I thought you were smarter than that, Cuz. You know exactly why I am here. I can't let you have that fortune. I will contest your marriage to the reaches of my abilities.'

Sutton snorted. 'It will be difficult to go up against a legal will and a peer of the realm.' Which was exactly what his uncle intended, no doubt. Sutton tested the waters. 'I can't imagine Imogen Bettancourt's father allowing such a contest to stand. His title is legitimate…his daughter is legitimate. He'd call you out if you dragged his daughter and wife into scandal.'

Bax, the insufferable bastard that he was, made a show of considering the information. 'I suppose there is merit to that. Wharton, the Viscount, the Marquis would all be formidable opponents with the law on their side as well. But you don't favour their daughters.' He narrowed his dark eyes. 'While you've been out rusticating with all the pretty girls, we've had to entertain ourselves with the betting books. Word back in town is that you favour the Italian Principessa.'

Sutton schooled his features to give nothing away. He couldn't afford to after last night. He'd taken Chiara's virtue. In his mind, they'd unofficially committed themselves to one another. If that came out too early, though, it could be used against them, could spark the rebellion of upset fathers his mother had spoken of. If the peers aligned with Bax, it might create enough of a tangle to keep Sutton from the fortune, to see it revert to Bax on a technicality.

'If I did, it changes nothing. She's of noble birth and that is all I have to show.'

'It would be a shame if you couldn't show it in time, though.' Bax allowed him a glimpse into his strategy. 'I think Lord Wharton and the others, along with myself, might want to have proof of her royalty on the grounds that she is a foreigner. That might take time.

Not very much time, surely. But perhaps more time than you have.'

Sutton knew how Bax's threat would play out. They would simply question who the Principessa was, knowing full well she would satisfy their claims. It was ridiculous to think she wouldn't. But to send for Italy for verification would be time consuming. Time he wouldn't have before the four weeks ran out and the funds would revert to Bax. After that, it wouldn't matter when the verification came. It would be too late. Not for him and Chiara. Nothing stopped them from being together. But too late to keep the money from Bax, the whole reason he'd started this bridal quest to begin with. He would have failed his uncle and, in some ways, society at large.

Bax finished his drink. 'I'll just leave you to think about your options. If you don't mind, I'll join the gathering. It's been a while since I've enjoyed a good house party. I'll be sure to say hello to my dear aunt.'

Sutton wanted to shoot him. A bullet between the eyes wouldn't be good enough for his cousin. This was just the sort of dilemma Bax liked creating, the sort with impossible solutions: the girl or the money, but not both, not if Bax could help it. Yes, his heart wanted Chiara, but the cost was enormous. So many would suffer if he could not bring Bax to heel. How could he consciously choose a solution that would allow a monster to run loose when he'd been picked expressly to stop it? It was like Bax was blackmailing him with his own heart. Unless…

Unless he found a way to beat Bax's timetable. What

if verification could come from somewhere closer than sending to Italy? For the first time since he had left Chiara, a smile settled on Sutton's mouth. He might have an ace up his sleeve after all. His friend, Conall Everard, the alpaca-wool genius who'd revolutionised wool production in Taunton, had married the former Marchesa di Cremona a little over a year ago. Cremona was in the Piedmont. Sutton went to his maps and spread one out excitedly. There it was! He found Cremona and traced his finger north, west, south until he found Fossano. Three days' ride from Cremona— less if there was a train.

Sutton returned to his desk and drew out a piece of stationery. He would send it with all haste. It would be a two-day journey to reach Taunton and then two days back. The letter would have to travel from Taunton to London and then from London through Cambridge to Newmarket. And there was the issue of the newborn. He didn't expect Sofia and Conall to come physically, but Sofia could verify through a letter. And if her presence was necessary, there would be time for that later.

One word from Sofia, Viscountess Taunton, formerly the Marchesa di Cremona, and Bax would be thwarted.

Chapter Eighteen

There was nothing Bax liked better than thwarting well-laid plans, except for perhaps ruining the righteous and beautiful. That was another kind of 'well laid' altogether. How delicious it would be to do both in one fell swoop. It was his first thought upon espying Chiara Balare, sitting alone in the garden, dressed in lavender and surrounded by flowers. The perfect picture of a perfect virgin, her blonde hair and lavender gown the ideal foils for the myriad colours of his aunt's summer blooms. A painter could not have created a better setting. It was also the ideal opportunity to approach her. She was sitting alone, but not truly alone. Guests had moved out to the garden for luncheon and lawn bowls. She was in plain sight of the party, which was exactly what he was counting on. He wanted everyone to see them together. He wanted Sutton to come out and see them together. He would not surrender the fortune simply because his father wished it. He would threaten Sutton from every angle. Bax tugged at his waistcoat and strode over. Time to be charming.

'I can see why my cousin is smitten with you.' He stood to her side, intentionally startling her and forcing her to turn in order to look at him. He hadn't wanted her to have time to think, time to see him coming. He wanted to control all aspects of the conversation from the outset. 'Not just him. Louie Fenworth speaks highly of you. It seems you've captured every young heart at the party,' he flattered shamelessly. How many women had he flattered into doing exactly what he wanted? It was easy. People were desperate to be loved, especially lonely ones.

But the Principessa wasn't so easy. She turned, shading her eyes to look up at him, and rose, unwilling to be quite literally in a one-down position. 'Cousin? You must be Baxter Keynes,' she surmised shrewdly. He'd give her points for quickness.

'You've heard of me, as well.' He smiled charmingly, taking her hand and raising it to his lips for a kiss. '*Enchanté,* I am pleased to meet you at last.' He did not release her hand. 'I think we might have even more than that in common. Would you care to walk?' When she hesitated, Bax laughed, low and conspiratorially. 'Don't believe everything my cousin has told you about me. Surely no one can be as bad as all that.'

'It's just that I thought to wait for Mr Keynes,' she hedged politely but directly.

Bax leaned close. 'You might be waiting all day, then. He was inundated with paperwork when last I saw him. Come and walk with me until he arrives.' It would be the last time he'd ask nicely. He would have his moment alone with her. He hooked her arm through his and decided on the walk for her.

He turned her down a path featuring a sweet-smelling arbour at its end, artfully draped in lilac the colour of her gown. He'd love to take her right here, up against the lilac sprigs, her bodice shoved down, her skirts pushed up and him thrusting into her hard until her body arched and she cried out for him. She'd resist at first. Women like the Principessa, good, virtuous women, always did, always felt they must. But they were always glad to have relented in the end. 'I want to get to know you better since you'll be my cousin by marriage soon, it seems.' Bax gave her a warm, brotherly look designed to thaw, designed to inspire trust.

She did neither. 'But not yet. Which is why I must insist we return to the party. It isn't appropriate for us to be off on our own.' She turned to start back, but Bax stopped her with a firm grip on her upper arm. Oh, it would be delicious blackmailing her. Money would be easy for her to give. Perhaps he would exact payment in another fashion, something less simple for her to give, this virtuous paragon his cousin believed he'd found. He wondered what the chances were of having her first. If he could put a child in her belly before his cousin did, so that she would wonder for ever whose seed had got there first, that would be a lifetime's worth of leverage if he failed to stop the marriage. Or if he needed to force the marriage in order to manoeuvre Sutton into forfeiting the fortune. If she were pregnant, Sutton wouldn't abandon her even if she didn't have a title. His cousin was noble like that.

He drew her back to him, his face close to hers. 'All of London is talking about you. All the betting books feature your name as my cousin's most likely match. Yet, no one recalls you before the party. It's as if you've appeared out of thin air, created for the very purpose of marrying my cousin.' He smiled wickedly. 'Is that true, Chiara Balare? Are you a figment of my cousin's imagination?'

She wrenched her arm away, her face wreathed in indignation. 'What exactly are you implying, sir?' He released her arm. She wouldn't leave now, not with information at stake.

'Only that I find it interesting there is no social record of you in London. Here you are, a princess and lovely, yet the society pages at the height of the Season seem to have overlooked your presence.' Bax shrugged, watching her face for any betrayal.

'That's easily explained. We'd only just arrived in London. There'd been no time to establish ourselves.'

'Where did you stay?'

'I don't recall. My father's secretary made the arrangements. I just show up.' Either she was telling the truth, or she was thinking on her feet.

'Your father is not listed in any of the hotel registries.' He knew, his men had checked.

'We use an alias when we travel. It's more discreet,' she replied quickly.

'I beg your pardon.' Bax made a small bow of apology, but wasn't sorry, not in the least. She had possibly made a small slip there. 'It appears I am seeing ghosts where there are none. It's only that I would not like to see my cousin duped.'

Her eyes narrowed in speculation. 'Wouldn't you?

You'd have the most to gain if he was. I believe the fortune reverts to you if your cousin fails to marry appropriately within the allotted time.'

'Me and all my wickedness. I don't even have to raise a finger to claim it.' He stepped forward, crowding her between himself and the lilac arbour as she answered with a step back. He reached for her then, his hand cupping her face. 'Care to join me? Wouldn't it be ironic, after all this posturing, if you could just marry me and get your hands on the fortune whether you were a *principessa* or not? You could simply be yourself, whoever that is, *miss*.' He was sure she was lying now. The ticket seller at the station had said the Prince announced himself very clearly when he'd purchased the tickets and the name Prince Lorenzo Balare di Fossano was the name he'd very legibly signed in the traveller's manifest. There'd been no mistake he and his daughter were on that train. That didn't sound like a man who sought discretion or used an alias.

She pushed at his chest, trying to move him away. 'What do you think you're doing?'

'Claiming payment, my dear,' he murmured, standing his ground easily against her efforts. She was no match for his strength. He'd wrestled larger women than her into compliance.

'For what? I have nothing to hide.' She was struggling hard now.

'For keeping your secrets. It's not so onerous of a price, is it? A few stolen kisses from a competent lover. In time, perhaps a little more. Kisses are satisfying for only so long. You might decide you like it.' He pinned her arms in a hard grip. It was best she knew who the boss was from the start. 'I'd settle down and accept the offer, my dear, before I feel less generous. I won't warn you again. Don't try me on this. I will not hesitate to tell my cousin of my suspicions, or anyone else who will listen.'

'What suspicions would those be? What proof do you have? Sutton will laugh at you.'

'That you're a fraud, my dear, a lovely face gussied up in silks and satins. I don't need proof, just logic enough. I think the lords here whose daughters are being slighted in favour of you would grasp at those straws if it kept their hopes alive.' He kissed her hard then, a bruising, punishing kiss meant to dominate and master, to remind a woman she was powerless. Finally, at last, a flicker of fear in her eyes. Was it fear of him or fear of what he could expose? But she wasn't entirely defeated. Not yet, although she would be, given time.

He stepped away from her, out of range of her foot, and tugged at his waistcoat. 'Very good, my dear. A satisfactory first instalment. I think we understand each other now. I'll go back to the party and give you a moment to think things over.' He made a mocking bow. 'Remember, Chiara, *I know*. And I will tell.' What a pleasant day this was turning out to be: his cousin threatened, a woman blackmailed and Louie Fenworth with the pretty sister waiting to be fleeced at cards. He wondered how long it would take to have Eliza Fenworth in bed in exchange for Louie's gambling debt. A fabulous day indeed and it was only noon.

* * *

Elidh sank on to the arbour bench, trembling. It was him. The blackmailer who'd sent the note was Baxter Keynes, not one of the jealous girls. Somehow, he'd found out something, enough to build his case. Her father would say his case was tenuous at best. What did he know? What could he prove? But her father hadn't seen the joyous evil in his dark eyes as he cornered her, hadn't been felt the threat of his body pressed up against her.

Now that it was over, she didn't know what scared her the most: what Baxter threatened to expose or what he wanted from her to keep silent. She touched her lips gingerly where he'd assaulted them. She could hardly call what he'd done a kiss. There'd been nothing gentle about it. He'd meant to teach her a lesson—that she was outmanned, outgunned and overpowered. If she didn't pay the price for his silence, he would shout his suspicions to anyone who would listen, and people would listen. He wasn't the only one making enquiries, he was just the only one they hadn't stopped.

Elidh clenched her hands in her lap, willing them to stop trembling. She couldn't go back to the party like this or Sutton would know something was wrong and he mustn't know this; he mustn't know his cousin had threatened her. He had so many other people to deal with, all those angry fathers who'd hoped their daughters would win the coveted prize. No wonder he liked working with animals better than people. She shut her eyes. This was all her fault. She had done this to him.

She was going to betray him. Even leaving would be a betrayal, only a kinder one.

Kinder? She'd leave him to what? A loveless marriage? Trapped for life with a partner who didn't understand him? That, too, was unfair. Sutton Keynes was a good man. Why should his life be sacrificed for the fortune? Now that she'd met his cousin, she understood better why he felt the need to not walk away from it. But it didn't make the idea any more palatable.

Elidh drew a breath, feeling her thoughts steady themselves, the initial fear of her encounter subsiding. Nothing was done yet that couldn't be undone. Baxter had only threatened her, only kissed her roughly. Nothing damaging had been exposed and, while she'd been frightened, she'd not been hurt. She needed to put everything into perspective. She needed to set her priorities. What mattered most was protecting Sutton. But she could not protect him entirely. She saw that now. Leaving would only mitigate the hurt. Elidh stood up and shook out her skirts. The game was in motion and it was her move.

She found Sutton, his head bent low in conversation with a footman near the French doors leading out to the garden. The footman bristled with restrained urgency and Sutton's posture was tense. She knew the moment he looked up and saw her that something was wrong. Elidh quickened her step, closing the distance between them. 'What's happened?' She reached for his hands without thinking, without caring how the gesture might look to those around them.

'It's the colt. He's not nursing. Or the mare isn't producing enough milk for two. If that's the case, then the other foal is in danger, too, if they're both sharing milk for one. It's hard to know, though.' Hard to know because he wasn't there. Instead, he was here, placating jealous fathers, protecting her, running out the clock until he could announce fairly and publicly his choice for a bride at the ball.

She could see the pain in his eyes at the thought of losing the foal. 'Oh, Sutton, I am so sorry.' She could see the dilemma he struggled with, too, how he wanted to be with the mare and her foals. 'Go to them, Sutton. You saved them once.'

He shook his head. 'I can't leave again so soon. There's been trouble with the fathers. You were right. I should not have kissed you in front of everyone. I have fathers pushing for a declaration I am unready to make and now my cousin is here. Have you met him? I hope not. Stay away from him if you can. He's making trouble and we must talk.'

'Those foals are important, too,' Elidh argued, her stomach tightening. What had Bax already insinuated to Sutton? She would not have him give up those sweet babies for her. She did not want those horses on her conscience, too. There was so little she could give Sutton, but she could give him this and maybe she could protect them both a little longer. 'I am going inside and calling for your horse. Meet me out front in twenty minutes. Let these men and their petty daughters do their worst. I would rather have them malign me than have those babies die when you could have saved them.' When all of this was over, she might not be able to save herself from exposure, from loving Sutton, or from the broken heart that would follow. She might not be able to save Sutton from the consequences of her deception, even if those consequences never became public. But she could give his beloved horses a fighting chance.

Twenty minutes later, Sutton settled in the saddle behind her and they were off, her lavender-chiffon dress rucked up about her knees, her legs bare as they galloped towards the stable. His voice was low at her ear as he whispered, 'Thank you. For your selflessness, for your courage to put other needs ahead of your own. This is why I love you, Chiara.'

Elidh leaned back against his chest and closed her eyes, savouring the words. If only they were true. If only he wouldn't hate her for it in the end.

Chapter Nineteen

Sutton did not regret going to the stables. He believed there were moments that defined a man's life, times where a life and what would become of it hung by the thread of those decisions. This was one of those moments and he'd nearly missed it, nearly let the moment define him instead of the other way around. He'd nearly let more than one life slide through his fingers this afternoon, including his own. But Chiara had pulled him back from the brink, made him see sense, made him see what mattered.

The mare was exhausted from the delivery and from nursing two foals. She rested as they took over. Chiara passed him a fresh bottle of camel's milk and smiled softly as he fed the foal. She settled on a hay bale across from him, offering a bottle to the other foal to make up for any milk he might have given up to his brother.

Sutton savoured the quiet intimacy of watching Chiara with the foal, love for the little creature shining on her face as if it were the most natural thing in the world for her to spend her afternoons in barns, sitting on hay bales in pretty lavender dresses. The dress wouldn't last. It was the second dress she'd ruined on his behalf. The delicate fabric wouldn't survive the prickly hay. But she didn't mind. In fact, she'd insisted on helping.

This is why I love you.

He'd been overcome with emotion when he'd spoken those words, but they were no less true now, surrounded by far less panic. Now, he couldn't stop thinking them. Everywhere he looked there was a reason to love her. The biggest reason of all was that she'd saved him today, with her insistence he come down here. The foals had needed him desperately. He'd feared on arrival that he was already too late. The first foal was restless and hungry, his appetite outstripping his mother's ability to provide. But at least he was still on his feet. The smaller foal, however, was curled in a ball and listless. The grooms reported he hadn't moved, hadn't tried to nurse for two hours.

For a creature who was supposed to nurse seven times in an hour, it was an alarming amount of time to go without nourishment. Sutton had gone to him, pushing a bottle into the foal's mouth and massaging his jaw to stimulate a sucking response. It was a slow process and a frustrating one. At times, he thought he got more milk on the hay than in the foal's mouth. In the end, it had taken both of them to help the foal before he started to drink.

That in itself would have been enough to make the trip down to the stable worthwhile. But there'd been more. Sutton stroked the foal's soft head as it dozed off for a milk-drunk nap, its belly full for perhaps the first time since birth. This was what mattered. This was who he was: Sutton Keynes, camel dairy owner and thoroughbred-horse breeder. He was a simple man when given the choice.

He'd lost sight of that since the day in the solicitor's office. Money changed people, even when they didn't want it. *Have you thought of giving up the fortune?* Chiara's words whispered through his mind as he watched her. That damned fortune had almost cost him this. Maybe, in the end, it didn't matter if Bax had the money or not. His cousin was going to continue his nefarious ways with or without it until someone stopped him in a very final manner. Perhaps he took too much on himself when it came to saving the world. He smiled, indulging in a little fantasy—of walking into Barnes's office and telling the man he was marrying Chiara. If that sufficed for the fortune, great. If not, well, that was just fine, too. Of course, the flaw in that fantasy wasn't him, it was her. It wasn't enough that he wanted to marry to Chiara. Chiara had to want to marry him, too.

'What is it? You're smiling.' Chiara blushed self-consciously under his stare. The blush made her look maddeningly innocent and provocative.

He set aside the empty bottle and held out his hand. 'Come with me? The horses won't need us for another hour. I want to show you the hot springs.'

And I want to show you how much I love you, what our lives will be like when all this nonsense is behind us.

She rose and took his hand, but she was hesitant. 'Sutton, where are we going? We need to talk.'

Sutton nodded. They needed to talk about a lot of things: Bax, marriage, what all of that would mean. 'Walk with me. Not here.' Not where they could be overheard.

He didn't speak until they were on the path to the hot springs, well away from any listening ears. 'Since last night, I've been thinking about how all of this ends and who I want to end it with. I am done with this house party and the search for a wife. I've found her and I don't care, do you hear me? I simply do—not—care what any marquis or baron has to say about it. They can make their protests and they can make their threats, but it doesn't matter. I've given my uncle's little game too much of my time and worry as it is.'

Chiara had gone pale. It wasn't exactly the reaction he was expecting. 'Who have you decided on?' Even her voice was pale. Did she think his choice wasn't her?

'You, Chiara. I choose you. Surely that doesn't come as a surprise?' How could she even think he'd choose another after last night? Or was it because she knew he'd choose her and she didn't wish to respond in kind? A new kind of anxiety replaced the upswell of happiness he'd felt a few moments ago. He steeled himself, preparing counterarguments and rationales. She would refuse the first time he asked, of course. There were practicalities to work out. But he would press his case and she would accept, eventually, because she knew in her heart, as he knew in his, that they had chosen each other long before this moment. He had not misread her. She was not Anabeth Morely.

'Oh, Sutton.' Everything was in those two words; the hope he wanted to hear, the regret he didn't, and something else he didn't understand—fear. Fear for him. What did he have to be afraid of? In the next moment he knew.

He needed to fear teary hazel eyes and soft words that murmured rejection. 'You know I can't possibly accept, no matter what my heart feels.'

'If it is only practicalities, we will overcome them,' Sutton tried to argue without sounding as if he were begging.

'It is not only practicalities.' She shook her head, but said nothing more.

'Tell me. What obstacles do we need to overcome? I will find a way.'

'That's what I'm afraid of. That if I tell you, you will be relentless and you can't be, Sutton. There are things I cannot tell you, except this—I am not worth it.'

They'd reached the hot springs, the smell of sulphur acutely appropriate for this hell suddenly racing through him. He didn't understand any of this except that she was refusing. 'How could you not be worth any effort I might need to make? Chiara, I love you and you love me. I see it in your eyes when you look at me, I feel it in your touch, I felt it in the tremble of your body last night. We belong together. Never mind that you're from Italy and I'm from England. Never mind that you are a princess and I am a man without a title.'

He paused, the nightmare of Anabeth Morely coming back to haunt him one last time, the old fears rising. 'Is that it? Is the lack of a title what bothers you?'

She should say yes. She would not be offered a better *congé*, and what was one more lie after all the lies that had been told? Her father could not have scripted a better opportunity. But Elidh would not do that to Sutton. There was anger and hurt in his eyes now that went beyond this conversation. She understood now. This had happened before. 'Is that why the other woman threw you over?' she asked quietly. It seemed that all their ghosts had come out to play here in the little glen: her lies, his past, all conspiring to drive their response to this moment, all things interconnected.

'Anabeth. Anabeth Morely. And, yes, it's why she jilted me at the last.' Sutton's voice held a hint of steel now, trying to protect himself. Against her. It felt awful but necessary to know she was forcing him to arm himself. 'She was an earl's daughter, destined for more than landed gentry with money.'

'I am not her,' Elidh whispered. Sutton would always be enough for her in himself alone. But she could claim no part of him.

'Then why do you refuse?' He would not give up. She'd come to expect no less of him. He'd not given up on the mare or her foals. She knew empirically he would not give up on her until he understood all was lost. She hazarded part of the truth.

'I will cost you everything. Your cousin...' She hesitated, fumbling for words to explain Bax's threat without giving herself away. Anabeth Morely's betrayal would be nothing compared to the one she'd hand him if he discovered it. He'd be furious, and vengeful. He would exact retribution. She had to prevent that and if she couldn't, she had to protect herself and her father.

Sutton pressed a finger to her lips. 'My cousin? Is that all? Bax cannot hurt us. Why would you think he could?' A cloud of thought crossed his face. 'Did he speak with you today? He did, I can see it in your face, Chiara. I can guess what he told you. I spoke with him as well. We needn't fear him.' Sutton smiled, appearing to relax. That worried her. It was a sign Sutton thought the discussion over, that he'd resolved their problems when nothing could be further from the truth.

'I can imagine what he told you, though. He and I had an unpleasant discussion in the office earlier. He thinks to make us prove your nobility. He has no proof because his claim is ridiculous. He knows that. His real hope is in running out the clock. But I have that well in hand.' Sutton's brow creased as he thought. 'Is that the same argument he used with you? I can't imagine what he thought to gain. You would be even less concerned with his threat than I. He would have no leverage there because you do not doubt who you are for a moment.'

'I do not want to cost you the fortune, Sutton. He is right. Proof will take time to send for. Mails are unreliable.' Elidh thought quickly. She spent too much time these days grabbing at argumentative straws to keep the ruse afloat, another clear sign the ruse was very nearly up. The sands in the hourglass were running out for her as assuredly as they had for Cinderella. The end was finally beginning and it hurt far more than she'd ever imagined because she'd *had* more than she'd ever imagined with this man. 'I am sure he was thinking that if I truly loved you, I would want to protect you and the fortune. Perhaps he thought I'd give you up in order to do that.' And perhaps Sutton would remember that logic when he discovered she'd left. She could hardly tell him his cousin knew the truth and had tried to blackmail her with kisses to keep the secret.

Sutton ran his hands up and down her arms in reassurance. 'That figures. It's just like Bax to try to use even something as wondrous as love to divide us. But he won't win. You needn't waste another thought on it.' Steam rose from the pools, beckoning invitingly, and Sutton smiled. 'Now that's settled, shall we have a bathe while we're here?' Apparently, it was a rhetorical question. Sutton pulled his shirt over his head and tossed it aside, making it clear he'd already decided on the answer.

Well, why not? It would be the perfect farewell, the last bit of good to come out of this whole disaster. He bent for his boots and desire began to hum through her, desire for him, for one last time. Good lord, how she loved to watch his body, all that rippling muscle and healthy, tanned skin. She wanted to memorise every line of him. When he finished with his boots, Elidh gave him her back. 'Help me with my laces? I wasn't planning on undressing when I put this on this morning.'

Sutton came up behind her, sweeping her hair aside and kissing her neck as he worked her gown loose. 'I'm sorry this one is ruined. It was pretty, like a summer

day,' he murmured. 'But I think you look best like this.'
He let the dress fall to the grass and helped her with
her undergarments.

Even in July a breeze could be cool when it fanned
across bare skin. Elidh shivered with the novelty of
it, of being naked out of doors, of feeling the summer
breeze on bare skin, of Sutton's hands on her body. She
leaned her head against his shoulder, her body pressed
to his, back to groin, her breasts in his hands. 'I feel
like Eve,' she whispered. 'And this is our garden.' And
he was her Adam, rising strong and proud behind her,
every inch the primal man. They had one last evening
before they were evicted from Eden.

'Hot springs first,' he whispered teasingly. 'Then,
we'll make love in the grass.'

The hot springs were a revelation. The pleasant
warmth of the water lulled her into relaxation. The
feel of Sutton's fingers at her neck, at her shoulders,
kneading away the stress of the day, was exquisite. Had
anything felt as good? She was happy enough to simply
be held against him, his arms wrapped about her. She
wanted to savour every moment of this. It was hard to
argue she and her father should never have come here.
How could she regret meeting Sutton when he'd given
her such a treasure? She only regretted the hurt they
would both pay for it. *Later.* Only later was approaching much sooner than she liked.

When they finished bathing, Sutton scooped her up
and carried her to the grass. 'All I want to do is make
love to you, right here. Lovemaking out of doors is dif-

ferent than making love anywhere else.' He was playful and hungry, and oblivious to the thoughts in her
head. She wrapped her body around him and held him
close. She would protect him with all she possessed.

He was right. Lovemaking out of doors was full of
sensations: the tickle of summer grass at her back, the
occasional breeze on her skin, the warmth of Sutton's
body over hers, the smell of him, all clean male mingled
with the scents of summer, all intoxicating. He made
love to her with a certain languor, lingering over her
with each kiss, each touch, each glance until he took
her in a long, slow thrust, as if they had all the time they
needed, as if the foals weren't waiting for their dinner,
as if she wasn't going to creep away at midnight and
disappear for ever. But that was hours away.

Elidh gave herself over to the fantasy; all that mattered was this moment when they could set aside their
cares; that Sutton Keynes loved *her*. Those words today
had been a stake to her heart. Because of those words,
her betrayal would hurt even more. She would find
comfort in knowing the betrayal of leaving would be
far less than the betrayal that came with discovery of
her lie. Perhaps someday he'd understand she'd chosen
to leave in order to protect him.

Chapter Twenty

They lay in the grass, wrapped in each other long after pleasure had had its way with them and the moon began to rise. She smoothed his hair back from his face. 'You're so handsome, every time I look at you, you take my breath away.' She didn't think there was a finer man in the world than the one lying naked beside her right now.

'As do you.' He grinned and levered himself up on one arm, facing her as he ran a hand over the slight curve of her hip. 'Do you feel better now, Chiara? Are you convinced Bax is no cause for alarm between us? That we can decide to marry without any pressure from external sources?' he murmured, leaning close, his mouth at her ear.

They'd come full circle. This time, however, she felt no sense of panic, only the impending weight of the inevitable. There was nothing to argue against because arguments would not sway Sutton; they would only fire him to fight back. Sometimes the only way to win an argument was to leave the room—in this case, to leave the house party. To leave the man who made the arguments.

'You never did tell me how you managed him,' she whispered as she kissed his jawline.

'I have a friend, Viscount Taunton. He is married to an Englishwoman who lived in Italy. Her story is complicated. She's divorced now, but her former husband was the Marchese di Cremona.'

Her kisses stilled. *Cremona.* Her father's map of northern Italy flashed through her mind, a web of cities connected by rocky roads through foothills and valleys. Asti, Milan, Turin the capital, Genoa, Pavia, Fossano, and Cremona, only a few days apart on horseback. A cold fist of fear took up residence in her stomach as Sutton continued. 'I don't think you would have known her. It was a difficult marriage, her husband didn't allow her to socialise much, and she's older than you, old enough that you would still have been in the schoolroom when she was there. But she would have known of you. She and her husband most certainly would have known of your father. Prince Lorenzo and Il Marchese would have met in the capital or at court, if not at regional gatherings.'

The fist in her stomach was a sharp-tipped icicle now, stabbing her hard. Her father had designed this ruse precisely to avoid the relevance of anyone possibly knowing them. But their luck had run out. She'd fallen in love with the only camel dairy owner in England whose friend had married nobility from the Piedmont. What were the chances of that? But Sutton wasn't done.

'I've written to her, asking her to provide validation in case Bax makes good on his threat. I sent the letter out this morning. It will reach Taunton in two days and I can have a response in my hand in four, with plenty of time to satisfy the will and to satisfy anyone here who might protest. Peers can't question the word of other peers without demeaning their own standing. If a peer can't take the word of another peer, what does their honour mean?' Sutton's smile was wide and relaxed. 'You see, there's nothing to worry about. Bax can protest all he wants, but he can't touch us. I've thought of everything.'

And she hadn't. Her father hadn't. Never in her father's wildest imaginings would he have accounted for Sutton Keynes having a friend from Cremona. Not that it mattered to her decision. She'd already decided to leave. But it mattered in a different way.

The comfort she'd reasoned on earlier in knowing that leaving was the less painful betrayal compared to discovery was gone now. In just a few days, he'd know the awful truth of her deception in full. He would be crushed. He wouldn't understand that she'd not meant for it to happen, that she'd not come to trap him. The Viscountess would write back that she'd never heard of Prince Lorenzo Balare di Fossano. Then, Sutton would know just how thoroughly he'd been duped. Nothing about her was real: not her name, not her history, not her title.

It was probably for the best he knew nothing real about her. If he did, he'd be able to find her and he'd be furious when he came after her. Maybe he wouldn't care enough to come after her. Maybe his devastation would be so complete he wouldn't bother. He'd have other things on his mind, then, like who to pick next and how best to protect his fortune. She should hope for that, as much as it hurt to want such an outcome.

Goodbye was imminent. She played it out in her mind: they would make love here, one last time, they would feed the foals, and she would have him take her back to the house. She would kiss him one last time and hope that some day he'd understand. But above all, she couldn't cry. Not until she was alone in her room, her trunks packed and her getaway assured.

Elidh reached for him, her hand curling around his rising shaft. She stroked him, relishing the contrasting hardness of his length and the tenderness of his tip. His body was a fascinating maze of mysteries she'd only begun to discover. He gave a groan of delight and she kissed him with a laugh. 'Let *me* pleasure *you*. This time, I will be on top.' She straddled him and he chuckled, his hands at her hips to steady her, his blue eyes laughing up at her.

This was what it felt like to fall in love. Elidh took him deep inside her, knowing in her heart that despite the risks and the worries, she would do it all over again just for these moments even though they had never been meant to last. She bent forward, her mouth finding his with a whisper. 'Remember this, Sutton. I love you.' As for herself, she wanted to remember him, *them*, like this—perfection for a moment.

* * *

Something was wrong. The moment Sutton entered the breakfast room the next morning, he could feel it the way one can sense an oncoming storm in the air. The room was crowded, far more people eating an early breakfast than the norm. Usually, he had the place to himself with the exception of a few other early male risers who also preferred to eat in quiet. Not so today. This morning, young ladies and their mothers made up a considerable amount of the population and as such the chatter seemed abnormally loud, a veritable cacophony of conversations going on in little clusters about the room and on the terrace where the French doors had been thrown open to accommodate the overflow.

'Good morning, Mr Keynes,' Wharton joined him at the sideboard as he assembled a plate. The man was fairly bristling with energy and good humour. Given their last few interactions, the latter came as a surprise. Up until yesterday, Wharton had been quite displeased with him.

'Good morning, Wharton. Lovely weather. I thought the men and I might get some fishing in while the ladies shop this morning.' A bark of male laughter rose briefly over the conversations. Sutton scanned the room for its source and found it. Bax. He was up suspiciously early for him and sitting with Eliza Fenworth. Where was young Fenworth? Louie ought to put a stop to it right away. Miss Fenworth was no match for Bax. At the very least, she ought not be sitting alone with him. That was a recipe for disaster. Having Bax here at all was the very embodiment of letting the fox into the henhouse. Fenworth was nowhere to be found and neither was Chiara. They were the only two not present, it seemed. 'If you would excuse me, Lord Wharton? I think I see a damsel in need of rescuing.'

Sutton made his way to the table in the corner where Bax sat, entertaining Eliza. 'Everyone is up early.' He pasted on a smile for Eliza's benefit. 'Even you, Cousin. A rare occurrence, I hear,' he said pointedly, wanting to imply to Eliza that Bax was not appropriate company. 'Where is your brother, Miss Fenworth?'

Eliza looked down at her plate with a blush. 'He is still asleep. He was up very late last night.'

Bax broke in with a good-natured *mea culpa* that didn't fool Sutton. 'It is entirely my fault. We got into some intense card playing.' Bax dug in his pocket, coming up with a gold filigreed brooch. 'I won this off young Fenworth, a pretty piece of jewellery, or so I thought, and I have to believe he thought so, too, when he accepted it as a stake last week.' Bax gave Sutton a veiled look. 'Fenworth won it off Prince Lorenzo. The Prince told him it was gold. Fenworth told me it was gold.' Bax rubbed at it, revealing a leaden surface beneath. 'It's not, as you can see. It's a fake. Makes one wonder what else might be fake.'

Sutton didn't care for the implication at all. His cousin was being less than oblique about his insinuations—insinuations, Sutton might add, that would fuel a mutiny of sorts against Chiara. He could only imagine how Bax's private accusations gone public would inflame the nobles if he didn't choose one of their daughters. 'I hope all ended well?' he asked with a benign coolness.

'Oh, it did for me.' Bax smiled at Eliza. 'Thanks to the fake brooch, I've made the acquaintance of a lovely young woman, whom I find far more entertaining than a piece of jewellery. How was your evening, Cuz? You were missed.'

Apparently so. Bax had taken the opportunity of his absence to clean out Louie Fenworth's pockets the moment his back had been turned, and now Eliza Fenworth's virtue seemed very much in danger. Sutton knew it would fall to him to clean up this particular mess since Louie was incapable of doing so. There was no chance to scold Bax. Yet. Isabelle Bradley and her father approached the table, taking the other two seats. Sutton would have preferred the chairs be taken by any other two people. Of all the girls, he liked Isabelle the least. She'd been spiteful to Chiara and she had a tendency to cling to his arm, to his every word. But he was in no position to decline. The room was full, the terrace crowded.

'I am surprised to see everyone up so early.' Sutton searched for neutral conversation after pleasantries had been exchanged.

'I think all the girls are looking forward to shopping before it gets too warm this afternoon. With the ball fast approaching in a few days, the excitement over your choice is mounting.' Isabelle leaned forward, gushing. 'You've made a fantasy come to life for all of us these past two weeks, Mr. Keynes. We've been treated to this lovely estate, waited on hand and foot by an impeccable staff and you've given of yourself so generously. I don't think there's a girl in this room who hasn't fallen in love you, me included,' she dissembled. 'I hope you don't think I'm too forward in saying so.' No, but she was a liar. He hadn't given generously of himself.

'Not at all, Miss Bradley. I appreciate the compliment.' Sutton took a forkful of eggs, unable to think of anything more to say. He scanned the room again, looking for Chiara.

'We're all so excited to see you who might choose. It's like a fairy tale—a prince holds a ball and chooses his wife at the stroke of midnight.' Miss Bradley was colouring it a bit too brown now.

Sutton coughed. 'I'm no prince, Miss Bradley. Just a man.' A man without a title, too. Funny how these peers forgot that when there was an obscene amount of money at stake.

'Well, it's still a fairy tale,' Isabelle insisted. 'It could be any one of us who's chosen now that the Principessa has forgone the festivities.' Isabelle's eyes sparkled dangerously with gossipy mischief.

'Has forgone the festivities? I'm not sure I understand what you mean, Miss Bradley?' Sutton tried for calm as his insides began to roil. *Remember, Sutton, I love you.* At the time, he'd not questioned those words. Now, the phrasing of them struck him as odd.

Isabelle feigned wide-eyed shock. Sutton was conscious of her hand overlaying his in a too-familiar gesture. 'Don't you know? She left. In the night, apparently. No one saw her go, but my maid said her maid was gone this morning and her room is empty.'

Gone. Chiara was gone? That wasn't possible. Just last night they'd made love beneath the sky, they'd bathed in the hot springs. *She'd* made love to him as the stars came out. He'd resolved Bax's threat and she knew it. Viscountess Taunton would put his preposterous claims to rest. Was there something more that he'd missed? What could it be? Was there a reason beyond Eliza Fenworth's company that Bax was so chipper this morning? His gaze landed on his cousin.

'May I speak with you alone, Cousin?' Sutton didn't even bother to make polite apologies for abandoning the table. He strode into the hall, taking the first quiet corner he came to, confident Bax was behind him.

He wheeled on Bax, grabbing him by the shirtfront and hauling him up against the wall. 'What have you done? And for the first time ever, tell me the truth. I know you threatened her yesterday. What else did you do?' Had Chiara not told him the full extent of Bax's threats? If he discovered Bax was at the bottom of this, he would kill him. A duel would suffice. Anger raged through him. 'This feud is ours and ours alone. Innocents are to be left out of it.'

Bax had the audacity to laugh. 'Your princess was no innocent, Sutton, as I warned you yesterday. I could see you didn't take me seriously so I went to the source. You should be thanking me. I have saved you from a terrible mistake and from public embarrassment. If anything, I've kept your hopes of claiming the fortune alive, come to think of it. Choose one of those girls in there and there's nothing I can do.'

Sutton shook Bax hard. 'You would never do anything so selfless. You knew I loved her and you forced her away. We had nothing to fear from your threats. Viscountess Taunton will vouch for her. I've already written.' Rage was riding him hard. Chiara, gone! Fled into the night without so much as a goodbye or a reason. But there had been a goodbye. His brain slowed. That last time, there'd been a delicious edge to it, something different. He should have known, should have been suspicious. He released Bax, remembering everything they'd said, everything they'd done. He'd told her about Viscountess Taunton.

She'd fled because of him… Something broke open inside him, darkness swallowing him up like ink spilt from a bottle. He did not want Bax to be right, but his cousin was relentless. 'Think about it, Cuz. A *principessa* who leaves in the middle of the night? What kind of sense does that make? She has no need to slink away. She can leave whenever she pleases. In fact, daytime would be so much easier. She didn't arrive in a carriage of her own and the trains don't run much before morning. It's not like she had a timetable to make. Unless, of course, she did have a schedule to keep, one that involved being gone from here before Viscountess Taunton's letter arrived. There's something else. No one in London had heard of her before she showed up here. She appeared out of thin air, Sutton. I hired runners. They couldn't find her.

Face it—the Principessa is a fraud, just like her father's brooch.'

This was wrong, all wrong. Chiara was not a fraud. The frauds had been thrown out of the party. Frauds were selfish charlatans preying on innocent victims, duping them, taking their money. 'I can't believe it,' Sutton said resolutely. 'She is like me.' Chiara was kind. She loved animals.

'Of course she is. Don't be naive. Good lord, Cousin, you've been on the farm too long,' Bax barked. 'She's the only one who figured out how to play the game. She knew it wasn't about her, that it was about *you*, and she set about knowing you better than anyone else here. She figured out what you wanted and she gave it to you.'

No, that could not be true. It simply couldn't be. He would not accept that. Bax was evil. Bax wanted to hurt him, wanted to ruin something that was all goodness and light. Of course he would say these things. 'I have to find her.' Sutton's mind was racing. He didn't want to hear any more of Bax's revelations. If he could find Chiara, she alone could set everything straight. This was all just a big misunderstanding. It had to be.

'Why?' Bax gave a cruel laugh. 'She left. She doesn't want to play any more. She chose to end it. You should be thankful she cared enough to protect you at the end. She left before you could choose her and look like a fool, before you could lose the fortune over her. Can you just imagine the headlines? "Heir to thousands gives up fortune to pursue fraudulent princess!" Take comfort in knowing she set you free. It was quite generous of her. No damage done.' Bax was wrong there. There was damage aplenty, starting with his heart, his poor, logical, scientist's heart.

'Be angry, Cousin. You should be furious,' Bax growled.

'Why?' Sutton glared. 'Because you would be? Because you want me to do something rash? Because my anger serves you more than my hurt?'

'Because any normal man would be, damn it!' Bax spat. 'You've always thought you were better than the rest of us. Smarter, wiser, above the social fray the rest of us slog through. My own father liked you better than he liked his own son.'

He released Bax and stepped away, getting a grip on himself. It would be easy to be angry. To throw a vase or a decanter, to see it smash against a wall and shatter into a thousand pieces like his heart. But it would solve nothing. It would give Bax pleasure. Sutton refused to cater to such dark humours. There was no logic in them and he needed his logic more than ever if he was to see his way through this.

A footman cleared his throat, warning of his approach. He held a basket in his hand. 'Sir, the gentlemen are ready to fish. Shall I tell them you'll meet them at the river? This was left for you, as well. The Principessa's gosling. There's a note inside.'

'Thank you, tell the men I will join them shortly.' Sutton took the basket, his heart pounding at the sight of the note, but he'd be damned if he was going to read it in front of Bax. 'If you'll excuse me. I'd like to read my mail in private.'

* * *

The gosling cheeped as Sutton set the basket down on the desk in the estate office. Sutton turned the note over, hesitating. What if he opened it and Bax was right? What if he opened it and discovered she'd simply left out of some misguided notion to protect him? He knew the reality before he opened it. Whatever was in this letter wouldn't change how he felt for her. It would only change how much it would hurt. Had he been betrayed?

Chapter Twenty-One

The shaking of his hands betrayed how much the contents of the note mattered as Sutton tore open the paper—another reason he'd not wanted Bax present. His feelings made him vulnerable. The note was short, disappointingly so, but not without meaning for a man who read between the lines.

Please return the gosling to its natural habitat and let it rejoin its family.

Sutton crushed the note in his palm. He was meant to let her go. To set her free. It was what she wanted. Which meant horrible things. It meant that Bax was right. She had something to hide. That she'd lied about who she was.

The anger he'd kept under a tight rein surged, pulling on his restraint now that there was no one to see. His logic mocked him: If an angry man threw a decanter and no one heard it shatter, had he really thrown it? Rage tore through him. Rage for himself, for falling prey to yet another Anabeth Morely; rage at Chiara for leaving, for not telling him; and rage for what had been lost when she'd made her choice. There'd been something beautiful and rare between them and now it was gone.

There was a quiet knock on the door and his mother entered, concern etched on her brow. 'Your worthless cousin told me you were in here. Is the Principessa's leaving his doing?'

Sutton shook his head. 'Not entirely.' It was, ironically, quite his own doing. If he hadn't told her about writing to the Viscountess, Chiara might still be here. But for how much longer? If she was a fraud, the letter from the Viscountess would have exposed her. Even if he'd been willing to countenance her lie, the threat posed by Bax would have scared her off eventually. If she was a fraud, he'd been wrong yesterday in assuming Bax had no leverage over her. Exposing her would have scared her into desperation. And yet, even if that were true, he couldn't help but feel a protective anger rising on her behalf. If Bax had threatened her with bodily harm, he would call him out for that alone. There were so many 'ifs'.

What did such thoughts matter now? Chiara was gone. He would know soon enough as to why she'd left. If she hadn't known about his letter, all it would have allowed was for him to have had her a day or two longer. That seemed like an eternity right now. He'd give anything for a day or two more of Chiara in his arms, for the blind bliss of thinking she was real. Dear lord, was he truly believing she wasn't real? That she was the

fraud Bax accused her of being? What was he supposed
to believe? She'd left him in the middle of the night.

'I am sorry, my son.' His mother sat down gingerly
on a chair, unsure how to proceed. 'I know you were
enchanted by her. This *will* pass. It must pass. There
is still a bride to be chosen.'

'I'm not in the mood for platitudes or brides, Mother,
if you don't mind?' Sutton ground out. Why hadn't he
listened? How many times had Chiara told him she
was not what he thought? Had she been trying to warn
him? But that made no sense. If she wanted to win the
competition, why would she drive him off? Was there
another reason for her having been here? Was falling in
love with him an unintended consequence? He remembered that first night in the gallery—*are you avoiding me?* Perhaps she truly had been. But that raised
other concerns. He thought about the faulty jewellery
Bax had shown him. Had they been here to steal? To
cheat at cards? He hated the direction his thoughts
were headed.

'Then maybe you're in the mood for logic,' his
mother said sharply. 'I understand you're hurting, but
there's no time to lick your wounds. The party ends in
three days. You have precious little time after that to
satisfy the will's requirements with a wedding and your
cousin is trying to seduce every virgin in the house.
We need to bring this to a close, for everyone's sake.'

'It will never be closed for me, Mother. Don't you
see? Whatever happens here will be with me for the rest
of my life. Everyone else gets to go home and pick up

their ordinary lives. But not me. I have to live with it for ever.' With it, without it…no matter what he chose to do, that decision would follow him.

'Yes, precisely,' his mother snapped. 'Thank goodness she had the sense to leave. Can you imagine what choosing her would have meant? Public humiliation. People would have been sympathetic eventually, felt sorry for you once the truth came out and once you officially distanced yourself from her.'

'Is that what I would have done, Mother?' Sutton fingered the obsidian paperweight idly. What would have happened? What would he have done if the nobles and Bax made good on their threats and actually had proof? If Chiara had been exposed? Was that even her real name? He would have felt betrayed, as he felt now. But would he have distanced himself? Would he have walked away from her? Was he willing to distance himself even now?

'How could you have done otherwise?'

'What if no one found out? What if any claims against her were discredited? Or silenced?' Bax wasn't the only one who could play that game. Bax had little credibility on his own and he'd have even less once Sutton got through with him.

'You would dirty yourself for her? Live a life of lies and blackmail to protect her secret? That's no life, Sutton. It makes you Bax's equal. I always thought I'd raised a son who was a cut above most men.' She paused, eyes narrow. 'You should be thankful Chiara left when she did. If she'd actually succeeded in marrying you, you would have had no choice in the matter. You would have been forced into complicity to protect your good name, to protect the fortune, to protect any children you might have had. The Everards, the Viscount and Viscountess Taunton, would have been required to avow the lie as well. The only avenue left might have been a divorce and that's a whole other scandal, one that would cost you the fortune after all you'd risked for it.'

His mother was right. A life of lies was no life at all, a fragile house of cards easily toppled that would consume whatever happiness they'd found. It would destroy them as assuredly as Chiara's departure had destroyed him today. A marriage needed honesty above all else. It's the one thing Chiara could not give him. Logically, there was nothing else to do but to give her up. Yet, his heart was already arguing otherwise. Logic had never so thoroughly failed to bring him peace as it had this morning.

Sutton got through the day. Thank goodness, fishing was a solitary pursuit even with other men on the river. Somehow, he survived tea on the terrace, finding the wherewithal to listen as the girls chatted about shopping, raving over the shops in Newmarket's High Street. He made sure to keep Eliza Fenworth in sight in case Bax tried anything untoward. He managed appropriate responses to the conversation at dinner and even to partner Wharton's daughter, Miss Hines, to victory at cards afterwards. He could barely concentrate as Wharton rambled on about his disappointment over the Prince leaving before they could arrange for him to meet a playwright the Prince highly recommended. He was numb, a machine going through the motions of living. It was as if the light had gone out of the world. He couldn't think straight. He could only think of her.

It wasn't much better the next day either. In fact, it was worse. The ball was closing in. Who did he choose in Chiara's place? It hurt to even think of the possibility. It hurt even worse to spend his day contemplating comparisons. No one was as funny as Chiara, no one as direct, no one as daring. He stole away to the stables for a couple of hours in the afternoon, thinking to find peace only to discover she'd stolen that, too. This was where he remembered her the most. 'She's left us,' he murmured to the foals.

He wished that were true. But despite her physical absence, she hadn't left. She was imprinted on everything around him. For a woman who didn't exist, she took up a considerable amount of his thoughts.

The darkness of his thoughts swamped him with two emergent truths in the solitude of the barn; the first was that he would give anything to have her back, whoever she was. And that was the problem. People who appeared out of thin air also disappeared into it. Chiara Balare was gone for good and for the best. For a man of logic, he was having a deuced difficult time accepting that. Why had she done this? Was she safe now? Did it hurt her to leave him as much as it hurt him to be left? Who was she? Where was she? And if he knew, what would he do about it?

* * *

Chiara Balare was gone. Elidh had never felt less like a princess than she did right now, jouncing along a dusty country road on the tailgate of a farmer's wagon, the July sun beating down on them, melting away the last of their ambition like Icarus's wings. She sat between Rosie and her father, all of them dressed once more in their old clothes, brown and grey and drab. Their fine garb was packed away in a trunk, the rest of it sent to Rosie's sister in Upper Clapton for safekeeping.

Elidh swatted at a fly with her hand. Oh, how the mighty had fallen. A day ago she'd had every luxury to hand, including a lacy fan to swat errant flies. A day ago, food had been no effort either, the tables at Hartswood had groaned with its largesse three times a day and two teas between. Shelter had been an after-thought: canopies on the lawn to shield guests from the sun, a beautifully appointed chamber with a white coverlet she'd miraculously managed not to stain. Now, each meal was a calculation, the night's lodging dependent on her father's persuasion with an innkeeper.

It was no less than she deserved. She'd reached too far above herself. The higher one flew, the harder the fall. She hadn't just fallen, she'd crashed. The luxury and security of Hartswood was far behind them. The reality was bleak. The sum of her entire world was contained in this wagon: her father, Rosie and one trunk between them. And it wasn't even their wagon. This wagon bed was provided on the good humour of a stranger, as was their destination. They would simply go wherever the stranger took them.

Beggars could not be choosers and they were surely beggars now. She'd squandered their last hope and now they could not squander their remaining funds on train tickets or mail coaches. Not that it mattered, because it didn't. What did it matter where they were, or where they went or how long it took them to get there, as long as they were out of reach of Viscountess Taunton's letter. Even her father had understood that. They'd had to disappear before it arrived so that Sutton couldn't find her.

Yet, she'd found herself looking up, hopeful, every time she heard hoofbeats on the road until her father had scolded her. 'Don't wish for it, Daughter. The man who comes to fetch you back won't be the one you knew,' he'd cautioned. He was right. How silly to think otherwise. If Sutton took the effort to find her, it wouldn't be out of love.

Rosie had taken pity on her, giving her father a scalding look. 'Men are ten different kinds of fools all at once. They don't see what's true and real right in front of 'em.'

Rosie wrapped an arm about her now, but that only engendered tears. Everything had been a fog since she'd kissed Sutton goodbye. Her father was right. Sutton would be angry before the Viscountess's letter arrived, frantic perhaps with worry. But after the letter? He'd be furious then. He would think… Elidh swiped at her tears as unsuccessfully as she'd swatted the fly. She knew too well what he'd think with Bax whispering poison in his ear. Only it wouldn't be poison, not all of it. Quite a lot of it would be truth. But

Sutton wouldn't have the luxury of sifting through all of it and determining what was real. He would think she'd lied about everything: who she was, what she felt for him. Worst of all, he would think she'd left because she hadn't loved him.

He'd be wrong there. She'd left because she *did* love him, because it was the right thing to do for him. He would never know how much it had cost her. So this was love, too, this hurt, this ache whenever she thought of him and whenever she thought of never seeing him again. Doing right shouldn't hurt so much. There should be some comfort in it, something to offset the pain.

The wagon stopped in a busy inn yard and her father jumped down, a spark in his eye. One might think this was all a lark to him. 'I'll see if the innkeeper will let us perform monologues in exchange for food and lodging tonight.' If he was angry with her, he didn't show it. She'd cost him a patron in the end as well. They could have no connection now with Sutton or anyone at the house party. After all the risk, they only had a small bag of card winnings to show for it. He winked at Rosie. 'Just like old times, eh?'

Her father was back shortly, rubbing his hands together in glee, already making plans. 'We can have supper and beds in the hayloft and we can even pass the cup for whatever coin we can get. It's market day and the tavern will be busy. Elidh, you can wear the blue gown and Rosie will put your hair up. You'll do the Juliet monologue. I'll do Macbeth tonight.' Never mind that she hadn't done Juliet in years. Her father would simply say there were two hours to refresh her memory and if that wasn't enough, no one else would know if she made a mistake. She envied him the way in which he just forged ahead, blindly ignoring the fact that the world was falling apart on all sides.

Dost thou love me? I know thou wilt say 'Ay,' And I will take thy word. Yet, if thou swear'st, Thou mayst prove false. At lovers' perjuries, They say, Jove laughs.

She couldn't do it. Elidh paced behind the grey flannel blanket serving as a curtain. She couldn't go out there and say these words. She couldn't think of love without thinking of Sutton. Her father came around the makeshift curtain, looking royal in the clothes he'd worn as Prince Lorenzo.

'Are you ready? We have a nice crowd, Elidh. We can make a little money tonight. You look splendid. Rosie has outdone herself on your hair.'

How many times had she heard him give a similar talk to his troupe backstage before a performance? For a moment, she saw him as he used to be: younger, more vibrant, his stomach perhaps a bit more taut, a man who had people to command, a man who would be King for a night, who would drink in the adulation of an audience and his troupe, all of whom believed he could conjure magic. How reduced he was now, older age upon him, no troupe left, just a reluctant daughter with no particular talent for the stage, certainly nothing to rival his dazzling wife, a man with no home, a man with nothing to his name. Did he see that man or did he still believe he was the Actor King? That the next great thing was just around the corner?

'I can't do it, Father,' Elidh cut off his speech.

'Yes, you can, because you must.' Her father fixed her with a stern stare. 'It doesn't matter if you mess up the lines. These blokes won't know. Besides, they'll be too taken looking at you to pay close attention. Dazzle them and they will follow you anywhere.'

'No, I can't,' Elidh pleaded. 'I am not like you, Father. I can't just plunge ahead as if the world isn't going to hell around me, as if my heart isn't breaking.' There was anger in her tone, resentment even. 'You have to face reality!'

He grabbed her arm, claiming all her attention. 'Face reality? Do you think I don't? I face it every day as best I can. When your mother died, she took the best of me. Plunging ahead is all there is.' The sternness left his features. 'What else can I do? I am fit for very little in this world besides acting, maybe a little writing. I am doing the best I can with what I have: a modest talent for that stage, for charming a crowd, and a broken heart. They are not amazing assets. But every so often, I get lucky and there is magic. For a few moments, I am allowed to forget my troubles and the crowd forgets theirs. That's all I can ask for.'

She heard the lesson in it for her, too. Move forward, find joy in the moments if the days eluded her in that regard. Be thankful for small mercies: a meal, a roof, a place to perform, and a chance to earn her way. It would have to be enough. She had to find a way forward because there was no other choice. She couldn't go back. Her father was right. If she ever saw Sutton again, it wouldn't be the man who'd held her beneath the summer stars and whispered words of love at her ears. There would be no love for her in those blue eyes, only hate. He could not possibly forgive her for what he thought she'd done, nor would he have reason to understand the truth. A man like Sutton Keynes, a man with everything, couldn't understand what it meant to be desperate.

Sutton was desperate. He didn't want to believe it. But it was hard not to, when empirical, objective truth stared him in the face. He fingered Sofia's letter, his gaze looking beyond the words. He had them memorised by now.

Sutton,
I regret to tell you that there is no one by the name of Balare among my former acquaintances in the Piedmont Kingdom. I do not believe there is even a principality that goes by the designation of Fossano, although Fossano is certainly a large town—the fourth largest in the area.
If I am not mistaken, Fossano belonged once to the Principality of Achaea.
I am sorry, since I sense that your heart is committed and this information may affect that commitment.
Sincerely,
Viscountess Taunton

Chiara had lied to him. Used him. No, not Chiara. She existed no more than her principality existed. Everything about her was a fiction from her name to her title. Yet, somehow, in some deep, integral part of him, those lies had ceased to matter. What *did* matter as he stared at Sofia's letter was why.

Why had she done it? *What* had she faced that seemed so insurmountable in her own life that masquerading as a princess seemed like a good option? Surely she knew the odds were stacked against her from the start? Apparently, they were not as enormous as whatever she faced. That made him worry. Was she in trouble? Danger? Did she owe money? Maybe it wasn't even herself who was in danger, but her father? She'd not been alone in this. What had driven them to this level of deception? Of risk?

Sutton crinkled the damning letter in his hand. He would give anything to talk with her one more time, to ask her. To *help* her. Bax would laugh at him, call him weak, foolish, for wanting to help a woman who'd lied to him, who'd nearly ruined him publicly. Certainly, the scientist in him could find no logic in the desire. But the man in him could. He'd seen those hazel eyes look at him with love. He knew she'd surrendered her body to him and only him. She'd chosen to be with him, intimately, her soul as naked as her body.

There'd been no lies there. Which prompted the second question. There had been lies between them. He could not deny that. But how many lies and regarding what? If her feelings represented the truth, did those other lies matter? Lying about a name, about a title, seemed superficial against larger truths. He didn't know her name. He didn't know where she came from or where she'd gone. He *did* know she loved animals, she had a heart full of kindness for the weakest among them. That she loved him. That couldn't be feigned, no matter what Bax argued. Still, he could make the claim that she'd loved him all day long, but without proof it was just empty words. Claims needed evidence to support them.

The proof was there in his memories, the way she'd acted the night the foals had been born. She'd not hesitated to dirty her dress, to participate in the messy process of birth; he'd seen her face when she'd nursed the foal later when the baby had nearly died. He'd seen her clutch the little gosling to her chest, determined to nurse its bad foot back to health. He'd seen her wade in the water, crash through the woods looking for a croquet ball, he'd seen so much of her in those unguarded moments; the girl who laughed, who spoke her mind and her conscience thoughtfully, tactfully, not like Isabelle Bradley or Imogen Bettancourt.

Then, there were her kisses. She'd been thoughtful with them, too. She'd not kissed him on a whim. She'd warned him against it and against her. He'd not been wrong in believing that she put others before self. His mind stalled on that thought. *She put others before herself.* Other words came to him, words spoken as they'd walked the ailing mare. *That's who we are. We collect those in need.*

He understood it all now. She'd left to protect him, not because she'd failed to win him. Bax was wrong.

Chiara had not been trying to trap him into marriage. She was, in fact, the only girl at the party who hadn't been. But he didn't want to be protected, not if it caused her pain, because that's who *he* was. He took care of those he loved and he loved her. Beyond fortune or misfortune. Beyond the fear engendered by his past failures and hurts. She was not Anabeth Morely. She was his heart and, if he ever wanted to reclaim himself, he had to reclaim her.

The clock on the fireplace mantel chimed. He hadn't much time left before he'd be expected for dinner. There was action to take. He strode to the door of his study and summoned the waiting footman, purpose making him brisk. 'Send for the best grooms in my stable. I need fast riders. Then, send for my mother.' His mind whirled with lists. He needed to retrieve a solicitor from London and find a bride. If London wanted a spectacle, he was about to give them one. He hoped. There was, in fact, a lot riding on hope and luck, two things logic detested. It was not a position he was used to being in.

Chapter Twenty-Two

At last, a little luck! Sutton swung off his horse and tossed the reins to a boy waiting in the inn yard at Wicken. He glanced at the sky. It was late afternoon and evening was coming fast, but with a little more luck, she would be there and he would take her home. If he was unlucky, well that didn't bear thinking about. This was the first decent lead he'd had.

When the ticket seller at the All Saints station recalled no one by her description on an outbound train, Sutton had his grooms spread out, combing the villages of Suffolk for her. Chippenham, Barrow, Dalham, Icklingham, Kirtling, Lidgate, Burwell and more, all of them within an eight-mile radius, and all his riders came back empty. There'd been no sign of her, her father, or her maid. Until early this afternoon.

His last rider had come in from Fordham with a report of a blonde girl and her father who'd performed a 'theatrical' in the pub the previous evening. They'd left in the late morning. Sutton had saddled up immediately, Fordham was five miles from Newmarket and

Wicken, the village beyond that, was another four. He'd made good time. It was evening, but it was summer and daylight was his friend. It was possible they could even make it home before full dark. *If* he was lucky. He had to be. The ball was tomorrow night.

Sutton stepped into the taproom. It was crowded and warm, full of men and women. He saw the reason for it; a grey flannel curtain was hung up behind a makeshift platform acting as a stage and his hopes soared. 'Are we expecting entertainment tonight?' He approached the innkeeper, who surveyed him with a sharp eye, no doubt assessing his quality and his coin.

'Yes, we are. A travelling troupe has stopped for the evening and have offered to perform. They'll be starting any minute. Perhaps you'd like to eat and enjoy the show? We have chicken pie and peas and a very good ale, unless you'd prefer wine?'

A travelling troupe? Sutton thought the innkeeper's claim was a bit exaggerated. If it was Chiara and her father and the maid, three people did not a troupe make. His stomach growled and Sutton took the innkeeper's suggestion. He had to determine it was her before he could do anything else. Would it really be her? Was his Princess Chiara an actress? Something about that sat oddly with him, trying to poke holes in arguments he'd carefully constructed: that she loved him, that she hadn't been acting about that at least. Doubt began to niggle. Had he been swindled entirely? Had he come all this way for nothing, even if it was her? It wouldn't be the first time his tenacity in romance had served him poorly.

A serving girl came with a tin plate of chicken pie and a mug of ale. He pushed his doubt away. He couldn't live in the past for ever. He had to move beyond the damage done by Anabeth Morely. He took a bite of the chicken pie and the flannel curtain moved. The man he knew as Prince Lorenzo stepped out, bowed low to the crowd's applause and Sutton's appetite was forgotten. They were here! *She* was here. Prince Lorenzo made a little speech Sutton didn't hear, his mind was too busy processing the reality and the relief. He'd found her.

Prince Lorenzo made a flourishing gesture towards the curtain and Chiara emerged, dressed in a blue evening gown, her hair done up, her cosmetics subtle, looking as if she were about to grace the drawing room at Hartswood. The crowd whistled and hooted. Not Sutton. He just stared. She looked as she'd always looked, beautifully put together. But he saw the artifice now, the cheapness of the jewels at her neck, here where there wasn't any luxury to hide among and there were no assumptions to protect her.

Well, she'd certainly had the last laugh. People really did see what they wanted to see. Moving among the wealthy debutantes, flaunting a title of her own, no one had expected to see her as anything other than what she claimed. As such, no one had questioned her jewels, her gowns. Still, this woman was lovely, but it was not the woman he wanted. He wanted the woman who'd been with him in the barn, who'd bathed naked with him in the hot springs. That woman didn't need jewels or hairstyles or cosmetics. On stage, she began a speech he recognised from *Romeo and Juliet*, one of

Juliet's monologues—the balcony scene, he thought. Sutton found himself leaning forward with the rest of the audience, hanging on each of her words, as if they were spoken just for him. A little stab of jealousy jabbed at him. Was that same thought running through the minds of every other man in the room?

He knew the moment she found him in the crowd. Her gaze lingered on him, her line faltered just a little from surprise. She'd not expected to see him. He saw her eyes go wide with emotion before fear, perhaps that he was here in anger. He saw the tremble of her lip and knew it wasn't artifice. Before she'd remembered to be scared, she'd been moved. She'd wanted him and he knew his journey hadn't been in vain. His instincts had been right. She'd not left because she hadn't loved him, but because she *had*. He was right to have come. For the first time in the days since she'd left, Sutton felt the darkness begin to lift.

The moment the performance was finished and they took their bows, Sutton made his way forward, only to be met with a wall of her admirers with the same intentions. If this had been London, he would have roses ready and money to bribe the guard to her dressing room. He would have had her all to himself. As it was, he came to her empty-handed and he had to wait, sharing her with a taproom full of people. He had come this far; he would be patient. He might not be able to bring roses, but there was something she might like more. He gestured to the innkeeper and slipped coins into his hand. 'A private parlour and dinner, please, and your finest wine. Tell the young lady and her father they are my guests when they're finished with their admirers.'

Sutton was here. It was the only thought that ran through her mind as Elidh stood at the entrance to the private parlour. But not the only emotion. Elation warred with fear. He was facing the window in a strong stance, legs spread shoulder-width apart, hands clasped behind his back, shoulders straight and broad. Was he here out of anger? Was he here to punish them? Or was something else possible? In the crowd, he'd not looked like an angry man, but a desperate one, a hurt one.

Her heart began to pound with ridiculous hope. Was he here for a different reason, a better reason? Was he here because he loved her and had found some impossible way to forgive her for what she'd done? 'Sutton, I am so sorry.' She stepped forward, the fabric of her blue skirts rustling. 'I didn't mean for...'

He turned and her words faltered. He was so handsome, so compelling when he looked at her, she couldn't go on. Speech failed her. It had only been a few days, but it was as if she hadn't seen him for ages. She stood and simply let him happen to her—his blue eyes, his smile, the tenor of his voice as he said, 'Hello, Chiara.'

'Elidh,' she breathed. 'My name is Elidh.'

His smile broadened. 'Elidh. That's a beautiful name. I was wondering what it was. Elidh what?'

'Easton.' She worried her lip, butterflies fluttering in her stomach. 'You're angry, of course. You have every right to be,' she rushed on—perhaps it would be best to clear the air.

He crossed the room to her and seized her hands. 'Elidh, I am not angry. I am hurt. I am confused. I know only a partial truth. I am in need of understanding. I am all those things, but I am not angry.'

Not yet. He still might be before this was done. She searched his face, looking for the contradiction. That he was here at all was too good to be true. 'You should be. I lied to you, I pretended to be something I wasn't. But not to trap you. Never to trap you, to win you. I didn't lie about that. I never meant to have you choose me.' The words tumbled out.

'Shh. There is time for it all to be discussed. Come, sit and eat. Tell me, why? When I discovered you were gone that was all I could wonder. Why did you do it, the masquerade, I mean? Why did you think it was your best option? What did you hope to gain?' He led her to the table. He poured her a glass of wine and took the seat across from her. 'Tell me everything, Elidh.'

There in the candlelight, the story poured out: how her father had seen the announcement, how they'd remade her mother's dresses, how they'd boarded the train and headed to Newmarket in hopes of finding a patron, knowing full well they didn't have enough money to come back. She told him of her father's hopes she'd win his hand and of her own misgivings, her vow to avoid him, to not participate in that game.

'There I was, in the gallery that first night, practically forcing my attentions on you.' Sutton gave a self-deprecating chuckle. 'You must have hated me for that.'

'No, I think I was charmed from the first. Early on, I convinced myself there was no harm in it. I never thought there was a chance you would fall in love with me. There were so many other girls who were prettier and offered more. But somehow you did and now everything's a mess.' She lowered her gaze to her plate, desperate to hide her tears.

She felt his hand at her cheek, turning her head up to meet his gaze. 'Why are you smiling, Sutton? I've hurt you even though I've tried to protect you. Now you know and it changes nothing. We can't be together, especially now.'

'I'm smiling because you're wrong. The things I love about you, Elidh, were not lies. The life you and I want together can still happen. I am here for you because I mean to marry you. I mean to announce to everyone tomorrow night at the ball that I will marry Elidh Easton.'

Elidh swallowed, watching the reflection of the candles flicker in his eyes. 'What about the fortune? I am not noble. I have no title.'

'I do not care. I have spent too much time thinking about what everyone else needs and not what I need. I need you.' He took her hand between his. 'I am asking you again, Elidh—if I call your name in the ballroom, will you say yes?'

'Sutton, too much has gone wrong. Everyone will hate you, the fortune will go to Baxter, everyone will know I lied.'

'The last we can overlook. I am not claiming to marry Princess Chiara. There is no lie in that.' He took her hand. 'Fairy tales are full of innocuous deceptions—*Cinderella, The Princess and the Pea, The Princess and the Frog.* Surely this little deception simply adds to the romance of our own fairy tale if told right, and we can rely on my mother to see it done. As for the other two objections, I simply choose not to care about them, not if they cost me you. I've been miserable wondering where you were, if you were safe, wondering why you'd done it.' He kissed her hand. 'I will find other ways to stop Baxter.'

Elidh interrupted. There was so much more to save him from besides herself. There were consequences beyond her, too. 'No, you can't simply say that. When I first met you and I asked you if you'd considered giving the fortune up, you were adamant that it was not something you could contemplate. You, a man who did not want to be forced to marry, was willing to consider such a marriage in order to stand in the breach and prevent your cousin from accessing that money. Marriage is no small thing and neither was your understanding of the sacrifice being asked of you. That was barely two weeks ago. So, no, Sutton. You cannot stand here tonight and blithely say you'll figure something else out. If there had ever been another way, you would have taken it from the start. Has that changed?'

'Everything has changed, Elidh.' He met her argument with swift confidence, proof of how thoroughly he'd thought this out. If she'd thought to take him unaware, or if she thought he'd forgotten this piece of the puzzle, she was disappointed. But in the tiny part of her that still hoped for the impossible, a flame began to stir, flickering slowly to life. 'Two weeks ago, I hadn't met you. I didn't know love. Elidh, love changes everything and it's worth more than anything, more than money, more than a fortune. I had no idea what I was sacrificing. When I began this quest, it was about money. It's not about that any more. It's a whole new equation. It's about love now, it's about you now and I will not trade you for Bax. My cousin isn't worth the cost of you, that's what it comes down to. That's what has changed.'

Sutton was magnificent in his defence, his confidence contagious, his eyes burning blue. 'So, that leaves us only your answer, Elidh?'

'You want to marry a woman whose name you didn't know until tonight?' she cajoled. As beautifully done as his defence was it was still an impossibility. She was so far beneath him socially. He was risking so much on so little acquaintance.

'If that woman is you.' Sutton's voice was low and private, for her alone.

'You will come to hate me.'

'I don't think so,' Sutton murmured, but his eyes had lost their glimmer. 'Elidh, will you come back?'

She rose. She had to be strong one last time and put herself beyond him for good. 'No, Sutton. I cannot do that to you.' She would lose him for good this time. This time, he would not come after her. They would have settled their accounts, explained their positions. She would go forward, knowing that he'd forgiven her.

He could go forward, knowing that she'd genuinely loved him. That would be enough.

He rose with her. 'Can you tell me why? Why is love not enough?'

'Because I love you, too. Love *is* everything, Sutton. I couldn't bear it if I lost yours. I love you enough to give you up, to know that it is selfish to keep you for myself. The world will never let us be happy.' She might never be happy again anyway. She could physically feel her heart breaking as she spoke.

'You mean that?' Resignation and shock registered on his handsome face—perhaps, she hoped, signs that he finally understood the battle was lost. 'Where will you go? What will you do?'

'I don't know.' Elidh rubbed her palms on her skirts. 'We'll manage somehow. We always do,' she said with more confidence than she felt. She was sounding more and more like her father. She was understanding him better these days. She'd misjudged him.

Sutton reached into his pocket. 'Will you take some money?' He passed her a folded packet of bills. She pushed it back. She would probably regret being stubborn about it, but she wouldn't take his pity, not when she was the one hurting him.

'No. It wouldn't be right. Sutton, I'm sorry.' Sorry for so much.

'Don't be. I'm not. I'm not sorry about the ruse. I wouldn't have met you otherwise. I'm only sorry that you won't come back with me and finish the story of us.'

He should be hating her, not absolving her. It only

made the hurt worse. It was her turn to ask questions, to give herself an epilogue to this ill-fated romance. 'What will you do? Who will you choose?' Who would end the story in her place?

He shook his head. 'I don't know. I didn't think I'd have to choose.' He paused. 'Elidh, if you won't come back with me, perhaps you will come on your own. It's not too late yet, Elidh.' He bent and kissed her cheek and then he walked past her, out of the room. Out of her life. This time for good. Elidh laid her head down on the wood table and sobbed.

All the candles had burned down. The room was full dark and still she sat. Unmoving. Unthinking, her head buried in her arms. At some point, Rosie came and sat beside her, her cool, motherly hand smoothing back her hair. 'Come, child, let's get you to bed. Everything will look better in the morning.'

Elidh lifted her head. 'He asked me to go back with him. He wants to marry *me*.' Her. Not the Principessa with her fine clothes and perfectly coiffed hair. Elidh Easton, who had nothing to offer him but her heart. The only thing he wanted from her was the one thing she'd denied him tonight. She'd given him penitence and apology, abject honesty when she'd poured out her story. But when he'd asked for her heart, she'd not given it. She'd wanted to protect him. Or was it herself she wanted to protect? Was she too afraid to face the last hurdles? Fear was a great immobiliser. 'Was I wrong, Rosie?'

'Only you can decide that,' Rosie answered quietly.

A new fear engulfed Elidh. Had she thrown away happiness out of fright, not once now, but twice? To love boldly she had to live boldly. Only she hadn't. She had nothing to lose and nowhere to go, yet she'd chosen to risk nothing tonight. She'd chosen to stay with nothing. Apparently, she preferred the status quo of the known to an uncertain outcome.

But Sutton had risked everything, *knowing* that he'd lose some of that amorphous 'everything' from the outset in the hopes of getting more in return than what he was giving up—the fortune, social avenues, influence, power. Yet he was willing to trade those things for her, she was worth more to him than anything the fortune and influence could give him. Because Sutton Keynes, scientist, camel dairy owner and lover of horses, believed love never failed, even though he knew empirically that it did. It was why he hated the house party, hated being trotted out like a fatted calf, a stud for hire, a placeholder for a fortune. Whatever one wanted to call it. There was no love there. It was a fancied-up business transaction trimmed in satins and silks and Sutton wanted no part of it. He couldn't find love there. But he'd found it with her and she'd turned him away.

'Rosie...' Elidh's voice trembled '...I think I've made a mistake.' A grave mistake. Love hadn't failed, but she had. She'd condemned each of them to a dismal future: Sutton with his money and loveless marriage to a woman he'd never wanted, and herself to the misery of endless poverty.

'Nothing that can't be fixed in the morning light,

my dear.' Rosie smiled reassuringly. 'There is still time.' That's what Sutton had said. Precious little of it, though.

'I'm going to need a ball gown, Rosie.' He'd come after her. Now, she would go after him.

Chapter Twenty-Three

Love never failed. Sutton clung to that simple thought as the hours of the day slid by, his grip on that hope growing more tenuous as the hours passed. Elidh would come. Some way, somehow, she would come. Nine miles was not an insurmountable distance. She would change her mind and she would come. She would see that her concerns didn't matter, that love was enough, that he would not come to hate her.

He started to look for her at noon, his pulse speeding when a puff of dust formed at the end of the drive, announcing the arrival of a carriage, only to find it was his own carriage bringing Mr Barnes, the solicitor, from the station. Mr Barnes had insisted on the heavily cushioned barouche—for the sake of his old bones, the solicitor claimed, gingerly stepping down from the carriage. 'Can't be jostling these joints of mine over country lanes in just any contraption. I'm bound to break something and at my age, that could be fatal.' Barnes patted his valise. 'I have all your papers right here. Everything will be shipshape tonight.'

* * *

Towards the late afternoon more carriages arrived. Hartswood took on a festive atmosphere as people disgorged from their vehicles for the al fresco supper and the ball to follow. All the talk of the last weeks was coming to a head tonight and everyone wanted to be on hand for his announcement, for the close of the fairy tale. Sutton greeted them all—it gave him an excuse to keep an eye on the drive, to see Elidh's arrival the moment she was here. But Elidh didn't come. There was only carriage after carriage disgorging a flurry of maids with dress boxes and pretty girls everywhere. None of them was Elidh.

Supper on the back lawn was a beautiful affair with lanterns and white canopies, the well-trained Hartswood staff moving effortlessly among the guests, serving a light summer repast and pouring chilled white wine from France into crystal glasses.

'Gorgeous evening, Keynes.' Wharton came by his table to shake his hand, no doubt feeling expansive thanks to the wine and the erroneous belief that his daughter, Ellen, might be named as Sutton's bride tonight. Sutton had spent the morning entertaining each of the four front runners individually as a way of passing the time. And perhaps, his rational side asserted, creating a backup plan. If love failed, if Elidh didn't come, he needed the next best thing. There were toasts and more greetings. Then dinner was over. Guests went to change into ball gowns, men went to drink his port and play billiards for an hour. His mother whisked him away to one more receiving line as dusk fell. More guests arrived, those who couldn't make it for dinner but who definitely wanted to be on hand for the big announcement London had waited two weeks to hear.

The receiving line was a special torture, hope rising anew with each face, only to be disappointed. There'd be a flash of colour, a movement out of the corner of his eye that triggered a memory of Elidh. He'd turn and his heart would falter again. 'She's not coming,' his mother whispered as the line began to ebb at last. In the ballroom, the orchestra was tuned up.

'She'll come,' Sutton said staunchly. But even he was running out of reasons to believe that. It was nearly full dark. Travel at night for someone without the right equipage was impossible and unsafe. Elidh couldn't go tramping through the roads and lanes of Suffolk on foot. If she wasn't here now, the chances of her being here at all were slim. He had to accept that. No, he did not have to accept that. Acceptance was resignation and admittance of defeat, of failure. Love never failed. There was no logic to back it up with, but he had to believe up until the very last minute. He *had* to, although his convictions were not ironclad. It was taking all his courage to screw his waning convictions to that sticking point. Past experience was against him, the clock was against him, logic was against him.

'It's time for the opening waltz,' his mother instructed. 'The girls wanted to draw straws.' He'd been fully reduced to a thing, something to be divided up like a prize. 'Lady Imogen won,' his mother continued. 'Fine choice, though. People will think she's the front runner anyway because of her father's rank.' She was trying to be encouraging.

Imogen it would be. He would be *and yourself*-ed to death by the end of the dance. But, thinking positively, he'd have dancing with her out of the way for the evening. He had to think optimistically. This was just one more thing to get through before Elidh arrived.

He danced with Imogen, with Isabelle, with Eliza Fenworth just to keep her away from Bax, who was prowling the sidelines with a gloating smile on his face as if the Hartswood ballroom had become his personal devil's playground. Who knew how many girls Bax would attempt to seduce in the garden tonight? Attempt was the key word, though. Sutton had instructed his footmen to keep a close eye on Bax. He'd also instructed a footman to keep an eye on the front drive and alert him immediately if there were any late arrivals. As a result, Sutton's gaze drifted rather frequently to the ballroom entrance, hoping to see the footman with news. But there was no footman, no news and no Elidh. Fairy tales weren't supposed to end like this, with the triumph of reality. In the real world, daughters of poor playwrights didn't marry gentlemen.

The excitement in the ballroom ratcheted up with each passing hour. Every pair of eyes was on him, watching who he danced with, fans flapping furiously as women gossiped and speculated behind them. His cousin came to gloat. 'You can stop looking at the ballroom door. She's not coming.' Bax downed a flute of champagne in a single swallow and set it on a passing tray.

Sutton flipped open his pocket watch, a gift from his father on his eighteenth birthday. 'Half-past eleven, right on cue, Cousin.' He steeled himself against his cousin's poison. He'd expected some last-minute effort from Bax and here it was.

'My father really stuck it to both of us, didn't he?' Bax posited casually. Anyone looking at them would think them friendly with one another, a final drink between cousins before the big announcement and congratulations unless one knew what Bax stood to lose momentarily. Sutton said nothing, refusing to be baited in the hopes Bax might decide against saying anything further. But neither luck nor hope, it seemed, had seen fit to grace him tonight. Bax continued. 'His money is a curse. Neither of us win tonight. If you marry, I lose a fortune. But if you marry, you give up the hope of finding love, something that apparently matters to you, after all, for what little it's brought you.' He laughed. 'I don't understand you, Cuz. You have thirty of England's finest virgins at your disposal, every last one of them wiling to spread their legs for you, and a fortune at your fingertips in enticement for taking their offer, and yet you hesitate.'

'Watch your language while you're in my home,' Sutton growled. After the emotions of the last two weeks, his patience was on thin rations. It would take little provocation to brawl in his own ballroom tonight.

Bax shrugged an insincere apology. 'But perhaps I overestimate your sentiments where love is concerned? Perhaps you've tired of love once more. You've the worst luck with women, Cuz. First, Anabeth Morely throws you over for a duke's heir and now your heart's been claimed by a fraud and a liar. Maybe you are better off with one of those white-gowned virgins over there, after all. Yet you persist in staring at the door. Are you hoping your liar will come waltzing in? What man wants a woman who's cheated him? Who will cost him a fortune?'

'Are you finished?' Sutton feigned boredom over his cousin's conjecture. He didn't want to spend these last minutes talking with Bax.

'Yes. I only want to say she's not coming.' Bax swiped another glass of champagne with smug confidence. 'Then again, perhaps it's best. How would you choose? Love or money? My father created quite the dilemma for you. I believe that was the very same dilemma your mother faced, was it not? Still, you'd think if she really loved you, though, she'd be here. Maybe she's the smart one. She's decided love isn't worth it. Or maybe without the fortune, she's decided you're not worth it.' He gave a mocking bow. 'Money is the only thing that matters in the end, Sutton. Always.' No. Bax was wrong there. Elidh loved him. Too much, it seemed. Love was working against him, there, but Bax would never understand that. Money. Love. Neither mattered at the moment. The only thing that did matter was that Elidh wasn't there.

At a quarter to midnight the footmen began to circulate with the champagne for the toast. Mr Barnes took up his august station at the foot of the dais, his valise by his side. Like an executioner with his tools,

Sutton thought, the dais looming like a scaffold. He was going to his death, Elidh his only chance at a pardon.

The only consolation was that soon all this would be over. The decision made, the guests gone and he could get back to his horses and his camels. His mother would plan the wedding. He would just show up. That would become the theme for his life. His mother and his wife would plan things—balls, suppers, parties— and he would show up. That was all he'd need to do. The rest of the time he could be in his dairy, remembering what had been and dreaming of what *could* have been if Elidh had come. If Elidh had believed.

That was what galled him most. She didn't believe he could make it right for her, for them. That he could and would face down anyone who challenged their marriage, challenged her place beside him. That she thought loving him meant giving him up, protecting him, and he'd been unable to convince her otherwise.

His mother arrived at his arm. 'Are you ready? After this dance, you can make the announcement. Have you decided?' She was all bright smiles tonight. Too bright. 'I am sorry she didn't come, my son.' He waited for her to follow it up with a platitude like 'it was for the best.' But she didn't. His mother was too smart for that. Whether or not she agreed with his choice, she supported him.

'When you chose Father instead of Uncle Leland, was it a difficult decision?' Sutton asked. 'Uncle was the older son, the one with the better prospects at the time. He had everything to offer a bride.'

His mother's smile softened. 'No, it wasn't difficult at all. Those things didn't matter. When I was with your father, there was a sense of rightness, that I belonged with him, in a way that could never be duplicated or replaced by Leland or anyone else's money. When you're with the right one, you just know.'

Yes. You did. But how did you convince that person it was enough? And when did you quit trying? The orchestra stopped. His mother squeezed his arm, in affection, in support, perhaps in regret that it had come to this. Sutton took a glass of champagne and mounted the dais. He looked out over the crowd as they turned to face him, giving him their breathless attention. To the right of the dais, the four front runners gathered, a pretty bouquet of pastel-gowned flowers, giggling nervously, supporting each other with false modesty. Near the dais, Bax stood ready to gloat at his demise. Bax might be losing a fortune, but he'd not lost sight of the price that loss extracted from his cousin. He'd take perverse joy in that. Sutton supposed Bax, like himself, might also be holding out hope until the last minute. Perhaps Bax hoped he might decline the fortune and marriage altogether. He wouldn't, of course. He wouldn't lose both Elidh *and* a chance to do some good, a chance to curtail evil. The battle between he and Bax would continue.

Sutton tapped his glass for attention and the remainder of conversation in the ballroom died. 'Ladies and gentlemen, welcome to the final night of our summer house party,' he began. 'Three weeks ago, Mr Barnes came to me with the contents of my uncle's will, which put this house party in motion and has led to the reason we are all gathered here tonight. In order to claim my uncle's fortune, I must choose a bride. You have all been very generous in helping me.' The crowd laughed. 'I appreciate everyone who has given of their time and efforts away from London to assist in that pursuit.' He took time to pay tribute to as many people as he could, acknowledging as many of the girls as possible. If everyone had their moment of fame, it would soften the blow of not being selected. If he could keep them laughing, it would delay the inevitable. Midnight neared. He could not stall any longer.

He looked at the girls. Not Isabelle. She was too catty. Not Imogen. Too shy, too young. He could not live with another enquiry of 'and yourself?' He'd turn it into a drinking game within a week of marriage and end up a drunkard. Not Eliza Fenworth—he had great hopes for her happiness with the violin-maker he'd written to. He would not take that from her. That left Miss Ellen Hines, Wharton's girl, whose only flaw was to have been out for three Seasons, to be too quiet, too mediocre to garner remark. She was neither above nor below reproach. Wharton would be pleased. But Sutton hated the idea that Wharton might think the choice was because of his bullying. Wharton had tried to bribe his mother. When that had failed, Wharton had tried to threaten him.

Outside the ballroom there was commotion, movement, strident voices, a flash of a brilliant blue skirt on the stairs, something full and frothy, the shade of forget-me-nots. Sutton's heart leapt as it had so many times already that evening. He raised his voice. He had to buy whoever was out there some time—time to get inside the room, time for him to see who it was. Just in case.

'We wanted to create a fairy tale these last weeks and I think we've succeeded admirably.' In the hall, the clock began to chime.

One. Two.

'As you know, fairy tales begin with once upon a time and they end with happily-ever-after.'

Three. Four.

'Not because a man held a ball and found a woman who checked off certain boxes on his list or because her father had wealth and standing, although it often starts out that way.'

Five. Six.

Bax arched a devilish eyebrow. *You're running out of time, Cuz. Will you risk it all on whoever is in the hallway?*

Seven. Eight.

The ballroom held its breath. Sutton continued, his own breath catching, 'But because a man found true love instead.'

A little ripple of 'ahs' ran through the ballroom. The flash of blue was closer now.

Nine.

'In between the beginning and the end, however, fairy tales are often full of surprises and trials.'

Ten.

Hurry, his mind cried.

'The Prince and the Princess in those stories aren't

always who we think. There are mistaken and false identities along the way with other sundry items designed to obscure the heart's truth. That has been the case here as well, but, as in all good tales, love has won the day and torn away veils that might mislead.'

Eleven.

She stood in the doorway, breathing hard, a hand pressed to the tight waist of her gown. She'd run. Her prettily styled hair had come down, dirt clung to her hem, but Elidh was here. *Elidh was here!* Sutton's throat constricted and he took a moment to collect himself.

Twelve.

'So, my choice is this. I will marry Elidh Easton and I will renounce my claim to my uncle's fortune in the name of true love.'

He held out his hand to her as the stroke of midnight faded. Amazement swept the ballroom in whispers and disbelief as Elidh swept through the crowd, cutting through the rumours and speculation. Who was she? Had she been at the party? Where did she come from? She hadn't been here all night. Dust-covered and dishevelled, she'd never looked lovelier to him, her head held high, her eyes fixed on him alone. Sutton smiled. That particular thought might become a recurring theme. He distinctly remembered thinking it before, down in the stables. He'd probably think it again, perhaps as soon as tomorrow, then again on their wedding day, their wedding night; the day after, and every day that followed; the day their first child was born, their second…and on *ad infinitum*. Sutton took her hand, drawing her up to the dais beside him, where she belonged.

'I didn't think I'd make it,' she whispered breathlessly.

'You made it just in time, that's all that matters.' He beamed. Bax was beaming, too. He had the fortune. But not for long, Sutton vowed. He would stop Bax's corruption. Some way, somehow. All things were possible with Elidh beside him. He turned to the solicitor who was rummaging madly through his valise at this turn of events. 'Mr Barnes, if you would please do the honours and read the legal paperwork here in front of witnesses.'

'Yes, I have the letter now.' Barnes brandished a document and made his way to the dais and cleared his throat. 'Sir Leland Keynes left two envelopes. One of which would be opened if Sutton Keynes, his designated heir, met the conditions of the will. Another, if he failed to claim a noble bride in time.' He held up the envelope and opened it, making a great show of unfolding the paper. 'Dear Nephew, if you are reading this, congratulations are in order. You have passed the test.' Barnes looked up, signalling a murmur of confusion around the room, and disappointment, to be honest. Sutton was well aware there were a few fathers in the room who would take pleasure in seeing him get his comeuppance for not choosing their daughters. Below him, in front, Bax's face had gone livid and then pale. But he hadn't time for Bax. He, too, was listening intently, confused along with the rest. And fearful. Elidh's hand tightened in his and Sutton froze, fearing another of his uncle's games. What more could his uncle do?

Barnes continued. 'If you have shunned my fortune in order to make your own choice, it can only mean you have chosen love over money. A very wise decision which I can attest to from the vantage point of my age. By doing so, you have shown the strength of your convictions and your courage in standing up for them. Your bride should be proud in knowing she is to marry such a man and she should rest easy in the knowledge that she is treasured for who she is and not what she likely doesn't bring to the table as a representative of her family's social standing. I am sure many bridal candidates were thrown your way shamelessly on the grounds of wealth and status.' There was a certain amount of foot shifting at the words. His uncle had delivered an excellent scolding to those who would turn marriage into an auction of brides to highest bidders. 'Because of this decision, I am awarding you full possession of the fortune regardless of your bride's birth along with the addition of the London town house and trust funds for each of your children. I also wish you something that eluded me in my lifetime—all happiness for as long as you both shall live.'

The ballroom was silent, expressions varying from soft looks of emotion, to harder, sterner looks of disapproval from fathers whose daughters wouldn't being going home with a husband or a fortune tonight. Sutton's mother took the dais, champagne glass raised. 'A toast, then, to the happy couple. It is clear they have found their happy-ever-after. Cheers!' She gestured to the orchestra to strike up a waltz. 'Dance with your bride, Sutton,' she whispered. 'Show them what happiness looks like.'

But Bax wasn't ready to give up. At the bottom of the steps he stopped Sutton, a hand firm on his arm. 'How dare you have both love and money? For as long as you both shall live?' he growled. 'How long do you think that will be if I have my way?'

'Quite a while, Cousin,' Sutton answered evenly. 'If any unnatural harm befalls either of us, you will be the first one suspected. You are our very best insurance policy for a long life. You can't spend a fortune when you're dead and you'd surely hang for murder.' He inclined his head. 'If you'll excuse me? I am going to dance with my bride.'

'This is not over, you bastard.' Bax stepped back, melting into the crowd. No, it wasn't. But for now, Sutton had something more important to do. He led Elidh out to the dance floor and swept her into the opening measures of the waltz, his happiness brimming over. 'I didn't think you were going to come,' he confessed. Around them, others joined in, filling the floor. He hardly noticed.

'I knew after you left I'd made a terrible mistake, not once, but twice. I feared the Viscountess's letter.' Elidh was breathless and flushed with joy. He wanted her to always look this way. He would do his best to ensure that she did. 'I almost didn't make it. The wagon I hitched a ride on broke an axel outside Fordham.'

'What did you do, then?' Sutton grinned.

'We looked for another wagon, but when we didn't find a ride, we walked.'

'From Fordham?' Sutton was amazed. 'That's six miles. That was dangerous in the dark.'

'Only five. I ran the sixth. I would have walked further for you, Sutton.' Elidh looked up, love shining in her eyes, and he saw his world reflected there.

'You ran a mile?' He was incredulous. 'In the dark?'

'Yes, I did. What choice did I have? You were here. I was nearly too late as it was.'

'Do you have another dress?' he asked, taking her through the turn at the top of the ballroom.

'Yes. Should I change?' she asked worriedly.

'No, you're fine the way you are. I was just wondering how long it would take you to have a dress ready.'

'For what?'

'For our wedding. I want to marry you as soon as possible. For the beginning of happy-ever-after.'

Elidh beamed, her eyes twinkling in mischief. 'Oh, that. I thought it had already started the first day I met you.'

Sutton laughed. 'Are you sure it wasn't the day you chucked my croquet ball into the woods?'

She cocked her head and pretended to contemplate the idea. 'Come to think of it, I'm not sure. It might have been the day you showed me the caves on the island, or the day we delivered the foals.' She gave a mock sigh. 'Your hypothesis might need further study, Mr Keynes.'

He kissed her then, his beautiful Elidh, his goose girl, his Princess. His everything. His world was in his arms. He didn't care who saw, didn't care what people thought. He knew what he thought, what he believed. Love never failed. It was empirically true. They'd proven it, together.

Epilogue

London—eight months later

The chandeliers dimmed overhead. The floodlights at the foot of the stage came up. The crowd inside Covent Garden's newest theatre, The Italian, quieted in the anticipation. In the richly appointed box to the right of the stage, Elidh and Sutton sat, hands linked in anticipation, a warm look passing between them.

'Do you think your father's play will be any good?' Sutton enquired, studying the playbill. 'It sounds dubious. *The Fraudulent Bride*?' He read the title with mock concern in his voice, teasing her.

Elidh laughed. 'I have it on good authority it's based on real events. A girl goes to a house party to which she's not invited, pretending to be a princess, and ends up married to the rich host.'

'After many twists and turns, of course,' Sutton supplied and she blushed.

'Of course, with many twists and turns. The path of true love never runs straight.' She sighed. The past eight months had been her own fairy tale come to life. The wedding had been a whirlwind affair, large and beautiful. Large to satisfy society's tongues that all was indeed legitimate. Beautiful to satisfy Sutton, who insisted on spoiling her. They spent their days at Hartswood with the animals, walking the property. Sutton taught her to ride and had bought her an agreeable horse for a wedding gift. They bathed in the hot springs. Spent the winter in the warmth of the barns with the foals.

It was a happy, idyllic life. But it wasn't for everyone. Like Sutton's mother, her own father preferred the excitement of London, and Sutton didn't disappoint, becoming the chief patron of a theatre where her father could write and direct to his heart's content, and where Rosie could dress a new generation of actress. She and Sutton had come up to town to celebrate the opening of the new play, her father's second since the theatre had opened its doors in December for the holidays.

'Would you like to stay in town for the Season? We have the town house at our disposal and things will get underway in a couple of weeks.' Sutton asked, his thumb caressing her gloved hand. 'We can have a new wardrobe made up for you.'

Elidh slid him a sly smile. 'I'm ready to go home. Besides, we'd only have to have the dresses remade.'

Sutton wrinkled his brow. She loved catching him off guard, loved surprising him. 'Why is that? Do you not like the seamstress? We can find another. My mother could recommend someone.'

'No.' She shook her head, her smile widening.

'Nothing's wrong with the dressmaker. It's me. I am planning on getting much bigger.'

Recognition flared in Sutton's eyes. 'Are you saying…?'

She nodded. 'Yes. I—we—are expecting a child.'

Sutton reached for her, kissing her hard and long, not caring who might see. She didn't care either. She was long past worrying over what others thought. She knew what she thought: she was the luckiest woman in the world because she was loved.

'Are you happy?' She laughed softly between kisses.

'What do you think?' Sutton smiled. 'Since we already know how this play ends, might we leave early?'

Elidh nodded. They might indeed. The curtain was rising on a whole new chapter in their lives. She wasn't worried. Love never failed.

* * * * *

*If you enjoyed this story
be sure to read the other books in
Bronwyn Scott's Allied at the Altar miniseries*

A Marriage Deal with the Viscount
One Night with the Major

*And whilst you're waiting for the next book check out
the Russian Royals of Kuban miniseries,
starting with*

Compromised by the Prince's Touch
Innocent in the Prince's Bed